Ente

The Program: Book 1

Enter Alexavier

Thomas Edward

Independently published through
Kindle Direct Publishing
Seattle, Washington

Enter Alexavier

Cataloging-in-Publication Data has been applied for and may be obtained from the Library of Congress.

ISBN 978-1-0862-0264-9

Text copyright ©2019 Thomas Edward, LLC
Cover picture by Sergey Nivens from Shutterstock

This book is a work of fiction. Any reference to historical events, real people or real locales is used fictitiously. Other names, characters, places and incidents are the product of the author's imagination, and any resemblance to actual events or locales or persons, living or dead is entirely coincidental.

Published independently in 2019 by Kindle Direct Publishing. All rights reserved. No portion of this book may be reproduced, stored in a retrieval system, or transmitted in any form or by any means, mechanical, electronic, photocopying, recording or otherwise, without written permission from the author.

Enter Alexavier

Acknowledgements

This book has been a long road of hazards, detours and construction cones. But through this journey, the book has found its destination, made possible by the help, positive feedback and constructive criticism by many: My wife Jean, for the many years of support, questions, reviews and putting up with this long and demanding process. As well as Megan Johnson, Roberto Corales, Ronnie Devlin, Julie Tibbott and Ming Chen for their help, reviews and information. Thanks to the many family and friends who've supported me, especially my kids: Andrea, Taylor, Ashley and Thomas, whose love of stories helped me to start writing. I'd like to recognize some others, who even without their knowledge, have inspired and entertained me: Chris Claremont, Rodney Dangerfield, Darrell 'Dimebag' Abbott, Bret 'Hitman' Hart, Adam Hunter, Paul Smith, John Byrne, Frank Miller, Stan Lee, Todd Mcfarlane, Jim Lee, Len Wein, Herb Trimpe, Neil DeGrasse Tyson, Steven Hawking, George Lucas, Gene Roddenberry, Glen A. Larson, Randy 'Macho Man' Savage, Rob Van Dam, Rhyno, the former Puma Prince and forever King Ricochet, Johnny 'Wrestling' Gargano, Will 'Aerial Assassin' Ospreay, Billy Lane, Indian Larry, Ian Bagg, Mitch Hedberg, Anthony Jeselnik, John Pinette, Steve Hofstetter, Ryan Stout, Sam Kinison, 'Roadside' Phil Johnson, Joe Machi, THE Greg (Romero) Wilson, Bob Zany, Chad Daniels, Foster Brooks, Don Rickles, B.J. Penn, Josh Barnett, Don Frye, Bob Probert, Darren McCarty, Pavel

Enter Alexavier

Datsyuk, Al Kaline, Kirk Gibson, Barry Sanders, Dennis Rodman, Kevin Smith, the Comic Book Men, the Ghost Hunters, the Street Outlaws, the Impractical Jokers, Producer Joe, Eric Zane, FBHW, Ryan Reynolds, Sheldon Cooper, Leonard Hofstadter, Penny, Raj, Mr. Wolowitz, Karen Walker, Jack Mcfarland, Will, Grace, Michael Westen, Fiona Glenanne, Sam Axe, and the music of Pantera, Guns N' Roses, Prong, old Metallica, old Machine Head, old Anthrax, Rancid, The Wildhearts, Testament, The Offspring, Soul Coughing, L.A. Guns, Ratt, Fasterpussycat, Skid Row, Tigertailz, Stone, Slayer, Slipknot, Rob and White Zombie. Finally, to anyone not mentioned who changed the direction of my life to where it is, whether good or bad, thank you. In memory of Nico, Jones and my little buddy Fred. You were taken way too soon, my friend.

Enter Alexavier

Welcome to the world of The Program!

Provided at the back of this book is a glossary to help familiarize yourself with the characters in this universe or as you need a refresher as to who is who and what they can do. Listed are all the characters that appear in this story. First are the people involved with The Program, listed in alphabetical order by first name with their hero names and abilities. That is followed by the names of the villains and their abilities, also listed alphabetically.

Thank you for purchasing my book. Hopefully, this story will bring you as much enjoyment and fun as it was for me to write.

Connect with me on social media:

Thomas Edward
Facebook: Thomas Edward
Twitter: @TEdwardWriter
Instagram: tedward_writer
Tumblr: tedwardwriter

Enter Alexavier

"They tried to instill fear. They tried to take away our way of life and even succeeded with the lives of some of our own. But, as much as they have tried to put us down, we will never stay down. We will always rise to fight for the rights, freedoms and the lives of all.

I promise to work hard to divert such threats and to pave a new path for justice. I will work toward building a better future. A future that is stronger, safer and brighter. And no, that future isn't so far out there that it's out of our grasp. In fact, that future starts now!"

Samuel Nelson, The Patriot Warrior
New York City, March 28, 1983

Enter Alexavier

CHAPTER 1

"I'm taking you down! One way or another, it finally ends here," Brad snarled, stalking his opponent.

"Sorry. You should know better than anyone that you can't beat me." A quick tug on his hood brought it behind his head. Plus a shake of his head removed his slightly long, dark hair from hiding his eyes, as he waited for the inevitable confrontation. His name is Alexavier Vankendreh'd, and he's ready for a battle.

"I know how to beat you, and there's nothing you can to stop me!" Brad Stryper made the first move by lunging forward. The young, Asian aggressor's hearty attempt to grab a leg came up short as Alexavier sprawled, backing his legs away and dropping down on top of Brad. Using his full weight to limit the attack, Alexavier secured a death grip on his opponent. It looked like this fight was over before it could really start.

Suddenly, ribbons of colored light emerged from Brad's body, as he immediately vanished with the light flying away. These streams of color gathered behind Alexavier, where Brad materialized, putting Alexavier at an instant disadvantage. Being quick to counter, Alexavier dropped down with a twist of his body and turning to his side to escape. Scampering back on his feet, Alexavier was out of the control of his unlucky adversary and back on top.

Frustrated, Brad tried another escape. With his body transforming into colored ribbons, this allowed him to move very quickly from place to place without being

Enter Alexavier

harmed. Brad took shape behind Alexavier, smirking as he was in control once again. Without hesitation, Alexavier dropped down. But this time he rolled back, taking his unsuspecting opponent along for the ride. Surprised, Brad dematerialized into light waves before he could be completely subdued. The cascading ribbons reformed in front of Alexavier, but not far enough away. Alexavier lunged forward, diving at Brad's legs, and they both wound up on the ground. Finding himself in another difficult position, Brad fled to a safer position.

Noticing Brad's calculated retreat, Alexavier said with much sarcasm, "I thought I was going down. Looks like somebody is getting beat at his own game." On his knees, Alexavier rolled backward, extending his body upward and performing a handspring into a standing position.

An annoyed look washed over Brad's face, as he jumped forward again. "I'm going to beat you at least once!" With the same precision, Alexavier easily evaded the aggressive attempt. This physical altercation was part of their usual daily workout, a sparring match of sorts. As the friendly war of exercise and training continued, a visitor stood stoic, observing every throw and submission attempt. The flowing movement of the friendly hand-to-hand combat kept him enamored. He is Major John Constantine, the appointed leader of this facility and others like it.

A member of the facility's managing staff arrived to greet him. "Are you enjoying the display, Major?"

"It's quite impressive."

"Wait 'til he goes on missions and starts handing those baddies their asses. He'll graduate from your segment of The Program in no time. Any kid who dominates people as he does should be taking down villains in droves. See how each move of Brad's is met with quick, decisive counters? He literally doesn't have to think to put Brad at a disadvantage."

"Like I said, impressive." The Major didn't blink.

Enter Alexavier

"Well, Alexavier is more than impressive. He's actually showing off right now. Brad is one of only a couple of people who will actually spar with him. Alexavier makes every move count, and any attempts by his sparring partners make them look like they're half-assed, second class recruits. There is no one here even remotely in his league. Even though he's not super powered like Union or Intergalactic, only having heightened speed, strength, agility and awareness, his combat skills are so advanced that he instills fear in others."

"They don't fear him. They dread him." A smile of content slowly overtook the Major's once expressionless face.

#

Back in the locker room, Brad, his opponent for the day, as well as another up-and-coming hero, Brian Haveman, the magically empowered Brindlehaven, joined Alexavier. Alexavier was in the middle of packing everything he had, while Brad changed back into his regular clothes. The exhilarating combat and colorful banter back and forth carried over from the battlefield into the locker room.

"It's kind of convenient," Brad stated, "that our rematch got cut short so I can't get payback for all of those times I got my butt kicked."

"It's not like that was going to happen. You haven't beat me so far. Why would you start today?"

Brian, who was usually the more serious member of this small group, joined in. "He has to have a purpose in life."

"Hey! You didn't get in there. You won't take him on," Brad stated.

"I'm smart. Without my powers, I know he'll win."

"Yeah, but I used my powers today."

"And you still lost." The laughter from Alexavier nearly drowned out Brian's

Enter Alexavier

words.

Alexavier quickly looked back, sensing something. Through the joking, the increasing sound of footsteps came from the doorway, ending with Major Constantine watching the heroes in training. The Major had a muscular yet slender build, particularly for being around 60 years old. Possessing a strong face and gray hair, he is always dressed in his Army best. Just like his uniform, he was all business. "Gentlemen, if I could have Alexavier to myself?"

"I guess that's our cue." Brian stood up, grabbing his towel. "When you get there, put in a word for me."

Brad quickly responded, "You? Aren't we a team?"

"We are, but no one is going to help you unless you help yourself."

Alexavier smiled and shook their hands. "If I can do anything, you know I will."

"Sleeping in, catching rays, we know what you'll do," Brad joked.

"Probably forget our names by next week. Say goodbye," Brian added, pushing Brad out of the room.

"Take care, guys!" Alexavier said, with one last wave.

Looking around the room, one wouldn't have thought much of it. Everything appeared to be as normal as any other workout facility. However, the building that this room resided in, was nothing but extraordinary. It is the home to the initial phase for training recruits. This secret government operation called The Program develops young people with extraordinary abilities to one day become superheroes and fight for the common good of the government and its citizens. Many remarkable, young people resided here, and at the top of the list is young Alexavier. For quite a while, the people in charge have been paying special attention to him, keeping a watchful eye on his progress. Right now, only one man was looking on, as the Major eyed his prized pupil.

"It was an intriguing workout today." Alexavier frantically continued getting

Enter Alexavier

ready, sliding on his black work boots and tying his laces while listening to the Major speak. "Your progress has become something of a case study for the docs. I, for one, am very pleased. The strides you've made, both in your skill set and physical development is phenomenal." Alexavier looked up. "You may be the final piece of the puzzle that I've been looking for."

"Thanks. I hope so." Alexavier looked back down and straightened his pant legs. He was less nervous than he should have been. Having spent so much time at this level of The Program had left him with a lot of doubt and uncertainty, almost as much as it had improved him as a hero. Through it all, he worked hard and stayed on course, finally accomplishing his goal of graduating and moving one step closer to becoming a hero.

The Major asked, "Still having the nightmares? Did the doctors prescribe anything yet?"

"They keep telling me the drugs should help, but they don't feel like nightmares. They're more like visions or dreams, so I didn't take them."

"If they persist, you should do something so you're not affected for the long term. I don't need you to be half the hero when we get to the complex."

"I was thinking I was going to be stuck here forever," Alexavier stated, as he stood up, placing the last of his workout clothes in his bag.

"Even though you had some struggles, I knew eventually you would prove to be worth the effort. You are going to make an impact. I have some special plans for you."

"I just want to get out of here and see Beth and Dave." Alexavier finished, tucking a journal in the bag. With most of his gear packed, he turned for what would be his final task, to take down the pictures lining the inside of his locker. Most young men his age would have had pictures of hot women or hot rods and muscle cars, but being part of The Program did not bring about normal dreams and aspirations. Starting at

Enter Alexavier

the top, he removed various pictures of heroes and stopped at the last one, which was his favorite. It showed a man who looked like Uncle Sam, pointing in his face. It was his idol, Sam Nelson, the greatest hero of them all, also known as The Patriot Warrior. After carefully taking it down, Alexavier carefully placed the stack of pictures in his duffel bag and zipped it up.

"Just so you know, this isn't going to be easy, son. Those skills you've got are going to be your meal ticket and your survival. So keep your eyes open at all times. This is no classroom you're heading to. That's all getting left behind. So far, you only had tactical simulations and battled fellow recruits. The next time you're being called upon will be against actual villains. The dice are in your hands, and it's time for you to roll them, son. You've been the lucky one so far. Whatever you've done with that rabbit's foot, keep it close. Sometimes, luck is all you need." The Major walked toward the hallway. "Grab your gear and follow us to the conference room for your exit interview. We have guests waiting."

Alexavier watched him leave, contemplated for a moment what his graduation really meant, the opportunity to become that hero he had dreamed of being. With renewed enthusiasm, he put on his favorite grey, hooded sweatshirt, turned and caught an image of himself in the mirror. So often, he looked in that mirror, staring at a face he did not know. Due to the processes used to amplify his abilities called Sessions, his face had become something so familiar to him, but yet foreign because of them. Leaning in for a closer look, he stared himself down. But this time, there was no mental fog clouding the view that sometimes happened after a Session. He knew who he was. There was no blinking or use of cold water. There were no more vitamins and supplements. He did not have to document his every breath in his journal just to remember his whole life. Now, it was on to better things. With a feeling of anticipation of his new life energizing him, he picked up his bags, throwing them over his shoulder and headed out the locker room door to join the Major.

Enter Alexavier

CHAPTER 2

The journey had taken a sort of locomotive feel, with a single file line of men snaking the hallways toward the conference room. As they approached, a man in a suit quickly opened the rather large door that lead to a conference room. The enormous room became more visible, with a group of military and civilian personnel gathered around a massive table. The chatter among them ceased upon his entrance. The parade route circled most of the room and ended at the head of the table, backed by a screen that was loading information. The Major motioned for Alexavier to stand to one side.

After a moment of preparation, the Major pushed a couple of buttons and turned to inspect the screen behind him. Slowly, an image popped up of Alexavier, accompanied by a sidebar of general information such as age, height, weight and other descriptors. Taking a last glance to the podium in front of him, the Major started the introduction.

"Welcome everyone, including our newest members of The Committee on Super Human Affairs and Development, aka COSHAD. Also, I'd like to welcome Senator Frank Steinberg, who is taking time away from Congress to be here. It's a pleasure as always." The Major made eye contact with the Senator, who nodded back. "My name is John Constantine, former Army Major, coordinator for The United superhero team and head of this facility, part of The Program. Absent from this introduction is Sam

Enter Alexavier

Nelson. You all know him as The Patriot Warrior, possibly the greatest hero the world has ever known. He is our primary consultant for recruit readiness, as well as for strategic planning for The Program. Also absent is Jonathon Bender, formerly known as The Time Bender, who has retired from active duty to be my second in command. Both of them as you know were members of The United, but when the team was called The United Superheroes of America, but now are actively involved in The Program operations."

"This is The Program, only known to a select few of you, as well as a handful of others throughout our government, possibly by the codename, The Secret Garden. We are at one of several satellites, entry-level, development facilities located throughout the country. This facility is the one of our government's recruitment and development programs for young people with extraordinary abilities. We are dedicated to providing the best outcomes from their training and releasing these young men and women into the world to carry out the good deeds set before by many of our world's greatest heroes. Our track record includes developing such heroes as Union, Intergalactic, Riva, Golden Wing, Alpha Dawn and Omega Knight, Mr. N. Sayen, plus the iconic, but oddly named hero, The. Not to mention, there are other countless heroes who are fighting crime on the streets as we speak."

"Can you explain why one of our heroes only has the name of The?"

The Major didn't like the question from one of the new COSHAD members sidetracking the meeting. "The history of his name has been questioned on social media with some reliable answers, so we'll leave it for another time. If you would like to ask The about it, I can refer you to him. If he's in a good mood, he'll answer your question."

"Also, with that question, we do have some new members of this committee, so I'll give a brief history and the mission that this Program adheres to. Following the events of the terrorist attack in New York City in the early 80's where a nuclear

Enter Alexavier

device was detonated, our government thought it necessary to start a program to develop young heroes to combat the evils that were quickly growing around the world. Every year, more young people were developing extraordinary abilities, but most of them were turning to crime. Seeing a need to provide an avenue for these gifted youngsters to do the right thing, The Program was created. We develop their abilities and provide them with the tools to make these young men and women into truly fantastic heroes. Each one starts in one of our satellite complexes, like here, and eventually making it to our main complex in Virginia just outside D.C. for finalization of their development. These varying levels of facilities have many layers to them for our recruits to use to reach their full potential."

"Knowing the importance of all of the complexes and everyone's safety involved in its operations, we also created The Elitesmen Guard, headed by the team captain, Dirk Henderson. This highly technical group of individuals has several levels of suits and armor that make each man into a formidable weapon. For lesser security duties, they wear an exoskeleton suit that provides adequate protection for these complex duties. For more intense situations, each man has full battle armor that can be worn. These suits are more than capable of handling whatever any emergency situation may arise, even if attacked by The Terror Tribe."

A General spoke up quickly, "Can you tell us a bit more about The Terror Tribe? We've read the reports, but the information presented to us in Washington is a bit vague. I don't think everyone has a true understanding of this organization."

"The Terror Tribe is a group of villains formed from the ashes of Major Disaster's team, once called The Squadron of Evil. They are led by a man who now calls himself, The Infamous One. Some of the individuals under his command include, Natural Disaster, who is Major Disaster's son, Game Over, Everlorne, Nib, Silver Shockwave, Dasher, Mega Conductor, Killing Joke, Carnevil, as well as numerous other villains all around the country that happen to have an affiliation from time to time. It is believed that there are more than a hundred active members at any time. At some point, presumably sometime before the New York attack, The Infamous One took over this group and masterminded the first detonation of a nuclear weapon on U.S. soil. Our heroes from The United engaged the villains, but were unable to stop the detonation. Although there were many causalities, our heroes were able to contain it from causing wide spread destruction. The original Human Battery absorbed much of the energy, but enough of the blast was released to harm and kill several thousand people. The Human Battery continued to absorb as much of the radiation as possible, eventually enough to bring levels down safe enough for the city to rebuild and repopulate. Unfortunately, the radiation eventually brought an end to Human Battery. Since then, The Terror Tribe has robbed countless banks, businesses and wealthy individuals. They have murdered numerous important people, including a couple of politicians and some of our bravest heroes. Their list of crimes continues to grow with each passing moment. Slowly, we have come to know that they have multiple locations being used as hideouts throughout the country, with the main base of operations somewhere on the east coast. We are closing in on these and hope to have one in the near future to provide us with important intel. One overwhelming fact remains. Their financial scores have grown larger, and certain crimes are being centered around facilities being targeted for specific items, with speculation that there is something big on the horizon. We have reviewed their pattern of heists and cannot at this time conclude what their plans really are. Top priority should be given to further the development of these young heroes, in preparation for the worst possible scenario."

"Now, as much as things have advanced, we realized that we had a couple of issues to address. One being that we needed to set up an end goal for the heroes in training. Once our early recruits have developed to the point of graduating and needing to venture out on their own, we set up and established the premier hero team,

Enter Alexavier

The United, which actually came from the ashes of The United Superheroes of America. This team's priority was to battle the major threats put forward by The Terror Tribe and any villains who dared to commit big enough or public enough crimes to require our attention. As time passed, more threats emerged, including new and more mysterious groups, like The Anarky Riders, Death and Debauchery and the highly secretive Order of the Right. This brought about another issue. Since we had new threats to combat, the core of the team at The Program needed to be overhauled, becoming much more specialized. Our needs changed, and we looked to select very special individuals that would make this team into the premier hunting weapon to finally make a difference in a much stronger and direct way. The young man we have here today is the result of many years of preparation to finally develop a super recruit in hopes that he will finally put this team over the top. He is the most accomplished and progressive recruit in the history of The Program. Ladies and Gentlemen, I give you the newest member of our team, Alexavier Vankendreh'd, the young hero known as Dread."

Amid lots of stares, Alexavier remained still as the Major held up a folder. "Please open the folder labeled Dread, #0920 where you will find detailed information.

Pointing to the LCD screen behind him, the Major continued, "Alexavier is a graduate of The Program complex in Philadelphia. He is nineteen years old, six feet tall and weighs one hundred and ninety-five pounds. He has a classification as a Non-Meta Human. For the people new to COSHAD, Meta Humans possess powers that are beyond normal human capabilities; super human powers like flight or energy blasts. Non-Meta Humans, sometimes referred to as Mutates, simply have standard human capabilities, but they far surpass the normal human range. Common abilities include extremely enhanced speed, agility, stamina and recovery. These powers are well beyond most notable human counterparts, but not in the realm of being classified a Meta Human. What all of that means is that as a Non-Meta, Alexavier's powers are all natural, physical abilities which have been enhanced through our advancements in training and use of Sessions."

"Originally enrolled in The Program at the age of six, Alexavier stood out early in his development. Trainers and instructors found his learning and adaptation skills well beyond all other recruits. Within a couple years, he was accelerated into the advanced classes with other qualified students. With his particular skill set, combat and defense were the focal point of his extensive training. He is fluent in every known martial art, as well as use of weapons in all forms, but he does not usually carry them. The equipment he does employ starts with a special pair of glasses that provides him a multitude of viewing options, including night vision, thermal, ultraviolet, flash protection and telescopic and microscopic functions. These have proved extremely useful for his roles of recon and stealth. He also wears a small belt that hides necessary tools that might be needed during missions. His training has been further enhanced with battlefield and tactical simulations, guerrilla warfare training and stealth techniques for covert spy and reconnaissance missions."

"While most other Non-Meta recruits would plateau with their powers, Alexavier has continued to improve and is still on the upswing." Turning to see the screen, Major Constantine hits a button, making a complex graph appear. "As you can see, the improvements of his performance numbers are steady, yet increasing. The only hitch in his progression has been due to a couple of specialized training events that he was sent to participate in, like combat evaluations and stealth exercises. Otherwise, he has had Sessions leading to regular enhancements and has responded exceptionally well, even retaining memories, which required less backtracking for his training."

A new COSHAD official raised her hand, "Explain to me about the Sessions and what they are."

"Sessions are the main process for maximizing our hero's abilities. Our recruits are given treatments that help amplify their powers and advance their development.

Enter Alexavier

Everything happens in the Session Chair, which when recruits are strapped in and receive prescribed treatments from our doctors. These include sound waves, mild radiation, light pulses, injectable drugs and various other stimuli. Although there are both physical and mental side effects, the physical ones are considered minimal. Whereas, we have noticed that the mental adverse reactions center on memory loss. Long-term memories seem to be affected with permanent loss happening, but don't hinder the recruit's development. Short-term memory loss is more noticeable, however with enough time and work, all recruits advance forward with minimal signs of rework and retraining. Amazingly, these issues seem to have a lesser effect on Alexavier. He makes advancements in all of his physical attributes, and for the most part doesn't lose his memories like the other recruits. Why Sessions do not affect him as much is still a mystery to our scientists." The Major looked around for any further questions.

The same official asked, "How often do they get a Session?"

"It can be utilized as often as needed depending on the recommendations from the team of doctors, psychologists and managing staff. Page six in your folder provides some further details about the process," the Major said, flipping through his copy.

A different COSHAD member asked, "Wait. I thought those Sessions caused memory loss to everyone. But you're saying he doesn't suffer from it?"

"That's what we've encountered for the most part," the Major explained. "One of the side effects from the power enhancement of a Session is the loss of memory. We cannot pinpoint the exact cause of these deficits. In most cases, some recovery time is needed, but the recruits eventually return to their duties with some retraining. The loss of memory is never so severe as to put a recruit in any state of mental distress. Once sufficient recovery time has passed, minimal debriefing is needed before they are back to active status. Even some of our best heroes in the past, who have handled the Sessions well, like Union, Intergalactic and Omega Knight, are nowhere near having

Enter Alexavier

the retention of memories that Alexavier displays. When we started working with Alexavier, we quickly discovered his recovery time was far less than everyone before him. Through all of his Sessions, he has retained almost all of his short-term memories. Some Sessions have occurred with no measurable loss of memory on any level. All he needed was minimal rest until the next day's training regimen and he had all memories restored. Since he has handled them so, we have been developing much more robust treatment Sessions, with Alexavier in mind. These new regimens have not been tested, and it is still too early to give the green light. At this point it is unknown how he or any recruit will tolerate a stronger Session. Previous incidents and issues have stalled any implementation. Until such time as the kinks can be worked out, we expect excellent results from Alexavier with his current Session treatment regimen."

An Army officer inquired, "What can you tell us about the fatalities that have happened during these Sessions? Are any of these related to the problems you mentioned?"

The question appeared to annoy Major Constantine. "The incidents in question were unfortunate, but were also unforeseen. We do everything possible to ensure the safety of our recruits through this difficult process, but as you are aware, problems can arise. We do not believe that the Sessions had anything to do with the deaths. These occurrences have been well documented. If there is a need to acquire further information on these incidents, please contact me. I will provide it for you later."

The Major looked back at the screen before quickly continuing with his presentation. "With new graduates, we have always had an endpoint, determined by the doctors regarding the cap on their powers. With the consistent gains made over the course of Alexavier's training, the doctors have declined to set any sort of cap at this time."

One of the military officers spoke up. "What does that mean in terms of his potential? So you're saying there's no ceiling to how far his abilities can go? From your report a few years ago, I thought the recruits top out."

"That was true from those reports. As for right now, we have no idea when or where Alexavier's powers will peak." A push of the button changed the screen again as the Major continued, "Here are some other Non-Meta recruits who have come through here. As you can see, Alexavier has performed and developed well beyond any of the others and past our projected goals. The development of most of our recruits stalls nearing the ages of thirteen to fourteen, with only slight improvements after that point. It takes consistent work and maximizing our efforts to get real results. Alexavier has continued to improve beyond our expectations. Until such time as this line on our chart starts to plateau, we will monitor his progress carefully, while moving forward with no thought of an end to his full potential. His training from here on shall include enhancements for combat and defense, but focused on specialized combat and stealth tactics that are not currently fulfilled by other members of The Program. My team is optimistic that Alexavier will rapidly evolve into the hero we urgently need."

"He has progressed further and faster than any previous recruit, with a performance record unlike any other." The Major hit the button on the podium, flipping through several screens until he reached the desired one to display. "In competitions between Program facilities, he has a perfect combat ratio with no losses. Every training goal has been met and exceeded by more than 70 percent. His ability to handle dangerous situations, although not tested in the field yet, is far beyond expectation. A true, front line, hand-to-hand warrior is a part of this team that we are currently missing. He not only fills that gap, but he may be the best to ever come out of the development facilities as a physical weapon. He has a long road ahead before going on missions, which are a necessity if he wants to become granted active status of The United. I have complete faith in him and his abilities. He is the shining star of

Enter Alexavier

The Program."

A General asked, "His record shows instances of insubordination over an eight-month period. Are we going to have issues now that he is here?"

"There should be nothing carrying over from his time in Philadelphia."

"How do you know that?" the General inquired. "Transgressions happening over such a long period usually mean a deeper problem, one that can easily resurface."

Major Constantine stepped away from the podium, standing a little closer to his star recruit. "Alexavier's behavior stemmed from frustrations of feeling stagnant. Those incidents, while wrong, were very minor and the product of a young man with such a strong desire to succeed. Being in one place for as long as he was, brought about a little frustration. Once he had time and coaching to understand what he needed to do and how to do those things, he became an overachiever in the best way possible. Other recruits might have made it here sooner. But for what we need of him, he accomplished all the requirements two years ahead of schedule. There should be no further incidents from this point forward."

Another COSHAD member wondered, "And what if he fails?"

The Major stared back defiantly, responding quickly, "He will not fail."

The Senator followed up with another question, "Will he be scheduled for hero training for public or civilian situations?"

"All recruits follow the same protocol for training in those areas. Once he has had sufficient training, and we can clear him for missions, then specific classes will be assigned to teach him how to deal with the public as a hero."

"What is his stance on becoming a hero and how is he going to achieve that status?" one of the Colonels asked.

The Major turned to the stoic, young hero. "I think Alexavier can answer that for himself. Son?"

"As far back as I can remember, I have always wanted to be like Sam Nelson,"

Enter Alexavier

Alexavier stated proudly. "All of the comic books I read of him and the Saturday morning cartoons I watched have influenced me to be like him. When you're so young and being trained to be a superhero, eventually you pick someone to emulate. Seeing Sam Nelson as The Patriot Warrior defeating criminals and saving citizens inspired me to do everything to be like him. I swore one day that I would continue his legacy. Everything I have done in training and classes has been to get to that goal. Whatever is needed of me, no matter the training or exercises, I will do it to the best of my abilities. My plan is to join The United sooner than any other recruit and bring down The Terror Tribe. I might have big dreams, but I believe I have the ability to make that happen, if you allow me the chance to prove it to you."

Senator Steinberg had a stern look on his face as he asked, "Are you ready and willing to commit to The Program one hundred percent?"

"I made that commitment when I was six years old. I am still committed to that today, sir." Alexavier's answer brought a collective, silent approval among the people in the room.

The Senator was first to exclaim, "I believe we have all we need. If I can say for the rest of us, welcome to The REAL Program."

CHAPTER 3

The audience of government officials rose from the table, with clapping overshadowing the small talk coming from the eager group. In a systematic manner, each person made their exit path past Alexavier to congratulate him. After many handshakes, the room had mostly emptied, leaving only the necessary people behind for him to meet.

"Alexavier Vankendreh'd, this is Senator Frank Steinberg." The Major began his formal introductions. "He's one of the main benefactors of the entire Program."

"I've been waiting to meet you since the stories from Philadelphia began trickling down a few years ago. How are you doing?" the Senator asked.

Alexavier replied, "Good, sir. I can't wait to get the training underway."

"I like the enthusiasm. You'll be under way very shortly. And don't be so formal. Call me Senator," he joked.

"Yes, sir."

"I'll be stopping by periodically to see your progress. Congratulations, Alexavier."

"Thanks again, sir." A last handshake, and Alexavier watched the Senator walk outside.

The Major finalized the meeting, allowing the mass of men in suits to leave before turning to his star pupil. "When they are done with you, our ride awaits."

After enduring a plethora of compliments and handshakes, Alexavier was more than ready to leave. Following a few last-minute instructions, he gathered his things and headed for the exit with the Major.

Pushing the door open to the world outside, Alexavier saw a courier vehicle waiting with the engine running and doors open. Carrying so much stuff made it slightly difficult to hurry, but each step put him closer to his long-term goal, and it drove him harder. Setting his bags down, he exhaled while turning back for one last glance at the complex. The look on his face was mostly relief, but with a little sorrow mixed in, knowing good friends would be left behind.

The Major was already in the courier vehicle, in the middle of an important call. "They may be gone when the team arrives. Update me as soon as you have any more information or when they are engaging The Tribe." He hung up and placed his papers on the seat. He quickly became impatient. "The time for sentiment is over. Did you bring the glasses?"

"Got 'em in the case, sir."

"Good. Grab your hero outfit and bring it with you. I might need to evaluate the upgrades to your suit." The Major turned to the driver. "Load the rest of his gear, so we can get underway"

The driver nodded, as Alexavier entered the vehicle with some reluctance, setting his duffel bag on the seat in front of him. He would never give up this opportunity. But from the first time he had met the Major, there was an overwhelming feeling of unease every time he was around this particular military man. An unusual sensation of dread had Alexavier keep the Major at arm's length. Still, with this journey leading to better things, he would do his best to enjoy the ride, even with Major Constantine sitting next to him. He leaned over toward the other side, just to lessen the feeling.

Once the driver had finished loading the vehicle and returned the driver's seat, the Major instructed him, "No disruptions during the whole trip. "Once we're outside the city, take some scenic back roads. Don't draw any unnecessary attention. Got it?" The driver nodded his head.

Enter Alexavier

The Major shut his door. "There are some refreshments in the fridge, in case we don't arrive by lunch. Help yourself to whatever you want."

"Cool." Alexavier sat back, trying to get comfortable for the ride. Even though he had finally nestled in the plush seat, he continued to be antsy, as they pulled away for what he hoped would be the last time. His saddened goodbye was camouflaged by the growing smile as the building slowly shrank in the distance.

For the next couple of hours, Alexavier stared out the window, soaking in the scenery and colors while taking in every little nuance of the countryside that passed in front of him. Green trees mixed with blue skies and every color of flower imaginable. Even though he's had opportunities to leave the complex, as limited in number as they were, this was his ride to his new home, and the world seemed more wonderful than anything he could have dreamed of.

#

Halfway through the uneventful journey, while looking over some of Alexavier's gear, the Major realized that not a word had been spoken. He glanced over to Alexavier, seeing him taking in the scenery that raced by. Wondering about the young man's state of mind, he inquired, "Enjoying the countryside? I know you recruits don't get really the chance to get out much, especially lately."

Alexavier continued facing the window. "We don't, except for a little time in the courtyard or when our training requires it. Plus, when we do, it's still downtown Philadelphia."

"Staring at buildings doesn't excite you when you're inside them all the time, huh?"

"That's why I try to sit in the shade of a tree on a nice spot of green grass whenever I can. There's one in the courtyard back at the complex, but nothing beats a nice field

Enter Alexavier

with a cool breeze."

"I can promise you, there will be plenty of opportunities to get away from the complex. There will be lots of chances to do recon and scouting. Missions happen quite frequently. But while on them, most of your time won't be spent sightseeing. I'm pretty sure this will be a change you will like."

"How soon before I can start taking on bad guys?"

The Major placed a boot on the seat next to him. "We usually ease new recruits into life at the complex. Since you've just graduated, we have a good idea of where you're at in your training. You're now here to hone those skills and add any necessary ones to complete your skill set. You're the exception with your already high level of skills and abilities. But in all fairness, graduates are brought here to use what powers they have and slowly work them into the missions. Essentially, if the opportunity arises to show your skills, especially to get to go on missions, make the best of it." The Major leans closer to Alexavier, "This is the big time. Everyone here is very close to becoming a member of the United, and it only takes a couple of really good performances to get there."

"Does everyone go on missions together or are there individual assignments?"

"Missions will involve most of the team, with the members chosen based on the needs of the mission parameters. If we are going in strong, those with strength and fighting ability will be priority. The team make up for each mission will be individualized."

"Working with others as a team will be a nice change. Hopefully I will be to see Beth and Dave again. I haven't hung out with them in forever."

The Major paused awkwardly, not wanting to continue the conversation, but luckily the driver called backed, "Major, I have an in-coming call for you."

He quickly picked up the phone. "Go ahead. Has the team reached North Carolina?"

Enter Alexavier

Alexavier continued to gaze outside while only hearing the one-sided conversation.

"Okay. Where?"

Alexavier could hear the change in tone and turned to look.

"No. We're on Highway 1, taking a less conspicuous route. Bel Air is only a couple miles from our current location." The Major paused, thinking hard. "How far are the teams?"

With his interest peaked, Alexavier now had his full attention on each spoken word by the Major.

"If it's only Mega Conductor and Glutton, this should be an in-and-out job. Suit up the tactical team. Divert the heroes on the mission in North Carolina, but have the cleanup crew take care of the aftermath. As soon as tactical is ready, let me know. With this just happening, we should catch them off guard and-" The Major looked over at Alexavier. "Wait. I think I have an idea. Plus, we're already here. Let me know immediately when the tactical team is on their way."

Hanging up the phone and with a slight smirk and handing Alexavier his mask, the Major announced, "Put your suit on. I guess your first mission is coming sooner than you had hoped, kid."

CHAPTER 4

A cloud of dust was kicked up as the courier vehicle skidded to an abrupt halt. The passenger door swung open quickly, with Alexavier jumping out in his all black outfit, pulling his hood over his masked face. An indiscernible shout from inside the vehicle caught his attention, he turned back to see the Major exiting.

"Here!" Tossing an earpiece quickly toward the young hero. "Put it in and listen for instructions."

With a bit of hurried fumbling, Alexavier reached under his mask, able to securely place the device in his ear. Turning to the scene of interest, he noticed a small hole busted through the wall at the rear of a building. Spectators began to congregate in large numbers with more approaching with each passing moment. Bolts of electricity shot out of the small hole every couple of seconds. Even with the possible danger, people wandered from the road to take a peek into the crumbling wall. A rather large individual stumbled out, carrying stacks of cash while swallowing them one after another. Dragging a few bags loaded with money, his partner in crime had electric sparks shooting out from his body with each step taken. Both halted once they saw Alexavier and the Major, looking at each other, unsure of what to do next.

"Remember your training," the Major said. "We have Glutton and Mega Conductor here."

Alexavier nodded, "One consumes things. The other emits electricity."

"Be aggressive. These are actual Terror Tribe members. Alexavier..." He looked

Enter Alexavier

back to hear the Major's energizing words. "Take them down."

With a tug of his hood over his head and a determined snarl, the hero began a fast sprint. The villains ceased their escape, with Glutton quickly trying to consume every bundle of money within reach. Mega Conductor threw his hands out, charging his body for the inevitable encounter. Alexavier approached the villains at high speed, focusing on the possible flash of electricity coming his way.

"Getting close to Mega Conductor will be hard and dangerous. Keep your distance and go for Glutton."

Alexavier ignored the Major's words, dancing sideways and slipping by the sparks that started erupting from the ground all around his feet. A look of surprise washed over the villain's face as the young hero was on him in an instant and shoved him in the chest. Mega Conductor landed on his back, with his body hurting as much as his ego.

Seeing his partner taken down, Glutton stuffed a few more stacks of cash down his throat and began to waddle toward Alexavier from behind. Feeling a bit uneasy, Alexavier turned to face the lumbering bad guy. Being so unimposing, Alexavier would have thought Glutton might back away, but he didn't.

Before the two could clash, the Major called over through the earpiece, "Be aware. From our last two encounters, Glutton has acquired the ability to absorb various forms of attack. It's as if he's become a human rubber ball."

"That makes it harder." Alexavier slowed up and took up a fighting stance, waiting for the encounter to happen.

Just as he felt the awkward sensation, a jolt of electricity hit Alexavier. He twitched and shook, until Mega Conductor eased up the attack. With an oddly sounding chuckle stemming from the money still in his mouth, Glutton began a slow charge. Making it close enough, he tried to leap into what resembled a belly flop. Alexavier easily rolled away and planted a kick to the side of Glutton's face. Just as

Enter Alexavier

the Major started yelling through the earpiece, Alexavier's foot bounced off as the obese villain's head bobbled around. Another shot from Mega Conductor landed close by, moving Alexavier several feet away.

"Don't take them both on! If they double-team you, you could be in big trouble. Go after one of them. Divide and conquer!"

Once again, the Major's words seemed inconsequential. Alexavier had confidence in his skills and charged them both. His path began heading directly at Mega Conductor. As he prepared to confront the oncoming hero, Alexavier changed direction, making a beeline for Glutton. With his heftiness working against him, Alexavier was able to close the distance so fast that Glutton couldn't get out of the way. But where Alexavier had hoped to the use extra force that would compensate for the elastic effects of the chubby villain, he simply bounced off and tumbled down the dusty alley.

With enough distance between the young hero and his partner, Mega Conductor released a heavy bolt of electricity. It nearly hit Alexavier, but he had rolled away, getting his feet back underneath him. The electrifying villain shot a few more bolts, slowly moving Alexavier back and creating enough distance to feel comfortable.

"What's your name kid?" Mega Conductor yelled, looking to gain a little bit of information about his new adversary.

"Remember, use your code name," the Major's voice rang out in Alexavier's ear.

"My name is Dread."

"Never heard of you. And nobody will ever hear of you if you don't get out of our way." Mega Conductor raised his hands, as if to issue a threat, while Glutton returned to stuffing wads of cash down his throat.

"Can't do that. You've committed a crime. Now you're going to pay."

"Oh, I'm scared. Glutton! We're leaving!"

From Alexavier's ear, he heard the Major say, "Call him Electrode."

Enter Alexavier

"Look Electrode, I'm not leaving until I have your face down on the ground."

That appeared to anger the villain. "I'm Mega Conductor!" A large bolt of electricity flew through the air, hitting the ground near Alexavier.

"That was his name when he was with The Program," the Major explained. "He hates being called that."

After side stepping the attack, Alexavier noticed the crowd kind of close to the battlefield and issued a challenge to keep the villains attention. "You missed again, Electrode."

The sparks and flashes started to increase with intensity as Mega Conductor shouted in anger. His attempt to finally land the one hit became an effort to throw as many shots as possible. Alexavier's ability to evade made the attack look more like a fireworks display. After dodging the onslaught, he sprinted hard for a full on assault. Putting both of his hands together, Mega Conductor unleashed the monster of all shock attacks. But Alexavier's quick reflexes had him sliding underneath, planting his feet right in front of the bad guy, coming up and jumping in the air, thrusting both feet to his chest. The exchange of energy sent Mega Conductor flying backwards. His landing was hard, causing him to shout out in pain.

Glutton spit up a few stacks of cash in disbelief. With a slightly determined look on his face, as well as trying to swallow more money, he lumbered over in hopes of helping his downed comrade. But with his lack of speed and quickness, any attempt was easily dodged allowing Alexavier to throw a few punches. Unfortunately, anything connecting with Glutton's body, easily bounced right off.

"Don't try any direct attacks. You're not going to hurt him."

"Got it!" Alexavier stood up straight, inviting Glutton to take another shot. He tried with all he could muster, but the hero simply ducked and weaved. Glutton stumbled along, trying to stay close for each swing, but each time he was just out of arm's reach. After throwing about a dozen punches, Glutton began to huff and puff,

Enter Alexavier

with every subsequent attack lacking energy. Finally, after having a difficult time raising his arms in between heavy breaths, Alexavier leaped forward, landing behind the winded villain and jumping on his back. Wrapping his arms around Glutton's throat, Alexavier grasped and squeezed, cutting off the oxygen, causing him to spew out money. Seeing his partner in crime struggle, Mega Conductor shocked them both, sending the hero to the ground with his muscles having spasms.

Alexavier scrambled to his feet, as he desperately tried to regain the use of his muscles. He leaned toward Glutton, but quickly changed direction and surprised Mega Conductor, grabbing his arm and tossing him into Glutton.

Glutton whimpered, looking back at his cohort for support. Mega Conductor's surprise was of little help. Not liking being beaten, Mega Conductor sprinted over, grabbing a bystander in hopes of changing the odds in his favor. "You can stay back! We'll just be on our way!"

"I'm not letting you go!"

"I don't care about this woman! She means nothing to me, and I'll shock her dead if you don't back off!"

"Just so you know, if you hurt her, I'll cause you so much pain and agony that you'd dream of a lifetime in a jail cell."

Although Mega Conductor didn't blink, hearing those threatening words scared Glutton, who stumbled closer to hide behind his comrade. The duo slowly started to move away, but Alexavier jumped ahead and cut them off.

A bit annoyed, Mega Conductor tightened his grip around her neck. He lifted his free hand and produced impressive electric bolts. "I'm not kidding!"

The standoff became more intense as Alexavier stood his ground. His eyes moved about, studying the situation.

"This is going to be on you!" A small shock was sent through the young lady's back, buckling her legs as she screamed in pain. Mega Conductor held on, smirking

Enter Alexavier

with confidence. "Come any closer, and I'll fry her!"

Feeling the situation deteriorate, Alexavier slowed up, cautiously moving his feet around him without taking his eyes off the villains. The fidgeting motion soon stopped, placing his left foot under a moderately sized stone. "I'm calling your bluff. Do it."

The words shocked the two bad guys freezing them in their steps. Not sure of whether to go through with their threat gave Alexavier the moment he needed. Flipping the rock into the air, he grabbed it. With one quick motion, he heaved it at the electrifying villain, nailing him in the shoulder most visible. Mega Conductor yelled out, releasing his hostage. She slumped to the ground, as both villains became confused and desperate. Mega Conductor threw his arm out, sending a massive electric bolt that splintered through the air, hitting Alexavier in the chest. His muscles contracted, until the bolt disappeared and he collapsed, twitching and shaking.

Mega Conductor raised his arms, generating tremendous amounts of energy that poured from his body, causing everything around him to explode. One such target was the wall from which the villains had escaped at the back of the bank. Several bolts tore apart the foundation causing it to break apart slowly and crumble. Suddenly, the entire wall broke free and started to collapse in the path of the once captive woman. Alexavier raised his head to see, yelling out to no avail. She stood there frozen with the falling wall nearly on top of her. Out of nowhere, she was snatched away by Alexavier, who flew through the air as if he had the power to fly. The wall landed making a thunderous boom, sending dust and debris into the air. As the cloud began to clear with the breeze that had been blowing, Alexavier rolled away from cradling the young lady, both appearing to be unharmed. After asking if she's okay and receiving a reassuring nod, he turned his attention back to the villains who appeared to have vanished. Before Alexavier could give pursuit, the Major called to him through the earpiece. "Hold on, Dread!"

Enter Alexavier

"But sir! I can catch-"

"Bring it in, kid! They're long gone. Plus, there's a growing scene of spectators. Head back to the vehicle. We need to get back on schedule for our arrival at the complex."

Halfheartedly, Alexavier complied while making his way to the vehicle, still scanning for the villains. Arriving quickly to the vehicle, he opened the door and slipped in. Still having that uneasy feeling, he leaned over to the far side, pulled off his hood, glasses and mask, continuing to catch his breath.

The Major had just made a call on the phone, bellowing orders to the people back at the complex. "I did try to disrupt them with Alexavier. Redirect the cleanup team. If anyone from The United is close enough, send whoever is available to track them down. With Glutton in tow, they can't move too fast, so you might be able to catch up to them. We'll be back on the road in a few minutes. I'll be expecting an update from you when I arrive."

Alexavier had been listening in, but played it off as if he wasn't. The Major hung up the phone, smiling from ear to ear. His star pupil had his first villain encounter, displaying his skills that reinforced his decision to advance him in The Program. None of this mattered to Alexavier, as he was still focused on capturing the villains.

"Are you sending a team after them, sir?"

"We have dispatched one of our best, with instructions to hunt them down. If we can capture one of them, it's possible to extract some valuable information."

"Haven't you captured Tribe members before?"

"We have. In fact, we did capture Max Towers just last week. But it's been over a year since bringing anyone back for questioning. Any information we've gathered back then is not useful anymore. And with Max Towers not being a close enough, regular member of The Terror Tribe, I'm not too optimistic about what we can get from him. It's imperative that we start making better progress toward bringing The

Tribe down. Getting any one of them, especially a core member, is our top priority."

"My skills would have allowed me to easily catch and secure them. If we head back now, I know I can-"

"I truly like your enthusiasm, but sometimes you need to know when the fight is over. You're going to do special things at The Program. But for now, we have to get you back so you can officially become a part of the team. Since you haven't been transferred yet with proper credentials and status, I really shouldn't have sent you to confront them."

"I've worked hard, sir. I've put in more time than anyone else to make myself better. You can trust me to do my best, including taking either one of them down."

"Don't worry. You'll have lots of chances to bring back a Tribe member. I'm counting on it. For now, relax from your encounter for the rest of this trip. We've got a little while before we arrive."

"Yes, sir." Full of adrenaline and stored up energy, it was a bit difficult to sit back without doing what he had been trained to do for so many years. But trying to divert his attention wasn't easy, even when watching the scenery pass by. All he could do was stare out the window and tap his fingers. Alexavier may not have been enthused about the end result, but the Major sporting a big smile was very thrilled.

Enter Alexavier

CHAPTER 5

Alexavier peered through the thick trees lining the long entry road. If this building was supposed to be kept out of sight, it was a job well done. After a lengthy ride down the stretched blacktop, an old gray building came into view.

"Welcome to your new home." The Major's words brought a sense of awe, but the building was a disappointment. Its appearance was that of a long forgotten factory, and Alexavier couldn't see anything pleasant among the old windows and weathered brick walls.

As the courier vehicle slowly pulled around the corner to the back of the building, life began to emerge. This back area was heavily fortified with guard stations surrounding the perimeter and a firing range that was currently in use. They pulled into a parking lot near the entrance to the building. There was no big fanfare for Alexavier's arrival, nor any big welcome signs or colorful balloons.

After finishing changing into his grey hooded sweatshirt and stretching from the long ride, Alexavier walked to the back of the courier vehicle, eager to get started as the Major emerged. "Don't worry about the bags. We'll have them put in your room. For now, we have something to take care of. It's time to meet your new family."

Alexavier followed Major Constantine ventured through the building offices toward an elevator. As they arrived, Alexavier looked around, trying to get a better sense of his surroundings. Not quite sure what to think, his eyes focused on the Major, which brought back that eerie feeling.

Enter Alexavier

For as long as he could remember, Alexavier had gotten certain feelings about the people he meets, a sixth sense in a way. When he encountered someone that could be suspicious or potentially dangerous, his body told him to become guarded. He had learned to trust these feelings a long time ago, and it had kept him out of trouble too many times to count, especially when taken out into the public for training purposes.

The elevator doors opened with the Major entering first. Alexavier paused for a second, held up by that strange sensation again. Major Constantine turned around with a glare of impatience, prompting Alexavier to join him.

The doors closed just before a warning alarm sounded, and the elevator started a slow descent into the lower depths of the building. Pushing the intercom button, the Major barked into the speaker, "Get all respective parties together in the W.A.R. Room for our arrival."

"Yes, sir."

The awkwardness ended as they reached their desired floor, allowing Alexavier to quickly step out. He was awestruck. The entire complex appeared to be an underground, mad scientist lair, crossed with a secret government facility. Being led down the main hall, he stared into the many glass walled rooms, the most prominent of which was the command center, filled with military and government officials.

Turning the corner to the next hallway, Alexavier peeked through a door and was startled with a sight he had hoped never see again, a massive Session Room, with an even more ominous looking Session Chair. Sessions were a big part of all Program recruits, as well as Alexavier's life in Philadelphia. These Sessions were used to heighten a young person's powers and help them to reach their full potential, but at a cost. It was routine to go through this process, producing good results. But for Alexavier, terrifying memories came with the harsh treatments that were given during them. His hopes of never seeing one again were broken. Distracted, Alexavier ran into one of the guards escorting him.

Enter Alexavier

"Sorry," he said apologetically, stepping around the guard, continuing down the hallway.

The Major slowed at an open doorway. "Wait in here."

Alexavier entered a sparsely decorated room, taking a seat at the conference table. The Major vanished, and several minutes passed, as the bland walls eventually allowed boredom to set in. Looking out the open door, he noticed that most of the people walking by were in uniform. Every so often, a much younger person passed by, wearing plain clothes. He kept his concentration focused, hoping to spot more. Could these people be his new teammates?

Suddenly, he noticed a blond girl accompanied by three young men. He leaned as far as he could to try to get another glimpse. Once she was beyond his field of vision, Alexavier jumped up and rushed toward the door. His head poked outside as he peered down the crowded hall, but numerous people blocked the sight of her. He couldn't be sure if that was Beth. His body swayed, as his gawking caused him to accidentally bump into the same guard again. "Sorry."

"Please step back into the room and remain seated."

Alexavier acknowledged the assertive guard, looking back one last time before going inside. Settling into the chair, he watched the doorway, just in case the girl returned.

Looking on from a secret room behind mirrored glass, several complex officials evaluated the young hero while he waited. They stared silently, waiting for something to jumpstart them into conversation. Major Constantine's entrance did just that.

"Gentlemen, here is our newest recruit." The Major closed the door behind him.

The men in the darkened room mumbled among themselves until a voice spoke up. "So, this is our golden child. Not much to look at."

"That might be," the Major responded, "but it's not his appearance we care about."

"And you still can't pinpoint the origin of his powers?" a grizzled voice came from the back of the small room.

Major Constantine continued to stare at the young hero. "Zero luck. All we can tell you is what he can do, but how is still a mystery. After we get him situated, further testing can begin per our doctor's advanced procedures."

The grizzled voice replied, "Maybe those standard tests need to be looked at as much as we're looking at this kid?"

Another voice chimed in, "He's too new to know whether or not he'll become a hero. How do you think he'll hold up?"

The Major replied, "We'll know soon enough."

#

Enough time passed, and Alexavier started to tire from watching people walk by. Thankfully, his sightseeing ended once Major Constantine returned and instructed the guards, speaking softly. Once finished giving commands, he turned to Alexavier. "Let's go, son."

Alexavier jumped up to follow the Major, as several guards took up the rear. They headed in the same direction as the blond girl and her friends. But then the group turned down a different corridor and toward a set of double doors, just behind the command center. As they approached, the soldiers standing guard quickly opened the rather large doors, not to slow down the caravan.

As Alexavier passed underneath, he read the words above the door that said, Workout And Reassessment Room, W.A.R. Room. His eyes moved down to see the vast space that was the complex training room, with various fixtures, objects and a set of steps loaded with all the heroes from The Program. He continued to scan the room while being lead just inside. Everyone stopped which allowed Alexavier to finally find those he had been hoping to see. Both Beth and Dave were near each other,

Enter Alexavier

mixed among a vast group of heroes. But even though he recognized them and had a delighted smile, they quickly looked over to him, turned back and kept putting on their gear. He kept staring, waiting for them to look back, but The Major shouted some instructions. "Okay, everybody! Our newest recruit has arrived! Be ready for a workout here with Alexavier in the next half hour to hour!"

The group gave a quiet acknowledgment before going back to their preparations, which disappointed Alexavier, as the Major guided him out of the room. He's so close to reuniting with old friends. But right now, the few feet of distance felt like hundreds of miles.

Enter Alexavier

CHAPTER 6

With the formalities having to wait with his new team, Alexavier stepped outside the W.A.R. Room to see a familiar face. The Major stepped in for another introduction. "Alexavier, I would like you to meet Mike Mackinaw. He is the main contact person here for the new members, so any questions can be directed to him."

"It's been a while, Alex," Mike said, shaking hands. "It appears your new regimens and training really paid off since I last saw you." Mike was an unassuming figure. His glasses, scruffy beard and less than fit body made him look more like a father figure, which was exactly his job at the complex, looking after the recruits.

Alexavier smiled. "Thanks to you. I worked my butt off with the plan you gave the doctors. When I met the goals, they were more than happy to recommend my graduation."

"I just gave them the gameplan. You did all the hard work, and it paid off"

"Thanks, but I still feel like I owe you."

"Are you getting sick of the hoopla?" Mike asked.

Alexavier laughed. "Somewhat. I hate having the suits around mostly. They just stare at you all the time."

"Just wait until you make it out of here and join The United," Mike said jokingly. "It will be even worse once you make the high level hero team. The United has Joe Public staring at them every time they hit the streets."

"I'd rather have them looking at me than the guys in uniform." Alexavier eyed the doorway, making sure no one could hear them.

"Be careful what you wish for," Mike said. "Not every citizen in this world is happy to see us. There are too many people who look at us as part of the problem and not the solution. I can't count how many times Sam or the Major has had to endure some crazed lunatic spewing garbage at him out in public, or even having things thrown at you when you're in the fight of your life. Well, when it happens to the Major it's kind of funny. But ask anyone from The United, and they will say it is much easier here."

Alexavier grudgingly accepted Mike's view. "I guess everyone here is supportive."

Mike placed his hand on Alexavier's shoulder. "Trust me. You'll probably have more support right now than any other time for the rest of your life. Everyone here wants nothing more than for all of the heroes to succeed. And I'm here for anything you may need. If you have questions, come to me. If you have any problems or concerns at any time, give me a holler. I help all of the recruits with getting acquainted to their new life. But right now, there are some other preliminary concerns. Have you had any labs done?"

"No. Not yet," Alexavier replied.

"That'll be one of your first stops," Mike explained. "I'm not sure when they're going to get measurements for your suit. I know they'll also have you go through the new recruit manual back in your room."

Alexavier sighed. "Sounds like fun. I hope there's caffeine. I'll probably need it. How soon before I get to try out for the missions?"

"That is all about your performance," Mike stated. "The better you do with workouts and progression in your training, the more likely that you can go. There's also the matter of you being needed for the mission. If your powers are to fly, but we need to go underwater, you might be staying back. Speaking of which, we should show you around so we can keep the train rolling. We've got a schedule to follow."

Enter Alexavier

Alexavier followed behind Mike, exiting the conference room and heading toward the center of the complex. The various rooms were described efficiently, as they passed them fairly quickly. For the time being, only a point of the finger showed Alexavier where he would spend his nights sleeping. The maze of corridors added to the unfamiliarity as they turned more corners. But luckily for Alexavier, their destination arrived quickly.

"Alright, here we are." Mike stood back, allowing the new recruit to pause close to the hangar. "I have to make a quick call. You're not afraid of needles are you?"

"Only big and pointy ones."

Mike smiled and rubbed his beard, but noticed the young hero pause. "Are you okay?"

"Yeah. I think it's starting to sink in that I'm finally here." Alexavier looked all around the vastly open area. "I had thought about this for years. And now I'm here."

"This is all you. You really wanted to become a hero. You put in the time. You overcame some obstacles. You did what you needed to do to get here. Some of the other recruits didn't put in the effort, and they're still back there. You worked hard, and you deserve it!"

"Thanks! Although, I might give you the names of a couple of people to consider."

"We'll talk about that later. I've got to make that call. Go get poked so this can all be official. Or, maybe the poke will wake you up from this dream you're having."

Letting out a chuckle, Alexavier turned away. "That's never going to happen." His appointment waited, although the stalling was just allowing more time for it to all soak in. A smile followed, brought about by that warm feeling of what was before him, the top level of The Program.

Enter Alexavier

CHAPTER 7

Cautiously, Alexavier walked towards the doctor's office, which had a large medical bay located adjacent to it and the hangar. Alexavier knocked on the door and waited. A few moments passed without anything happening, so he looked around the complex. It felt different than his former home in Philadelphia, but slightly familiar with similar colored drab walls. The hangar took on a futuristic feeling, with what looked like a jet helicopter straight out of a Hollywood movie. Its location near the infirmary was ideal for incoming injured heroes to receive necessary medical attention after intense combat. The sightseeing ended as the door to the doctor's office finally slid open and what he saw surprised him. Alexavier was used to working with older doctors from his experiences in Philadelphia, but today he was confronted with a much younger doctor. He judged that she was closer to his age and was of Asian or maybe Polynesian descent. He couldn't help but notice how young she was as well as being very attractive. She was at a table, finishing her prep work for his blood draw.
"Hi. How's the tour going?"
"Pretty good. Mike is a great tour guide, although I haven't seen everything yet."
"I'm Dr. Jean Dennis."
"Nice to meet you."
"Have you met the team?"
"Nope. I mean I saw them, but we're supposed to do that next. I'm excited to see

some friends I haven't seen in a while."

With a bit of concern on her face, the doctor asked, "You know everyone gets Sessions, right? And that they cause memory loss?"

"I know. I guess I'm hoping that maybe they'll still remember something."

"Don't get too discouraged if they don't. It's just a part of the process. Alright, have a seat right here, so I can get a blood sample." She patted the chair.

Sitting down and reclining back, he laid his arm on the armrest and waited for her to start. Checking out the office, he noticed a few degrees covering the walls. "You graduated Harvard? You can't be that much older than me."

"Actually, I'm only a couple of months older than you." She glanced at his file. "I started at Harvard when I was 12, just after I arrived at The Program. They discovered that I was exceptionally advanced compared to the other kids, as well as having very raw powers of healing. They decided to not only enhance these powers, but to send me to medical school to further the skills I needed for healing." She reached for his wrist, exposing the inner part of his arm. Grabbing a rubber tourniquet and wrapping it around his upper arm, she searched for the best vein to draw from.

Alexavier noticed how comfortable he felt when her hand touched him, causing the same sensation that swept over him before. "Do you make people relax and feel at ease too?"

She smiled, "You noticed. I had always had it, although it was very weak for most of the time. I developed it further when I found out how many people were so tense when they would be sent for tests or blood work, since so many people have a fear of needles. Does it help?"

"Yes. It's kind of a calming sensation."

"Okay. So, we're also going to get some follow up tests out of the way, and start to define the hows and wheres of your powers that no one can seem to define." She found the appropriate spot and reached for an alcohol swab. "Alright, you might feel a pinch or a small poke." He remained oblivious, as she took a syringe and pulled the cap off the needle, directing the syringe toward Alexavier's skin. For some reason, it became a bit tough at first. But with enough effort, a successful poke allowed the blood to fill the tube.

An interesting question popped into Alexavier's head. "Is this where you wanted to end up, being a doctor and not a superhero with the others?"

The doctor exchanged one of the tubes for another. "Sometimes I think it would be fun to run around saving people. There's not much excitement here, except when the injured come back on the helicopter. Patching up the usual bruises can get a little tedious."

"Did you ever ask about getting any kind of training?"

She switched tubes again. "I tried bringing it up once, but the Major didn't seem interested. I just let it go."

"If you want to, I can train with you. Anytime you feel like getting away from here and want to work on some technique, let me know."

"Maybe I'll do that. Even though I'm not in the action, I'm usually there. One of these days, I'm going to be cornered by someone. I need to know how to defend myself." Dr. Dennis removed the last tube and syringe from his arm. Quickly, she reached over, grabbed a swab and placed it at the needle puncture sight. "Okay, keep the pressure on." she stated as she finished collecting everything. After closing the case that housed the samples, Alexavier hopped down, allowing her to clean the chair with alcohol.

"So, one thing I was curious about is your memory retention. After a Session, you are able to keep memories better than anyone else. I've reviewed your files extensively. It's really quite remarkable."

"I don't know why I can. Well, I actually do a couple of things that seem to help. I had no clue how or why, or if they would even work, but over time these little things seem to help me. I mean I should be happy about it, but it makes me feel bad that everyone goes through Sessions and have to deal with all of that confusion."

"Don't feel bad. Most of the recruits don't have any idea who they are, where they are from or who their friends are. I understand that you've still retained memories of your parents?"

"I remember a bit about them, but what I do have is limited."

The doctor realized that she might be able to help. "I want you to come back in a day or two. I would like to see if you could recall some possible hidden memories with the help of a procedure that I have read about recently. It involves minimal sedation, and it works to clear your conscious mind, allowing your subconscious to open up. I've read some of the published clinical studies of how almost every participant was able to recover memories to some degree. I haven't been able to test it yet. But given your history, I think it would be worth trying."

"How much is there as far as drugs or treatments?"

She arranged more items for the next patient. "It will be just a mild sedative. The study showed that when participants are more relaxed, it was easier to recall suppressed memories. I think it might work for you. Are you interested?"

"Sure, I'll give it a shot."

"Great! I'll have everything I need in a few days after I review some of the case studies and the specific procedures used, but that won't take long."

Alexavier opened his arm back up, peeling off the unstained swab. "Thanks doctor."

"Call me Jean. It makes me feel old being called doctor all the time by people my own age."

"Okay. Thanks, Doctor Jean." He grinned.

"You're welcome." She returned the smile before continuing with her prep work.

Enter Alexavier

Alexavier looked down at the puncture site on his arm as he left her office with a smile. He started to feel really good that he might bring back part of his past that had long been lost.

Enter Alexavier

CHAPTER 8

As Alexavier stepped out of the doctor's office, Mike was still on the phone, although it sounded less like work. In mid-laugh, Mike turned around and saw that the appointment had concluded. A quick goodbye, and he was back at the doorway. "All good?"

"Yup. She wants to do try something to open up some past memories."

"Really? I didn't know she was into psychotherapy or dreams or stuff like that."

"She did say I'd need medications for it."

"Ah, that would make sense now. She's an internist and pharmacologist, but not a psychiatrist, although she is very talented. I wouldn't doubt that she could do anything if she got the chance. She moved up quickly after arriving here, and now she is the lead physician for the heroes."

"She seemed optimistic, much more than I am."

"Oh, one of the staff dropped off something. I have a new recruit manual that you will need to get acquainted with." Mike handed Alexavier a binder as they began walking. "After you get settled in your room later, you can read through it. I'm not sure if there's already one in your room or not. But right now, we'll do a quick introduction with the team. If you have any questions along the way, just ask? Any so far?"

"No, sir."

Enter Alexavier

"Well, that means I'm either doing great at my job, or I'm about to get fired. Just let me know if you see the Major looking really mad as he walks our way."

Mike's sarcasm had Alexavier laughing, enjoying Mike's sense of humor. General conversation between them continued as the maze of corridors led from one hallway to another. But luckily for Alexavier, they soon arrived at their destination, finally reaching the doors to the W.A.R. Room. Mike turned to Alexavier. "Let's do this."

With a slight hesitation, Alexavier walked into the room, noticing the gathering of people on some raised steps with the Major facing them. Almost everyone was about his age or slightly older. To his delight, he found a couple of familiar faces in the crowd. There was Beth standing near the back, which brought a smile to his face. He was thrilled to see her again, as well as Dave, who was standing next to her.

He followed Mike over to the Major. But before any formalities could happen, a Sargent entered the room in a hurry. "Major, we have yet to see Dwayne Cygnus this morning. In fact, he has yet to join any training sessions for the month."

A disgruntled rumbling left the Major's mouth. "Doctor, has he taken part in any scheduled events in his itinerary this week?"

A doctor replied, "No, sir."

"Excuse us, Alexavier. This will only take a minute." Major Constantine and the doctor vanished, following the Sargent outside. Standing alone in a room of unknown fellow heroes brought about some nerves. Although the familiar faces in Beth and Dave gave a little relief, something in his body started to scream very loudly. A feeling of extreme uneasiness made him turn toward a man hell bent on confrontation.

"So, you're the new brat, huh?"

Alexavier awkwardly said, "Hi."

"The name's James Killus, The Killing Machine."

"I'm Alexavier Va-"

"I know who you are. You're the Major's new puppy dog. Heard about your little exercise on the way here. I can't wait to-"

"Can't wait for what, Killus?" the Major queried with a stern look on his face, as he made his return.

Killus stepped back and smiled. "Just taking a break to meet the new guy before getting back to stomping people's faces in."

The Major stood next to Alexavier. "Take your place on the steps, James."

Killus walked away, but not before giving one last smirk. "Later, kid."

Major Constantine eyed the retreating hero while he flipped through the various pages contained in the folder. The slightly disorganized team had the Major wanting to begin the meeting, so he spoke up a bit louder. "Alright, everyone! Updates are as follows! Our efforts to halt monetary thefts by The Terror Tribe have been limited lately. Although we've been somewhat effective, they have been quite efficient at continuing their operations to illegally acquire funds from various financial sources. As of late, our usual intelligence gathering is no longer proving worth our time and limited financial backing. I have concluded that our intel gathering operations will be stepped up accordingly. Expect to be sent out at any moment." The Major turned to Alexavier. "We regularly send out members for recon. Our need to do so varies, but you could be sent out more than once a week, or up to weeks at a time. Readiness is a plus. For your first couple of recon details, you will be assigned a mentor or teammate. Listen and learn from them."

"The recent graduation of the former Elemental Mage, Ellen Tallmadge, who now goes by the name Riva, opens up many new opportunities for our tactical missions. As you know, every mission is a chance for you to prove your abilities to us, in hopes of joining The United."

The Major gave pointed looks at certain members in the room and lowered his voice. "Some of you have been trying my patience lately. Remember, the only way to show that you can handle the grind of a hero's life is through these missions.

Enter Alexavier

Listening to my commands, following orders, and supporting all of your teammates is essential. Use the recon time to solidify your teamwork skills. But remember, extreme caution should be used at all times. Wally was nearly discovered a few weeks ago. The media is looking for any morsel that they can about heroes, both good and bad. We don't need any unwanted attention for this organization. So watch your backs, as well as each other."

"The Terror Tribe activity has been sporadic lately. New leads have come in much slower. But with the little intel we've received, it suggests that they're planning bigger scores. Likely targets are banks, which Alexavier and I were involved in a heist of a bank this morning. Keep in mind, leads toward other avenues of gain are not out of the question. Hit your confidential informants hard. We need credible leads as to what they're planning. The low level of scores they've had in the past six months means that their financial status may have become dire. If we can choke them off of new money over the next month or two, they could become desperate and make a mistake."

"Any luck tracking Meta Wave Signatures?" Wally asked.

"Scanning hasn't turned up much. When using The Deerdron Scanner, it can detect Meta-Humans. Unfortunately, we haven't been successful recently in finding any signs of villain activity from their wave signatures. Apart from the obvious newly diagnosed Meta-Humans, we're pretty much in the dark."

"What about The Infamous One? Can you scan for him?" Alexavier asked.

Major Constantine turned to address Alexavier. "The Deerdron Scanner can only detect power signatures, particularly when they're using their powers. One would think being their leader would make him easy to detect. Unfortunately, The Infamous One's powers are not at the level of his cohorts. The former Midnight Thief has a limited power signature. One that doesn't hardly show, even when he's using his powers. Detecting the power signature of these villains has become very difficult.

Enter Alexavier

Each new generation of super-powered persons shows weaker power signatures, even if their powers are substantial. You could say that not only does The Infamous One hide in the shadows, but he can hide from our scanners too."

"However, we've had a little luck lately. The Cleveland incident was a big blow to their operations. Good job to Bobbie and Dave. Your tracking was picture perfect. And Beth, you did an outstanding job in protecting civilians, as well as capturing Max Towers. He is being handled by interrogators, as we speak. Although he isn't a regular core member of The Terror Tribe, we hope to have some information very shortly."

Major Constantine turned several pages, waiting for the ensuing applause to subside. "Now, we have to go over a few things before we really get down to business. First, we will be having updates to the security system over the next several weeks. This should not pose any real interruption, but be aware when you're exiting or entering the facility and rooms requiring card access."

"Second, we will be having visitors this week, including Senator Steinberg. It should be a standard tour, nothing more. Just remember to keep yourself to the rules of conduct while he's here. One wrong wise-crack, and you could be staying here instead of going on missions."

"Tomorrow, a Session is scheduled for Manny Batista." A quiet fell over the group, as the Major turned to Manny. "Be ready early, no later than 0800. We will be there to escort you to the Session Room for your 0830 appointment. See the doctor later today for the required blood work."

"Yes, sir." A solemn Manny bowed his head.

"Remember to help him in any way possible afterward," the Major said loudly. "Your support can make a difference."

Awkward silence ensued, before the Major spoke again. "Finally, let me introduce you all to your new teammate, Alexavier Vankendreh'd. All you need to know is in

Enter Alexavier

the packets that you received yesterday. If you haven't done so, familiarize yourself with the information on your own time, since I'll only be giving you a brief summary as usual."

"Alexavier is a graduate from the Philadelphia complex. He has high marks and progress that rivals or surpasses any grad so far. He's coming to us as a specialist in combat, both hand to hand and all forms of weaponry. He's also an expert in recon and intelligence gathering. Our assessment is that with minimal issues, Alexavier will be on missions and an integral part of this team very quickly. Welcome him as one of your own." Major Constantine motioned with his hand toward the new hero, as some of the group replied with hellos.

"Hi." Alexavier waved.

The Major began walking away. "If there are any questions that the packet can't answer, see myself or Mike. We have a full agenda for today, so let's not delay any longer. Alexavier, come over to the posts and hop up on the first one." The Major stopped near the first row of a strange field of posts and turned to Alexavier, who obliged.

Most people would be hard pressed to climb up onto a four-foot tall post. Having a higher degree of athleticism and greater strength in his legs than most, Alexavier bent down and jumped straight up, reaching the post in one strong vertical leap.

The Major continued, "This is our standard speed and agility test. We record the information and use it to mark improvements as your training progresses. All recruits receive this test, and it can be used as a benchmark in comparison to other recruits, and where they should and need to be. It can also determine the proper training or to make any necessary changes for each individual."

"Now for the test. The posts are three feet apart, from here to the wall. They stretch from each side of the gym as well. You can move in any direction, although there are a couple of restrictions. First, you have 30 seconds to get to the wall. Two, you can only hop on one foot, your right foot."

Some whispered comments came from the gathered heroes. Alexavier, on the other hand did not flinch.

"Furthermore, once you've reach the other side, you will have 15 seconds to reach this post you're standing on. You can do it by any means necessary. Understand?" Alexavier gave a nod. "This is pass or fail. If you fail, you might get the chance to try again next week, or you might be sent back to Philadelphia. If you pass, next week will include flaming arrows. I'm just kidding." Alexavier gave an odd look with Major Constantine's attempt at a joke being an obvious failure.

"I'll track the time," Mike stated.

"Remember, 30 seconds there and 15 seconds back. Good luck." The Major backed away.

Taking a deep breath, Alexavier crouched down, ready to spring into action. The Major looked back, slowly bringing an eventual hush to the room. Alexavier exhaled as he waited patiently, bowing his head while focusing. Eyeing his prized recruit, the Major waited a few more seconds to allow the dead silence to flood the room. Suddenly, he yelled, "Go!"

Alexavier leaped hard, hopping to the first post. Leaning forward to jump to the next, he gathered momentum as the crowd began to stir and cheer softly. He progressed along without incident. One by one, each post passed by effortlessly. Nearing the last couple of posts, a strange sensation came over him. Something inside his head screamed out loud, telling him to evade and get out of the way. In one fluid motion, Alexavier jumped in the air, twisting his body. A large steel block, suspended from the ceiling like a pendulum, nearly smashed into him. He successfully dodged it and landed solidly on the last post.

Turning quickly, he sprinted across the field of wood. More oncoming obstacles swung at different speeds, creating varying difficulties along the way. He traveled through the center of the field, looking to take the direct route. Out of nowhere, another hammer impeded his progress, forcing him to change his course. A quick spinning maneuver had him safely past the danger and keeping his hectic pace.

Disrupting his route to the final post was a set of three large hammers, swinging erratically. Alexavier pushed off hard enough to pass the first swinging hammer. Using his right hand to stabilize, he kicked with his feet. His legs cartwheeled over his body, barely bypassing the next obstacle. The move put him off balance, on a collision course with the last hammer. With all of his gathered momentum, he brought both feet together to spring into the air as hard as possible. The resulting burst of energy sent his body vaulting over the hammer's leading edge. Alexavier straightened himself out, landing squarely on the last post. He stood motionless as the hammer returned, swinging by only inches from his face and causing the breeze to blow his hair to the side. He turned his head, looking down at the Major.

Major Constantine turned to Mike, who exclaims, "14.58 seconds there and 8.1 seconds back." Exuberant talking erupted from the crowd.

The Major looked back. "Great job. I think that beats our current best times."

"Oh yeah! Sam's record was 68.3 seconds up and 31.2 seconds back!" Mike said with a smile on his face.

"Head over and stand next to Mike," the Major ordered.

Alexavier hopped down, following him while asking, "If it took Sam so long to do it, why was I given so little time?"

Major Constantine didn't look up. "I've witnessed your skills before and knew you could do it."

"Wait 'til Sam hears this!" exclaimed Percy, a very tall man of African descent.

Dave put his hands up. "I'm not telling him."

"The only one telling him is me." The Major walked past the excited team. Once he had his back to the crowd, he cracked a tiny smile, but only for a second.

Enter Alexavier

Alexavier received congratulations from a few of the group. Beth was overjoyed, while Percy nodded his approval. Dave and Wally continued their own praise, but the commotion began to grow too loud for the Major. "Enough gawking! Pick your jaws off the floor and get ready for combat exercises."

This portion of workouts had usually been a testing ground for members to hone their skills in either self-defense or combat situations. They provided good markers for evaluating new recruits to where they were in their training and development. It also brought some excitement, as it pitted one recruit against another. Today was one of those days as many were in anticipation of what was to come, having known the reports of Alexavier and his progress for quite some time.

"Agility, balance and decision making are just as reported, maybe better." Major Constantine flipped through a couple pages, eyeing some numbers.

Mike walked up, attempted to interject, "He needs more time through different obstacle courses and environments to know where he performs best or where he could use a little fine tuning."

"He's proved enough to me," the Major proclaimed.

"Combat exercises are scheduled once we establish baselines for all the criteria of his development. We haven't thoroughly tested his basic skills to document them at any level. You know once these kids make it here, we re-establish every skill level before moving forward with their training. If not, we have no way to know when they are able to go on missions, particularly if they hope to get Sam's approval," Mike added.

"I doubt Sam will have any problems approving him. I have my own requirements as far as this test goes. If he passes the combat maneuvers, he'll be scheduled for stealth exercises, maybe even more. Sam will have his own requirements that he can assess when he arrives later." The Major walked away shouting, "Percy, grab your gear!"

Enter Alexavier

Percy stepped down from the second row carrying a duffel bag and proceeded over toward the Major. "Yeah, what's up?"

"Stand front and center to face Alexavier. Use of your side arms is allowed, but no ammunition," the Major announced.

Percy opened his bag and pulled out his pistols, with the first being a chromed, semi-automatic pistol. The other was a dark revolver with a titanium chamber. He put both weapons in holsters on his belt. Once finished securing the belt around his waist, Percy looked up, displaying a sly smile.

The Major turned back to the combatants. "Both of you stand ready."

Alexavier did not take his eyes off Percy, waiting for someone to give him the go ahead. But before anyone could say to start, Percy drew his chromed, semi-auto pistol at lightning speed, bringing the gun up near Alexavier's head. Before Percy could attempt any further sort of offense, the gun was snatched from his grip at even faster speed. Alexavier brought the gun down and pulled back on the slide, pressing the magazine release. The magazine dropped out of the gun's handle, and Alexavier caught it before tossing the disabled gun back to Percy, followed by a hearty fling with the magazine as well.

Percy looked on in astonishment. No one had ever done that before. His only thought was to do what came natural, pulling out his revolver. Just as before, Alexavier grabbed the gun out of Percy's hand right as it was raised up to eye level. Alexavier began the same regimen of disabling the weapon. Once he was finished, Alexavier closed the chamber and threw the gun back to Percy.

Feeling humiliated and angry, Percy dropped the guns and bent down to dip into his bag. As he pulled out a highly modified, M16 assault rifle, the Major intervened. "Percy, stand down!" Percy hesitated, having a hard time not loading a magazine full of center fire ammunition in the weapon.

Major Constantine again spoke up, but this time with more forceful. "I said, stand down! Now! I'm satisfied by the results of this encounter." With a hate stare, Percy looked over at the Major, before lowering the rifle and putting the gun away. The short walk back to the bleachers gave everyone the chance to see him vent his frustration in a mumbling growl.

The Major followed up with a surprise call out, "Harvey, you're up next!"

Everyone in the room began to buzz. Harvey walked from the side of the steps, standing directly in front of Alexavier. A stare down ensued. Neither one flinched. Harvey was one of the team's most successful heroes, and one of their most powerful. If the Major wanted to test a new recruit's abilities, this was the man to do it against.

The Major stalled, watching the testosterone filled display before continuing. "Harvey, you and Alexavier are to battle each other with full use of powers. The first one unable to get back to his feet for combat is the loser. Is that understood?" The only response he got was their continued stare down to go with Alexavier's slight nod. "On my mark, begin your combat exercises. Ready." The room became deathly silent. Letting the anticipation linger long enough, the Major yelled, "Go!"

Harvey's concentration intensified, directing all of his power for a Brain Drain attack. His plan was simple, deprive Alexavier of oxygen, and he would pass out. Plus, a couple of cheap shots would not hurt either.

Feeling the unusual attack, Alexavier decided to shake up the exercise. Quickly, he turned and ran in another direction, up the steps of the bleachers closest to the door. The move appeared to confuse Harvey. Reaching the top, Alexavier jumped up, using the wall for a springboard to leap over the Major and Mike. He landed, rolling forward only a couple feet from his target. Alexavier righted himself, using the momentum to thrust his arms straight toward Harvey's chest. The resulting transfer of energy sent Harvey flying backwards, sliding across the floor.

Alexavier stayed low, watching a perplexed Harvey lie on the ground, confused by the unusual attack. After a brief moment to let the reality of the situation sink in,

Enter Alexavier

Harvey got back up, pausing for an instant before advancing toward Alexavier. Anticipating some sort of physical confrontation, Alexavier stood up and braced himself with Harvey only a couple of steps away. Then, without warning, nothing happened. Harvey simply turned toward the doorway, giving Alexavier one last look as he walked out.

Everyone was stunned. Chatter among the team started to build over the surprising turn of events, but Major Constantine was shocked most of all. "Harvey!"

"Should I bring him back?" Mike asked.

"No!" the Major responded. "I'll address the insubordination later, plus I've seen everything I need to see from Harvey. I've got other things to attend to right now." Upset and annoyed, the Major searched his folder, then the raised steps and the crowd that occupied it, finding the next opponent to test Alexavier. "James, you're up."

James Killus smiled, pushing his way through Beth and Wally. He flashed his knife, as well as sarcasm for them to see. "Too bad he's not going to last that long. I was hoping to have a beer with him later." Killus stopped short, about three feet from Alexavier. His lips curled into a smile, as the stare down felt more like a joke to him. Alexavier on the other hand remained serious, again getting more of that awkward feeling. He decided to put the hood of his grey sweatshirt on.

"Put away the knife!" Major Constantine ordered. Killus replied with a dirty look before placing his knife back in its sheath. He did not have the chance to look back up before the Major quickly yelled, "Go!"

The Major watched with high interest, knowing his new recruit's supreme fighting skills would be tested against The Program's top, lethal weapon. Alexavier braced for the confrontation, but Killus didn't budge. The Major became eager to see combat, but was quickly disappointed when neither made the first move. Both remained still, standing face to face. Bored with the two combatants in a staring war rather than throwing punches, he shouted even louder, "Fight!"

Enter Alexavier

Both men stood their ground, while Killus rubbed his hands together. The absence of action created an even stronger silence. The standoff became a war of wills, as everyone held their breath. Killus finally decided to break the stalemate and took his first jab, lunging forward. Alexavier backed off without any troubles, causing Killus to respond with repeated attempts to jab and swing. Alexavier dodged them all, but each attempt moved the two men farther away from the rest of the group and closer to the posts. Alexavier glanced back and decided to use them for his benefit, eventually getting behind the closest ones. Killus attempted a vague attack, while Alexavier sidestepped it, moving to the next post. Killus threw another swing, but Alexavier moved farther along and down the line. Killus was chasing his prey and quickly realized that his plan of attack was futile. Looking to take the initiative and trying to get ahead of the elusive foe, he swiped far to one side in anticipation. Alexavier blocked the attacking arm, spun around and moved back out into the open area.

Tired of the cat and mouse game, Killus took the direct approach by rushing in. Alexavier stood his ground, meeting the oncoming attack by grabbing a hold of Killus, twisting his body and throwing the would-be attacker. A small roll on the ground had Killus back up to his feet and charging again. This time, Alexavier sidestepped the head on collision, but Killus turned with a swing that Alexavier blocked. Continued punches and jabs were thrown, eventually with Alexavier using a front kick to Killus' stomach, sending him down to one knee.

Feeling angry and intensely frustrated, along with the need to escalate the fight, Killus drew his knife, holding the blade up to his face. Mike quickly wanted to step in and stop the unnecessary confrontation, but the Major held him back. "No, let this play out."

"This is-"

"This is the perfect time to see how Alex handles dangerous situations, especially if we want him to be on missions right away," Major Constantine stated while staring down Mike. "Plus, Killus needs to learn a lesson."

That devilish grin took its place on Killus' face. He methodically stalked Alexavier, who noticed the Major allow the use of the knife. Unfazed and almost inviting the challenge, Alexavier circled away from Killus, not wanting to be within striking distance of the blade. Killus enjoyed the thought of hurting his opponent and began stepping forward more quickly, taking a few swipes and jabs. Alexavier continued to keep his distance, but that feeling hit him again, and he turned to see the field of posts impeding his escape. Killus took advantage and rushed in, lunging with a stab of his knife that nicked Alexavier.

Reaching down, Alexavier felt his ribs and found only his sweatshirt had been sliced. Knowing the next swing could be deadly, he ducked behind the closest post to put an obstacle between them. Killus grinned, taking the maneuver as a challenge. He danced from side to side, matching Alexavier's attempt to get away. A quick thrust, and Killus tried to cut his opponent off. Alexavier stopped, but swung around the other way, hitting Killus with a backhand attack. Killus moved away to take a defensive position, allowing Alexavier to distance himself from the posts.

Killus rubbed his face, smiling as if to enjoy the pain, once again stalking his prey. The pace quickened as Killus got closer. Each swing became a closer call than the last. Each jab nearly hit its mark, until Alexavier planted his feet and met his combatant face to face with a death grip on the knife. Killus pulled the blade close, but Alexavier pushed back in a war of wills and strength. Slowly the knife came closer to Alexavier's neck. The maniacal hero's strength was much more than Alexavier anticipated. Rather than fight his brute strength, Alexavier dropped to one side, using the momentum to throw Killus across the floor and out to a safe distance.

Alexavier jumped to his feet, as Killus laughed. He used the knife to prop himself up, standing slowly while twirling the blade. This time, Killus walked over at a much more deliberate pace, holding back from needless attacks. Cautiously, Alexavier stood his ground, waiting for another attempt. But Killus slowed, delaying any swings. The space between them gradually diminished. Finally, within striking distance, Killus took another stab. This time, Alexavier blocked the arm away, countering with a straight right to the jaw. The blow stunned Killus, but not enough, as he continued another swipe. Now getting his timing down, Alexavier began blocking each attack, finally resulting in Killus trying to tackle him. Alexavier rolled to his back, holding onto the arm. He wrapped his legs over Killus' chest and arched his back, dislocating the attacking arm's elbow. Killus dropped the knife, yelling in pain. Keeping an eye on his downed opponent, Alexavier released the hold and stood up.

That awkward sensation came over Alexavier, so he turned to see Hank Malberg pushing through the crowded steps only to have Major Constantine shout, "Stand down, Hank! Back to your place on the stairs!" A reluctant Hank pushed his way back through the other heroes.

The feeling didn't go away, as something made Alexavier even more uneasy. He tensed up and braced for an attack, as Killus had regained enough composure to use his other arm with a vicious swing of his blade. Alexavier turned slightly to his right to see and spun quickly in the other direction. A well-timed spinning kick landed hard, impacting Killus' solar plexus, leaving the wind knocked out of him, bent over and vulnerable. Alexavier took a step back, winding up. Using every ounce of energy, he swung as hard as he could, connecting with Killus' jaw and causing his head to snap back so hard, he became unconscious before hitting the floor.

Breathing heavy, Alexavier turned around and walked back toward Major Constantine, shaking and flexing his hand from the pain of contact to Killus' face. The Major did well to contain his enthusiasm, but ever so slightly gave a small grin. He turned to Mike and said, "Executed with deliberate aggression. This is why he's here. This is why The Terror Tribe is coming to an end."

The Major walked over to Alexavier. "Great display, son. This is what we've been

Enter Alexavier

waiting for. You keep that up, and no one is going to beat us."

Alexavier let out a sigh, needing to be prepared for another battle. But before he could get ready, Major Constantine shouted, "Everyone is dismissed!" Some of the group took the opportunity to vacate the room, still buzzing about the proceedings, while others swarmed the tired hero. He was met with glowing praise, as he reached for his gear.

"Dude, you're my new idol!" Dave shouted. "You know how long I've wanted to smack Killus like that?"

"Thanks."

Wally added, "I wish I could have given it to him like you did. Boy, has he deserved it."

Beth showed her excitement. "That was amazing! You were awesome!" Alexavier became speechless, enamored with her standing right in front of him.

But that quickly changed, as Percy was not so impressed. "Don't get cocky. Wait 'til you get on the streets. Then we'll see how you do."

"Aw, somebody can't take getting beat. You need a hanky, Mr. Cranky?" Dave joked.

"Hey, you know it's just training. Would you rather him fail miserably, and then have to watch your back during a mission?" Wally said.

"He better have my back," Percy grunted.

"Chill man. He might save your hide. Then you'll owe him. You might have to name your kids after him," Dave cracked.

Beth stared down Percy. "This is how we know how each of us will do in the field. You should be happy he can hold his own."

Percy paused, looking at the body on the floor being attended to. "I guess we can keep the kid for now, but we need a rematch."

Enter Alexavier

This smaller group of heroes began poking at Percy. Some reluctant laughs finally came out at his expense, as Alexavier gathered his stuff. He looked over to Mike, who grinned cautiously and nodded.

Before Alexavier could join in further with the other heroes' conversation, Major Constantine interjected, "Okay. You'll all have time to get acquainted later. Now I need to get Alexavier to his room and finish the rest of the agenda for his orientation."

The team said their goodbyes, as Alexavier followed closely behind the Major. He gave one last look back. Seeing Beth wave gave him a warm feeling that he enjoyed better than any praise he received for his stellar performance.

Enter Alexavier

CHAPTER 9

Not much had been said, although everything that needed to be said had been done during the workout. The journey from the W.A.R. Room was quiet, just a very slow and silent game of follow-the-leader. The unofficial game ended only a few minutes after it had started, as they halted outside of a heavily windowed room on the corner of two hallways. From the outside it was uneventful, and the windows had the blinds drawn, giving no clue to what's inside.

"Alright, here's your room. Give me your right hand. We need to set up your room's security." Major Constantine reached over, placing Alexavier's palm on the small screen next to the door. A few seconds passed, until a slight beep sounded. "Now that it has accepted your palm biometric, it will let you in. The only other people who can access the room besides you are the medical staff, security and myself. You can also change the settings to allow easy access for visitors." Taking Alexavier's hand away, the Major pressed a button on the screen.

Finally, the door slid open, showing Alexavier his room for the first time. Accommodations at this location were much better than his previous ones. A computer sat on a desk near the far windows, as well as a digital camera. A large screen television decorated one of the walls near a table and a couple of chairs. There were plenty of storage cabinets. His new bed appeared to be much bigger than his previous one, and Alexavier made it a point to try it first. Comfortable was a word that did not do it justice. The softness of the mattress brought the first signs of how nice graduating could be.

Needing to get to an important meeting, the Major provided some brief instructions. "Go ahead and unpack. You have your manual, so familiarize yourself with. Visit the cafeteria anytime you feel hungry. We will have appropriate meals set up for you once we get your profile updated."

"Can I get something drink?" Alexavier inquired.

Major Constantine walked over to the desk's far side, opening a small door. "This mini fridge will be stocked regularly. For now, it contains a selection of water and energy drinks."

Alexavier joined him to take a look. "Water is good," he said, pulling out a bottle from the fridge.

Walking out, the Major turned back, "Mike should be by soon, and I'll be around to check on you a little later." Major Constantine eyed the young recruit one last time before leaving.

"Thanks." Alexavier nodded and looked around to survey his room. Once the Major had left the room, he sat down at the desk. "Wonder if it I can get online?"

Holding down the power button to turn on the computer, it roared to life. As it took a minute for the computer to get to its home page, Alexavier used this time to look at the camera next to it that he would surely use while on reconnaissance. Amazed at how much stuff populated the room, he glanced around the space that was now his, still in disbelief. When your previous accommodations included a roommate, you value the extra space not occupied by another human body.

Getting comfortable in the room was surprisingly easy. Alexavier spun around in his desk chair, taking in all that was his room viewed through the camera lens. He only stopped when he noticed the temperature to be a little cool and checked the thermostat on the wall behind him. Although everything appeared to work properly, he turned up the temperature slightly.

Enter Alexavier

Before the computer could fully start up, a knocking was heard at the door. Alexavier shouted, "Who is it?" but nothing happened. A few more seconds go by before he yelled louder, "Come in!"

A muffled voice replied back, "Hit the button!"

"Hold on!" A desperate search for the appropriate button had Alexavier freaking out. "Ah, give me a second!" He reached under the top of the desk, but felt nothing. A quick spin in his chair revealed no obvious buttons close by. "Um, open sesame! Is there a password? I don't even have a key!"

"Hit the button near the door!"

Embarrassed, Alexavier headed over quickly. A slap of the button at the control panel allowed the outside world to become visible, as well as Mike. "Major pain-in-our-butts never showed you how to set up verbal commands, huh?"

Alexavier walked back to the desk. "No. He seemed to be in a hurry. He did mention you would be stopping by."

Mike strolled inside, holding a folder. "That figures he'd check out early… not saying that's a bad thing. Great job in the workout today, although I think the use of force was a little premature and dangerous. But, you're proving just why they really want you here. Anyway, there's a heap of goodies that you haven't even discovered yet, like the self-tinting windows or the climate control that follows you to each area of the room. It's fully programmable."

"Really?

"Heck yeah! The back part of the manual has the instructions for all of the amenities. For now, we need to get your dinner ordered." Mike reached for the manual, opened it and pulled out the meal card in the front pocket.

Alexavier took it and studied the choices. "There's a lot to choose from."

"That will change once we get the results from your blood work." Mike adjusted his glasses, wandering over to a couple of particular doors. "Have you browsed the toys inside these?"

"Not yet."

After patting the doors, Mike made his way back to the entrance. "There's a nice assortment of weapons for training and real-world use."

"I'll check that out first when I get back." Finishing the card, Alexavier stood up. "Where do I put this?"

"It goes in the slot just outside the door. All paperwork can get placed there if it needs to be picked up, so you don't have to walk everywhere." Mike took it and placed it in the appropriate spot. "The kitchen staff should be by soon to process it. You won't have to fill them out for very long. Just let me adjust the door settings." A quick press of buttons and Mike said, "Okay, now visitors can enter when you give the verbal command to open. If you want to change it, hit the settings button on the menu. Okay. Duty calls. Review the manual, and I'll check back in a bit, unless I see you in the cafeteria."

"Cool. Thank you." Heading back to finally get acquainted with his room, the young hero looked about, locating his bags. Seeing the many cabinets and doors placed about the room was comfortably refreshing. A neat thought popped into his head. He might have so much room, there's no telling all the cool things the Major might have for him.

The first place on his list to investigate was the sliding double doors. As he opened them slowly, the view inside was awe-inspiring. Taking a step back, Alexavier reveled in the closet for clothes that was wider than he is tall. Having previously had barely any room in a four-drawer dresser, the possibilities could be endless, if he could ever think of enough things to hang inside.

Noticing the very heavy looking metal door on the adjacent wall, he ventured over to check it out. The handle had a solid feel, and it required a bit of effort to turn. After unlatching the heavy door and giving it a good, hard pull, he peered inside. Suddenly,

Enter Alexavier

Alexavier's face lit up. This was his personal vault for weapons and equipment, with some weapons already stocked inside. Knives, swords and staffs of various sizes adorned one wall. Taking a few steps, he noticed some drawers opposite the weapons. Pulling them out, he saw a plethora of gadgets lining the bottom of each drawer. Some were familiar, like the grappling hook and lock pick set, while others were mysteries that he would enjoy toying with later. Looking up, the back of the lengthy vault had another door with a keypad. Curious, he decided to try and open it. A hearty attempt to turn the handle came up empty. Not knowing the code, Alexavier exited to continue the exploration of the rest of his room.

The last place for storage was a long, lateral drawer system vaguely resembling a dresser. In opening each of the drawers, he was welcomed with emptiness. Taking hold of his main duffel bag and placing at his feet, he unzipped it and began pulling out everything. He held his special combat boots up, contemplating for a second before setting them on the desk. One by one, he extracted articles of clothing and neatly arranged them in the drawer. Posters, papers and other non-essentials were set on top of the dresser for the moment. Once the duffel bag had been emptied, he turned to stow the rest of his gear, including his many sweatshirt jackets.

As his hand reached out, Alexavier noticed only one boot was where he had set them. Puzzled, he leaned over, looking to the sides and beyond the desk to survey the floor, but came up empty. He dropped to one knee and looked under the desk. Getting the same results and completely stumped, he sat up and thought hard. He knew that he had not bumped it by accident.

Having no explanation for what just happened, Alexavier's first thought was the Major might have had something to do with it. Whenever he was around the Major, a feeling of dread always came over him, similar to just now. The feeling was slightly different. Finding no reason for the awkwardness, he chalked it up to nerves.

Unfortunately, his intuition kept telling him that something did not seem quite right. He stood up and looked around, trying to figure out what made the room feel stuffy. He glanced from side to side, seeing nothing out of place. After a few moments, he returned to the task of finding his boot. Out of the corner of his eye, he caught a glimpse of something moving. Taking a quick look, he noticed only the lamp and bookshelf. Suddenly, a noise came from the other side of the desk. He got up to look over the top, but saw nothing.

Alexavier reluctantly leaned back into his chair. A casual spin had him comes face to face with a young, Asian woman staring back at him. Startled, he fell over backwards, hitting the floor with a huge thud. The young woman giggled uncontrollably at the entertaining display.

Alexavier's head slowly rose up over the desk, again seeing no one. Somewhat frustrated, he cautiously picked up the chair. Looking up, he was startled once more by the young woman sitting on the back table. He stumbled over the corner of the desk and said loudly, "Hey!"

Regaining his balance, he looked to see that she had vanished once more. He quickly turned around toward the window to catch a glimpse of her, although her body was nearly transparent. Hoping to break the ice, he decided to introduce himself. "Hi. I'm Alexavier."

The image of the woman's face became quite clear, followed by the rest of her body. He could see she was attractive and obviously quite playful. He did not remember her from the initial meeting in the W.A.R. Room. She giggled a little and stated, "You're funny."

"Not that I was trying to be, but I'm glad you liked it," Alexavier replied.

"Call me Jennifer."

"It's nice to meet you, Jennifer." He leaned back against the desk.

"You're the new kid." She started to fade away again.

"Yeah. I guess I am."

Enter Alexavier

"Okay. See ya." Jennifer's image completely vanished.

"Wait!" With a disappearing act that would make any magician envious, Alexavier was alone again, except when he turned around to see his other boot on the desk in front of him. The sight of the boot brought a smile to his face. With the seriousness of the day's events, he enjoyed her playfulness.

Enter Alexavier

CHAPTER 10

With a shower and change of clothes, Alexavier made nourishment his next priority. Having submitted the meal card might have locked in his dinner choices, but he wondered if he could chance the cafeteria's other foods for lunch. Strolling in the cafeteria, he was pleasantly surprised to see a somewhat occupied room. Before choosing where and who to sit with, he needed to select from the appetizing dinner choices. Surveying the food, he quickly realized that the quality of the food might be a little suspect.

A cafeteria worker came up to the counter. "Are you Alexavier V.?"

"Yes, ma'am."

"Here's your meal card identification for your lanyard. All of your choices each day are by the color code from the card. For today, you're red. So, you can choose any foods with that color tag. This will change shortly, so be aware of that."

"Okay. Thanks." Nothing seemed like it would taste great, so Alexavier picked a variety and headed for a table. One corner had Killus and crew, with James staring down Alexavier, while hiding his bruises. The rest of the population was mostly general complex employees. Not wanting to chance any interactions with Killus, he strolled over to an open table farthest away and on the other side of the cafeteria counter. Setting the tray down and taking a seat, the sight of the thoroughly unappetizing egg substitute made him wish he had chosen the equally awful meat and poultry choices instead. The terrible food did little to flush away the feeling of not having company.

Finishing his path through the jungle of the food line, Mike looked around the room to find the next place he would grace with his presence. Initially, he saw a couple of techs from the hangar and headed their way. On his way over, Mike noticed Alexavier sitting alone. Being the resident goodwill ambassador, he took the opportunity to venture over to see how young Alexavier was doing.

Mike put his plate of food next to Alexavier's and sat down. "How's the room? Did you find all of the goodies?"

Alexavier looked up with a small smile. "It's great! I'm actually surprised about all of that stuff."

"Everything else good about your room?"

"No complaining. In fact, it's far beyond my wildest dreams. I had no idea it would be this nice, but I can't get in one door."

"You made it here, so you've earned the right to have an upgrade," Mike stated. "Oh, that must be your outfit locker. It will have your hero suits, once they're made."

"I did have a weird welcome from Jennifer."

Mike smiled. "You've met my favorite little prankster. I see you're not traumatized, so that's good."

"Why's that?"

"She loves to fool around and play pranks on people. She doesn't do anything too bad, mostly harmless fun."

Alexavier grinned. "She did hide my boot from me."

"That would be her. Good think she didn't zap you."

"Zap me?"

"Uh huh. Her name is Jennifer Xiaohan, known as Syphon. She can draw energy from several sources and has these bursts of electricity that she'll sometime use when you're not looking, her way of pranking you. You'd definitely know she's around when that happens. And don't worry about her being in your room this morning to say hello. She's good about giving you your privacy."

Continuing to grin, Alexavier looked around the room at the eclectic group of heroes in training as Percy, Dave, Wally, Beth and Harvey sat down at another table. "Is this everyone on our team?"

Mike stopped in mid-motion, the food dangling precariously from his plastic spork. "Most of them, anyway. I guess I should be the one to tell you about your new team members. So, you've sort of met Harvey in the workout earlier. His full name is Harvey Stringer, code named Heart Strings. He has a limited, magnetic control of only microscopic particles of iron. That means the only thing he's able to control is the iron in a person's blood. He can make you pass out by stopping your blood from circulating. Anything larger than that, he doesn't have the control, like a hammer or wrench. Although Sessions have not improved upon that, he can affect more targets from a much greater distance."

"Across from him is Percy Shottenheimer, called Precision Shot. He has an uncanny level of accuracy. Whether it is with a M14 rifle or paper airplane, he can always hit his mark. He's the most accurate shot The Program has ever had."

Alexavier looked over at the table. "Who else is at the table sitting next to Percy? Wally, right?"

"Yup. Wally Ryder is also called Wave Rider. Underneath that piercing blond hair and blue-eyed look is a hero who can use sources of energy to travel great distances. He can fly through the air on a windy day, riding the air currents. Or if it's calm outside, he can use an electrical wire's energy pulses to surf wherever he wants."

"I bet he saves a lot of money when it comes time for traveling on vacation."

Mike chuckled. "Then we have Dave Headley or Dead Head."

"Dead Head Dave, as he was called back in Philadelphia. He can die and come

Enter Alexavier

back to life."

Mike's eyes lit up. "That's right. You guys were in Philly together. Then you remember Beth Breckenridge, the Beacon of Light."

"Yeah, but we just called her Beacon for short, 'cause her powers are light based."

"She started shortening her name too. You'd be surprised at how much her powers have developed. She can intensify her powers to be used for extreme heat as well. She's not as powerful as Solarflare or the original Beacon of Light, but she can make things pretty damn hot."

"Next to them is Michael McKnight, one of two recruits of East Indian descent. He is the most interesting Metas that has come along in quite a while. Mecha, as he's called, can shape his body into metal plates, weapons and gadgets. He's kind of a human Swiss army knife."

"That sounds cool."

"Wait 'til you need cover fire," Mike said, the enthusiasm bubbling over. "The Starburst Missiles fired from his shoulders are amazing to see. And you obviously haven't met Bobbie yet?"

"No, sir."

"Bobbie Terpstra is called Booby Trap. She's actually on recon right now. That mighty little wonder of African descent is our favorite recon expert. She's expertly trained and better than anyone who's come through this complex. But it's her powers that really make her stealth missions great, especially if she's discovered and needs to evade capture. Whatever she touches with her bare hands can turn into objects to help her escape, just like setting booby traps. If someone is following her, a touch of a garbage can might have the can explode and confuse the pursuer enough for her to get away. She's also one of our best fighters."

"Man. Not having to fight some of the Meta villains could save you from some definite bumps and bruises."

Enter Alexavier

"Also missing is the new Human Battery, Manny Batista. They're prepping him for his Session in the morning. He's extremely valuable since he can drain the energy from any villain he chooses. It's hard to stand and fight against us if you don't have the energy to stand up. Our resident recruit of Mexican descent can also pull energy from sources to use as a weapon."

Alexavier looked over toward the far end of the cafeteria. "So, what's with that table?"

Mike turned around. "That is the gang of misfits that is headed by James Killus, the Killing Machine. They're just a bunch of voluntary outcasts. They don't try to mix in with the rest of us, no matter how much I try to get them to."

"That really makes for a great team atmosphere."

"Watch your back with Killus," Mike's face grew serious and lowered his voice. "He's a maniacal killer. Nothing but blood follows that guy."

"Does he have any powers?"

"Not that we know of, but the Major likes having a guy around who isn't afraid to do really bad things when the time comes. There's a reason he's called the Killing Machine."

"Good to know. I guess Hank fits in with him."

Mike's voice perked up with surprise. "How do you know Hank Malberg?"

"We had a couple of one on one sparring matches a while back when the different training complexes had to interact and do exercises. I won both matches, but he was a dirty fighter."

"Wait," Mike said with a grin. "If I remember correctly, he didn't take either one too well, did he? Well, he's now called Hack 'n Maul. He's just as dirty as Killus and twice as nasty. He's Killus' right hand goon and dumb as bag of hammers. I still wouldn't mess with him. His strength is amazing for a Non-Meta, and he's got some pretty good invulnerability that we didn't suspect he would develop. He can be extremely dangerous for anyone who messes with him."

"Who's that girl? She seems uneasy around them."

"She's April Dandridge, our other hero of East Indian descent. She's newer here like you, having only been here a couple of weeks. Before she got a chance to mix with the rest of the team, Killus took her into his gang. Now she's almost held away from the others because of him. She's a very unusual Meta. She has various arms, legs, and other body parts, even a pair of wings and a tail stored somewhere on her person that she can pull out and attach anywhere on her body. I believe that's why she was given the name Appendage. The crazy part of it is that once the limbs are attached to her body, they come to life as if they were her own. We've tried finding out her story, but she doesn't talk about it, no matter how much we try."

"Standing off to the side is Dwayne Cygnus, our newest African descent hero known as Sickness. If he touches your bare skin with his, he can make you sick or give you a disease depending on his mood or attitude. The more unpleasant he is, the worse the sickness he gives you."

"I hope he can control it?"

"Actually, not that we know. The people in charge throughout the various Program sites don't know how to handle him, so the Major brought him right here. We're still having a hard time working with him. The only place he's felt comfortable has been with Killus and his gang. Even then, he tries to be alone."

"They don't seem too social with him either."

Mike stirred his food. "It's hard when your power is so scary. A doctor touched him accidentally and was bed ridden for weeks. I try to talk to him whenever I can, but he's pretty quiet and doesn't say much."

"That's so depressing."

"Then there's Glu, Glen Euw. Just like his name, he makes things sticky. But, he's also the most annoying of the group. He even gets on the Major's nerves. Hey! Let's go meet the others!"

Alexavier grabbed his tray, following behind Mike, who sat down next to Percy. Alexavier cautiously set his meal next to Beth. Looking up, she smiled which gave him a smile of his own.

Mike interrupted the group's joking and laughter. "So, you've all met Alexavier."

A collective nod and howdy made Alexavier feel welcome, except for Harvey who remained quiet. Alexavier smiled, glancing over toward Beth. The awkward silence was broken by none other than Dave. "Nice job with the workout. I appreciate any time Killus gets his butt kicked, especially in such spectacular fashion."

"That was really exciting," Beth stated, bumping Alexavier's shoulder.

Wally waved his food around with his spork. "We've really needed someone with those kind of skills."

"Alex is going to take this team to another level," Mike responded. "I've said it for a while now that he's going to make an impact. Just help him get situated first, guys. The real work will begin soon."

"Anytime," Michael agreed.

"Sure," Wally said.

Dave disagreed, "No way, man. The new kid can hang with me."

"Just because you're hanging out with our next great hero doesn't mean it's going to make you look better," Wally stated.

Dave gave Wally a dirty look. "Hey! Don't start with me!"

"When have we stopped?" Beth joked.

"You can hang out with me. I'll need someone to carry my gear when I'm kicking butt." Alexavier reached over handing some books to Dave.

The look on Dave's face was a bit of shock, but in a funny way. "Great. Now I'm being relegated to carrying school books, and it's not even for a girl!" He sat them down, while everyone had a good laugh.

But Mike noticed Percy's scowl. "Hey, Percy. You're not that upset that Alex showed you up today, are you?"

"He didn't show me up."

Michael had a weird smirk. "Hold on. You were there, and you don't remember?'

"He schooled you like you were in kindergarten," Dave countered.

Wally giggled, "Hope you took notes for that lesson."

Percy closed up, not liking the extra poking being done. Alexavier threw a curve ball. "Maybe he just needs to know that he can trust the new guy, that he'll have his back no matter what."

"You have to admit he can handle extreme situations," Mike pointed out.

"Especially with what he did to Killus," Wally added.

A quiet fell about the table, waiting for a response. Percy's pursed lips finally gave way to an unexpected reply. "I did like the way you smacked around Killus."

Mike patted Percy on the back. Instantly, the air in the room lightened. Conversation opened up and became much more fun and engaging, with verbal jousting happening among everyone, except Harvey. With either a bowed head or staring straight ahead, he never looked to the rest of the table. His demeanor was poor and got worse with each bout of laughter. It went on unnoticed by everyone, which just made him even angrier.

Enter Alexavier

CHAPTER 11

It was a dreary, cloudy day in Manhattan's financial district, and the mood was just as gloomy inside one of the larger financial institutions. Patrons became impatient with the long lines that usually appeared during the lunch hour rush. Attitudes were poor, and grew worse the longer the wait times had become.

Suddenly, a blast shattered the glass windows, spraying piercing debris at everyone inside. Many close to the shockwave remained on the ground, knocked out. Confusion blanketed those unfortunate to be conscious. Through the smoke and broken glass stepped a wall of a man, Natural Disaster. His hair flowed and waved, distorted by the energy released from his body. The only armed guard not rendered helpless attempted to pull his gun, but received a concentrated burst of energy from the villain's hand that put an end to the guard's attempt to stop him.

In a panic, the manager raced toward one of the back desks, reaching for the silent alarm. As his hand touched the side, a strong blast of energy destroyed the entire structure, sending the manager scurrying. He quickly stood up, moving back toward the rear offices. From the shadows, The Infamous One, who was dressed in his all-black outfit, came up behind the manager and wrapped his arms around his victim's neck. With a constricting squeeze, the manager quickly fell unconscious, and The Infamous One unceremoniously dropped the limp body to the floor.

With a slight wave of The Infamous One's hand, several Terror Tribe villains stormed the bank's lobby. Game Over, Nib, Silver Shockwave and Mega Conductor

Enter Alexavier

joined Natural Disaster to start their heist. Mega Conductor shocked the few remaining customers and security guards who were left conscious. Game Over grabbed a granite pillar and began swinging it like a baseball bat, striking the hinges of the vault door. Pieces of the door flew off, but the structural integrity remained intact. Silver Shockwave opened his hands, slowly producing a silver, liquid sphere. Once it had reached the size of a basketball, he threw it at the vault door, which exploded, sending even more shrapnel flying. Having the vault door nearly free, Nib, the highly terrifying villain of African descent, strolled over and ignited a bright red blade of energy from his hand. With one sweeping stroke, he put the blade through the outer edge of the door, weakening the structure. Game Over reached for the handle of the door, pulled hard and removed it from its hinges. Like conducting an orchestra, with a few waves and pointing, The Infamous One had everyone scrambling to stuff stacks of money in various bags from the palettes on the floor.

"How much time do we have?" the Infamous One asked.

Mega Conductor shouted, "Four minutes!"

The Infamous turned to his crew in the vault. "Time's wasting, people!"

"Got it." Game Over acknowledged, heading for the vault.

Natural Disaster scanned the room for anyone hoping to fight back. "We're clear from being disturbed. I'll keep an eye on the exit."

The Infamous One watched all corners of the building. "Efficiency is the key, my friends. Like worker bees and their honey, waste no time and expend only what energy you need."

"I need some bags," Nib hollered, continuing to grab the cash and tossing it near his feet.

"Three minutes!" Mega Conductor yelled, not noticing a darkly dressed woman with a wide brimmed hat enter the bank from behind. She walked up in a very deliberate manner, becoming visible to The Infamous One, while a couple of other women in costumes stood outside. Mega Conductor saw the stare and turned his head to see her. "Glad you could join us, Cavalio."

She looked out of the side of her eyes, not turning her head. "As long as I get paid." She leaned in, kissing The Infamous One on the cheek.

"Did you take care of the police?" Natural Disaster inquired.

Cavalio stopped short of entering the vault. "The whole precinct is under my control, and Troublemaker and the girls are spreading havoc elsewhere. Unfortunately, we should have strays coming in with their squad cars at any moment."

Game Over leaned in to whisper to Nib, "She gives me the creeps."

Nib brushed him off as Mega Conductor shouted, "Two minutes!"

The stockpiling of bundled cash ended with everyone grabbing as many stuffed bags as their hands could hold, with Game Over using his gravity defying abilities to haul out the most. One by one, they exited the vault and made their way through the lobby with The Infamous One making a detour toward the computers situated on desks behind the crumbling counter. Clicking away, he searched for a certain program. Placing a thumb drive into the port, he hit enter once, holding down the Tab button. Pleased that the computer continued to process the software, he headed toward the front door. Looking back, he saw Nib lagging behind. "It's time we made an exit. After you, my dear." The Infamous One allowed Cavalio to leave before him.

Having no thought of going quietly, Nib stalked the bank manager who was barely conscious. Hiding behind the counter didn't save him. Seeing a reflection in some glass of the frightening villain searching for him, the manager scampered to an adjacent desk, before crawling back to where the vault was. The events of the heist and unconsciousness may have hampered his thoughts somewhat, but not enough to know he needed to get to the second emergency button. A desperate race culminated at the door, only to have a powerful energy blade pierce his back and chest. Falling to

Enter Alexavier

the floor, the manager turned over to see Nib standing over him.

"It looks like someone has a problem with our generous hospitality. I think we'll leave you a going away gift." Nib leaves the incapacitated man to squirm on the floor as he walks away, patting Silver Shockwave on the shoulder. Silver Shockwave opened his hands up to a small silver liquid sphere that started to grow. The shimmering globe expanded, achieving the size of the doorway. The smirking villain dropped the sphere and turned to exit the bank. Nib and Silver Shockwave were last to make it through the doors and started racing across the street and down the block. The activity at the bank subsided. A few bystanders began to slowly move closer to investigate. Their curiosity was paid in blood, as the huge sphere finally exploded, obliterating the entire first floor of the building.

Enter Alexavier

CHAPTER 12

Part of being involved with a team is having that feeling of belonging. Walking back from dinner with Beth, Dave and Wally was one of the best feelings Alexavier ever had. Although Dave and Beth did not remember him from their Philadelphia days, he was still welcomed into their small circle. The banter continued back and forth. But he remained a bit reserved with his comments, observing the dynamic of the team, both good and bad.

"What if we grab some snacks and watch a movie?" Beth suggested.

"Sounds like fun." Wally noticed Harvey staying back from them. "Aren't you coming along?"

"I don't need the company."

"You don't want to join us?" Beth wondered.

"Not you. It's him." Harvey replied, looking at Alexavier.

The response confused the group with Dave stumbling over his words. "Wait. Wha... you aren't serious?"

"If he's around, I'm not." Harvey walked away without looking back.

"I didn't even say a word," Alexavier stated.

"Look, I don't know what's got into your shorts!" Dave became frustrated. "He's not even listening."

"Let him go. He can be as moody as a girl," Wally joked.

"You're not talking about me, are you?" Beth wondered.

Wally's only saving grace was his ability to back pedal. "Not you. I'd never mean my favorite girl."

"I can hear the butt kissing from here," Percy said from behind them.

Mike smirked, "You know there's one talent Wally displays better than any other hero. I give you, Mister Butt Kisser!"

Wally began to blush, and everybody noticed. Percy was one to never let an opportunity to joke around go by without a wise crack. "Somebody's turning awfully red right now. Little Mr. Bashful doesn't like being embarrassed in front of the ladies."

"Hey, I have to stay on her good side. She can be kind of vicious if she wants to be. I see what she does to Dave every other day." Wally shied away from her a few steps. "I'd rather have a red face from blushing than getting slapped."

"I'd never slap you," Beth relied. "I have many more ways to get back at you."

"Great. Now I'm going to have to have my room scanned for any improvised explosive paint balloons."

"It doesn't matter what you use. You'll never find them." Beth smiled, looking at Wally out of the corner of her eye.

"Great. I guess we're not watching the movie in my room. Who's the guinea pig?"

"Well, I have the biggest television. So my place it is," Mike offered. "Bring all the munchies you want, and I'll see you all in about a half hour."

"Everyone good with it?" Wally inquired.

"I might have to pass." All eyes focused on Alexavier. "I've got a bunch of assignments that the Major has for me. Some need a bit of work, and I don't want to get on his bad side by not having them done and done right."

"C'mon, newbie. You're going to set a bad example," Dave said. "The Major's going to expect more out of me."

"Let the guy overachieve. It's what he does best." Mike's words warrant respect for Alexavier's dedication.

Wally gave his approval. "I'm not going to stop a guy who wants to get better."

"More popcorn for me." Percy headed toward Mike's room.

"Enjoy your textbooks," Dave patted Alexavier on the back. "Not the kind of company I'd want, but okay. See ya later."

"If you decide otherwise, we'll have a seat for you." Beth smiled.

Alexavier nodded, as the others headed off. Beth turned to look at him one last time. She saw that he was still looking at her, so she waved back to him. His wave was followed by a smile of his own, enjoying the temporary distraction from the work he had to finish. Although the meal was acceptable, the addition of having company made the bland taste fade away.

#

Life goes on. One moment passes, and the next will come. In between, there is homework. Walking back to his room, sorting through the numerous books he had to study, Alexavier hoped to be done with homework once he arrived at the premier level of The Program. With all his focus directed toward skimming textbooks, the rest of the world would appear to not exist, but you never know what is right around the corner.

Out of a side corridor stepped James Killus, accompanied by his band of misfit cretins, Hank, Dwayne, April and the odd looking Glu. Being the hapless little crony of the group, Glu did what he did best by hiding and taking refuge behind Hank. Dwayne voluntarily stayed off to the side.

Enter Alexavier

"Didn't think they let the little ones out of the nursery unsupervised," Killus said with a smirk.

The group started to chuckle as Glu poked, "How was dinner at the kiddie table?"

"I wouldn't know. You guys didn't invite me." Alexavier's comeback killed the laughter.

"Give me a reason to hurt you, loser," Killus threatened, pointing a knife.

Alexavier saw the escalating situation and knew it would not end pretty, but he would never back down. "From what I understand, you don't need a reason. I'm surprised you actually have to think about trying your luck with me."

Killus smiled, twirling his knife. "It's your bad luck when I stick this six inches in your chest."

Alexavier replied, still holding his books, "Six? I heard you only have two inches to work with."

The moment was at its breaking point. Killus smirked as he moved closer, nose-to-nose with his newest adversary, just waiting for the right moment to explode with anger.

"Do you really want to start this now?" From behind Alexavier walked a legendary man he had seen before, but only in comic books and television. Jonathan Bender, also known as The Time Bender, stepped in between the two men. He had a subdued physical stature, being shorter, with a less muscular physique. And although he was unimposing physically, he could more than handle himself with people like Killus and his band of thugs.

Killus barked back, "Not your fight, weasel."

Jonathon replied, "There isn't going to be a fight, Killus. If you can wrap your head around the thought."

"I'll wrap my hands around your weak little neck!" Hank's out-stretched arms gave an easy target for this well experienced hero. Jonathan's eyes turned black, with

Enter Alexavier

a small point of extremely, bright light shining in the center. Hank arms were within reach of Jonathan's throat, but never got a chance to grab hold. The already massive arms swelled up in size to enormous proportions. With the added size brought the added weight. Once Hack's arms became too large, they dropped to the floor with a thud.

"You son of a-" Hank tried lifting the massive pieces of flesh, but to no avail. "Don't think this is going to stop me from snapping your pencil neck, you geek!"

"There's time for us to really get acquainted, kid. The fun's just beginning. Right, Jonathon? We've got all the time in the world." As intelligent as he is deadly, Killus knew when to fight and when to leave. He motioned for the group to gather Hank's useless limbs, but was unsuccessful in trying to lift them. Their only course of action was to pull Hank along with his forearms sliding across the floor. Dwayne followed far enough behind everyone, so not to make physical contact.

Several seconds went by after they vanished from sight before Jonathan broke the silence. "I think this proves that the Neanderthals were knuckle draggers."

Alexavier laughed with a little outburst of relief. "Nice one. But any time they want to, I'm more than willing to-"

"Just keep your mind on the tasks ahead. Don't worry about them. They'll have to answer to the Major for this crap. Keep focused on what you need to do." Jonathon moved closer with a reassuring tone. "You have better things to do than worry about them. If you really need to expend some energy, get your gear and meet in the W.A.R. Room. Somebody is always available to do a little sparring. But for now, do what you need to take care of. The world is waiting to see its newest hero. So, don't be late."

"With all of these combat and strategy textbooks, I think I have a lot of homework I should do as well."

"Then get to your studies. Someone will always be around if you need to get a workout or some extra training." Jonathon pats Alexavier on the back.

Enter Alexavier

"Cool, thanks." Alexavier was in awe, as Jonathon left to find the Major. Although he did not get the opportunity to relish the encounter, he was thrilled that he had the chance to meet a true hero in The Time Bender.

Enter Alexavier

CHAPTER 13

A knock on the door interrupted the Major's morning. He reached over to the right side of his desk and pushed a button. The door slid open, revealing James Killus and two Elitesmen Guard. Before the chaperons could follow Killus in, the Major instructed them otherwise. "I need privacy."

Once the door had shut, Killus asked, "So, why the booty call?"

"You are to leave Alexavier alone. You and your cronies are all to stay away from him."

Killus snarled, "I'm not sure if you need glasses, but look at my face."

The Major sat his pen down. "You took the training session a little too far and suffered the consequences. You're lucky that's all he did."

"So, he's your new, star pupil?"

"He could be the greatest thing that has happened to this team in years."

"You mean to tell me he's more important than me? I'm the guy who's going to bring you The Infamous One's head on a stick."

The Major closed the folder that had preoccupied him. "That may be, but it may be Alexavier who gets you to that point. He is an elite fighter, just what we've needed for years. This team is finally coming around with the right pieces of the puzzle."

"All you need is me and not some punk who has no clue to what it's like to be out of diapers. For all we know he could be the one to screw up and let Infamous get away. And that I will not forgive."

"It's not your place to forgive. The only thing you do is exactly what I say."

Killus leaned forward slightly. "Threaten me all you want. But if the brat ends up in the morgue, he deserves it."

Major Constantine stood up to confront Killus on an even level. "He ends up hurt in any way, and I will make you miserable, including locking you away in a padded cell for the rest of your life."

Killus did not change his expression. "When you die and go to hell, I will be the first person to greet you at the gates."

"I'm already in hell. Now, get out of my sight."

The final comment made Killus smile. He righted himself and casually turned away. The Major reached over, pressing the button for the door, allowing Killus to leave without incident. The Major breathed in deep and exhaled through his nose, sighing heavily. Before he could bury his head in the never-ending stack of papers, Dr. Dennis entered through the still open door. "I've got the test results back on Alexavier, but I'm not sure if I can fill in all of the blanks about the mystery behind his powers."

"Some is better than none. What do we know?" Major Constantine sat everything down, giving her all of his attention.

The doctor opened her folder and sifted through various pages. "Well, not much actually. The test shows that the marker on the individual's genome, which identifies our subjects as either Meta or Non-Meta status, by the specific mutation in the one DNA strand does not match, both by digital analysis and chemical makeup."

With a blank stare the Major asked, "Can you explain that in English?"

"What we use to identify Metas and Non-Metas did not show up when we tested Alexavier, even though we had seen it in previous testing. Essentially, the usual test that we use to determine what he is and possibly where his abilities originate isn't

Enter Alexavier

there."

Major Constantine put his hand on his head. "I'm afraid to ask. The answer might ruin everything we've tried to do here. So, what does this all mean?"

"Actually, it doesn't ruin anything. This initial test is the most extensive one we possess, used on all recruits upon first entry into The Program to identify the mutation that gives us their status." The doctor flipped through a few pages. "Upon examining Alexavier's results, the expected anomaly wasn't present. So, the test doesn't help us with Alexavier's particular mutation. I say particular mutation, because the same DNA strand shows something unique at a different location, something we've never seen before."

"So, is there something there that the test picked up?"

"Yes. It found something new, but our test provides no clarification of the unusual alteration found in Alexavier's DNA. We've never been able to truly figure out the mystery about Alexavier and his abilities. I believe what makes him unique is this anomaly. The problem is we don't have anything that currently identifies or makes sense of it. I'd like to run some additional tests, particularly ones not yet approved by the FDA, but are being tested by the DNA medical field. This is a perfect time to find out the many things about him that we have absolutely no clue about. Even though Alexavier's case is a bit more complex and goes off into unknown territory as of this point, everything is still the way it was until we know differently."

"Proceed," the Major said emphatically. "In fact, you're authorized for every test we can do. If you're not authorized, see me, and I'll make it happen. We need a lot of answers. If we are to move ahead with him as one of our shining stars of this Program, we have to know where we're going. Having so many questions lingering for over a decade is unacceptable. Get me answers."

"Yes, sir."

Dr. Dennis was just about out the door when Jonathon entered the room in a much more serious mood. "You won't be happy to know The Terror Tribe just robbed a major New York bank, made away with several million dollars and detonated some sort of bomb, killing several bank employees and customers."

"Damn it!" The Major pushed all of the stuff on his desk forward and stood up. "When did this happen?"

"Less than ten minutes ago. We have preliminary reports from several members of The United who are at the scene."

Another loud sigh from Major Constantine showed his frustration. "Do we have an idea where they headed after the heist?"

"Eyewitnesses have various Tribe members headed toward Brooklyn. We have Booby Trap scouting in the lower Manhattan area. She could be there within minutes."

"Have her on their tail immediately. I also need the crime scene secured by whoever is there."

"I believe our hero The was the first one. He's now joined by Riva, Union, Mr. N. Sayen, Intergalactic, Metal Knight, Anthem, Statutory, Rumble and Big Hoss from The United. Local heroes lending support are Downtown, Apex, Epic, Giggle Stick, Livevil, DLX and Takeaway. I'll send our technicians out right away to process the scene. We should know more within the next few hours."

Jonathon exited the room quickly, leaving the Major to his thoughts and his rage. Another big crime had happened to the benefit of The Terror Tribe. The possibility of them getting away with a big financial score had the Major furious, and his work took the brunt of it. With a good, stiff push, all of his folders scatter across the office floor. The excessive display did little to help, as he rested his hands on his now clean desk with nothing else to take his frustration out on.

Enter Alexavier

CHAPTER 14

It was time for homework, and Alexavier took the elevator up to the library. Once he started doing recon missions, his classes would suffer, so better to get ahead of things now. He wandered through the door to a room full of books, but nearly devoid of visitors. The computer terminals were vacant, and the library custodian sat quietly, waiting for someone to help. Only a couple of complex employees were there, searching the shelves. Alexavier meandered down the aisles looking for a specific section. The library housed books for various educational purposes, ranging from regular school subjects to spy tactics, counter intelligence training manuals and battle readiness guides. You wouldn't find any sappy love stories or superhero, science fiction novels here. He traveled to the last rack of books before turning and stopping at the section labeled mathematics. Looking at the many populated shelves in front of him, he had no clue as to which book would be his best choice to help him with geometry. A casual selection had him grabbing at a mildly used textbook. Opening it to the middle and thumbing through a few pages, he gained a somewhat satisfied feeling. Knowing math problems did await his attention, he headed back to find a spot among the many tables up front to begin his studies. He received a pleasant surprise seeing Beth as a lone occupant at one of the tables.

He walked over, making a cautious approach. "Hi. They have you buried in homework too?"

"Hey, Alex." She saw his stack of papers. "What have they got for you?"

Enter Alexavier

Alexavier sighed, "Found this wonderful envelope with lots of tactical scenarios to get familiar with, not to mention geometry."

"We get those a lot. Your commitment to learning made me want to get some work done too, rather than the movie. Want to study with me?"

"Sure, if I'm not bothering your work," he said coyly.

"No." Beth cleared some space at the table. "It will be nice for a change to have a study partner. Dave and Wally like to hide in the corner by themselves. If I wouldn't know any better, I would think there is something up between those two."

Alexavier laughed, "Yeah. Wally apparently likes hanging all over Dave. Cute couple. What are you studying?"

"I'm trying to work out some of our battle strategies." She began shuffling through various pages. "The Major wants me to be one of our front-liners, so I need to work on the tactics and what my execution will be under different circumstances."

"Wow," Alexavier responded. "And I was worried about whether they'd want me to do more geometry."

"I'm going to impress the crap out of him. I plan on seeing him smile for once."

"That would be cool. Five bucks if you can get him to show teeth."

"Make it $20. And if he chuckles, you can clean my room," she confidently challenged.

"Deal. But your room is always so neat. I don't think cleaning it will be too tough."

"You might be surprised. It's pretty messy right now."

"Okay, we'll see. You were always the best at getting your work done. Once you left, my grades suffered."

Beth looked a little confused. "I wish I could remember more about my past. I know that we lose memories, but it's hard to think about what I've lost. I just can't remember. I really wish I could."

Enter Alexavier

"I could tell you about the good times. Little by little, you may get some of them back by reliving them with me."

"I would like that." A smile appeared on her face.

Alexavier ran his hands through his hair. "Maybe we can grab a snack later? I can talk about how you, me and Dave used to get in trouble all the time."

"Okay. You should grow your hair longer. I think it would look good on you."

He perked up instantly. "I got it cut after you left. I grew it out because you wanted me too."

"It's good to know you remember me."

"Nothing they do could make me forget, not even a Session." Beth's grin did little to camouflage her blushing. He smiled, opening his book to study, although something kept nagging him. "Do you think I impressed the Major enough to go on a mission soon?"

"If it were up to me, you'd be my first pick. I know the Major, and he always seems to have an agenda. We've been on several missions in which he left behind some of our best people. I worry that his bad decision making could get one of us hurt."

"I'll make sure you're safe," Alexavier stated.

She smiled, "You'd better, or I'm gonna hurt you myself."

"You're too nice to hurt me."

Under the table, she raised her hand. With a short, controlled burst of energy, she shot a beam of light at him.

"Hey!" Alexavier jumped up, his knees hitting the table. Beth laughed quietly, while he rubbed his leg. Both of them looked about the library, hoping his outburst did not disrupt anyone. Alexavier began to smile, as she joined him in subdued laughter. Even though they buried themselves back in their work, Beth kept looking

Enter Alexavier

back at her study partner. Both were content in the place they were at right now. Neither would change a thing.

Enter Alexavier

CHAPTER 15

Each step was careful. The movement from one area to another became an exercise in caution. For Bobbie, it was just a typical night out for the best reconnaissance hero The Program had produced. There was elegance to how she moved, so quickly, yet with deadly silence. If there happened to be any villains in the building she was scouring, they would never know her presence.

Moving through the last hallway, she finally arrived at a dark door that led up to the roof of the large factory. Getting up to the 12th floor so quickly, Bobbie was slightly out of breath. She quietly opened the door and rested while closing it softly. Taking in a few deep breaths helped rejuvenate her as she cautiously walked to the periphery of the roof. Getting close to the edge, she ducked down for cover, crawling the last few feet. Methodically raising her head, she stared down towards her intended target, a warehouse positioned just across the way. Turning back to take cover, she quickly dipped into her bag and produced a small pair of binoculars. Slowly, she raised them up to her eyes. Peering through, her heart started to pound in her chest. Excitement ran through her body as her gut feelings were confirmed. She had finally found a seemingly lifeless building with life in it.

Almost every building in this industrial district of Brooklyn had no activity for a few years now. This one was lit up however, particularly on the 5th floor. The activity was not the easiest to view, but when people came into view, they were unmistakable. They came in and out of sight through the windows in very odd fashion. The back and forth nature suggested that some kind of argument might be ongoing. Finally, a huge smile came across Bobbie's face. Turning back to sit, she placed the binoculars down beside her and tapped the call button on her earpiece. "Come in, headquarters. I've found them. I found The Tribe."

Enter Alexavier

CHAPTER 16

Time passed as Beth and Alexavier were getting reacquainted. The spark that had been buried long before slowly ignited again. The homework was an afterthought. Textbooks might have been open, but they served no purpose except as elbow rests. The only thing getting done was pleasant conversation, with Alexavier finishing a tale. "Dave ran like a lunatic. They didn't even hesitate to shoot when he didn't stop."

Beth laughed softly. "God. That is so him. I wish I could remember those times."

"I won't forget any time soon. You can always come to me and re-live Dave's mindless shenanigans."

"Promise?"

"I promise. Just don't get me started on the night you scared Brad Stryper. You had him peeing the bed."

"Oh my gosh! No, I didn't!" she gasped. "Why would I do that to anyone? That's not me."

"You got him back after he loaded your hair dryer with baby powder."

Before Beth could ask another question, an announcement came over the P.A. system. "Code Black! All recruits report to the hangar immediately! Repeat, Code Black! All recruits report to the hangar immediately! All operations and mission gear must be in hand!"

Confused, Alexavier wondered, "What's Code Black?"

Enter Alexavier

The grin on Beth's face vanished. "They found The Terror Tribe. More importantly, they found The Infamous One." She quickly gathered her things. "I bet it's Bobbie. Come on, get your suit and combat gear and meet in the hangar." Alexavier had little time to ask any more questions. Beth had vanished out the front door of the library. Feeling a bit left behind, he grabbed everything into one big heap and raced to get ready for what would hopefully be his first mission.

#

With a lightning turnaround, Alexavier arrived in the hangar before most of the others. He had his hero suit on, ready to go, while many of the team carried their outfits with them. He made his way to the ramp of the jet helicopter that was almost ready to take off. The only two who made it into the hangar sooner were Wally and Major Constantine. Bellowing, the Major directed each person as he or she entered the room. "Get all combat gear together, check functionality and board the chopper in the hangar! This is no drill people!" More team members filed in. Percy was next, followed by Killus. "We are a live go with no prep! Percy and Killus, check all your gear now!"

Alexavier double-checked the gear in his bag, as well. His current outfit consisted of a hooded sweatshirt with cape, mask, gloves with forearm shields, shirt, pants, belt with compartments, bags with compartments that strapped to his legs and boots with shin guards that were all black in color. He pulled out possibly the most important thing from his duffel bag, a special pair of mirrored glasses that were designed specifically for him with various capabilities. In no time, he was ready, waiting for his orders.

The room filled up quickly with nearly every hero in The Program as the Major continued to yell instructions. "Hank and April, suit up! We're not going in soft! This

Enter Alexavier

is a shoot to kill operation! Everybody clear? All hostile targets are to be terminated! If you can capture a hostile, it is a bonus, but not a necessity!" The Major looked around as Beth and Dave finally arrived. "Full briefing will be disclosed when we're airborne. Let's get going! We lift off in three minutes people! The following are to get on the chopper now! April, Percy, Dave, Michael, Beth, Killus, Hank, and Wally are cleared to board!"

A wave of humanity headed for the cargo ramp, carrying what they had. Beth stopped short of vanishing inside the helicopter, realizing who was still standing on the launch pad. Alexavier had not moved. The Major looked over, seeing his newest recruit in front of him. He marched up, looking Alexavier in the eye. "Your time here has been too short for the appropriate people to give their approval." A pause of silence was only broken by the sound of helicopter blades spinning faster, until the Major finally said, "Do not disappoint me. Get your gear and get on the chopper. You have one minute to get on board."

Without any hesitation, Alexavier picked up his bag and sprinted toward the helicopter. Beth smiled, quickly ducking inside. The Major tucked the folder away, joining his team in hopes of finally getting their hands on The Terror Tribe.

Enter Alexavier

CHAPTER 17

In the skies over eastern New Jersey, the flight had the team on edge. To call the team antsy would have been an understatement. Some fidgeted, while others adjusted their own gear. Killus enjoyed every moment running his hands over his knife, looking forward to getting his chance to hurt someone. Wally straightened his blue and white outfit, while Percy inspected his weapons. Alexavier on the other hand was very calm and soaked in the other member's pre-mission rituals.

In no time, they arrived in a truly abrupt fashion. As the helicopter swooped in, the pilot called back, "We've arrived, and I'm locating a drop point."

The words faded, with the replacement of the Major's own. "Masks and helmets on! Wave Rider and Mecha, secure the landing zone!"

The noise of wind began to roar when the rear door opened. Wally and Michael proceeded to the opening and exited the helicopter. Wally used the strong winds to soar high, surveying the area below. Michael dropped down, feet first. His body shifted into full metal plates with his calves opening up and rockets emerging that ignited and slowed his decent. Once on the ground, weapons emerged from his arms. He surveyed the landscape before signaling back for the helicopter to land.

As the helicopter prepared to touch down, Major Constantine barked out orders, "Check the immediate area when you step off! Watch your heads! Everyone put in your Com-Link phones, hold off on the chatter and wait for my commands!" He walked down the cramped isle. "Precision Shot and Killing Machine, take spots at the nearest high point within 100 feet! Scout for targets! Hack 'n Maul, I want you to carry your mace and ax! Proceed out from the perimeter and secure up to a thousand feet! Remember to watch for inhabitants! This place is crawling with wild animals and feral cats!" A mild jolt gave confirmation of the landing, and Percy and Killus exited quickly, while Hank chuckled as he lumbered off, "Feels like home."

Jonathon asked, "Any more strategic info about the hideout, or is it a blind entrance?"

Major Constantine pointed the remote at the monitor on the front wall and hit a couple of buttons. "Last visuals before the cloud cover rolled in had her right here at this location! We should be on top of them! Her last communication had her going for cover in a nearby building! Alexavier is to hold his position near base camp and wait for instructions! The rest of you can pan out slowly for the first five hundred feet and wait until we have a sure point of attack!"

Within seconds, the rest of the team exited with sculpted precision. Their location was the top of an empty, ten story building in the middle of the factory district near the waterfront, just a couple of buildings away from their intended target. Percy and Killus had situated themselves to the left, directly on top of the elevator shaft. Wally swooped in and picked up Hank to drop him off down below. The rest of the team headed to the stairs and made their way down. Alexavier proceeded directly to the edge of rooftop. Major Constantine, Jonathon and Dr. Dennis were the last to exit, allowing the helicopter to lift into the air.

Jonathon was the first to analyze the choice for a base camp. "Is there enough view from this vantage point? Should we spread out to other rooftops?"

The Major surveyed the landscape. "The building Bobbie used to spot The Tribe hideout is too small to land on. I don't want to hamper our extraction if we're only guessing at base camps, and we need a place for the chopper to land safely. Right now, we're perfectly set to take the hideout once we determine the correct building from the surveillance photos."

Alexavier straightened his mask, pulled his hood forward and turned to Dr. Dennis, "This doesn't feel right."

"What's wrong?"

"I'm not sure, but I've done enough urban warfare exercises to know that we are at a huge disadvantage, particularly from this building." Alexavier explained. "This is as close to any ambush scenario as I've ever run across. We need to regroup for a different plan. Maybe we should pull back and enter as one unit."

"Maybe you should tell the Major," Dr. Dennis replied hesitantly.

Alexavier walked over and interrupted the Major and Jonathon. "We're sitting in a precarious spot, Major."

"What's bugging you, son?"

Alexavier pointed to the skyline. "Without knowing the exact location of the hideout and how the various buildings are spread out enough to separate our people, the viewing angles are all blocked or highly distorted. They could be picking us off or diluting our numbers by separating us."

Major Constantine responded, "I don't think they know we're here, especially with the chopper in stealth mode."

"This was the only building with a roof big enough and clear enough to land a helicopter on. There could be a reason why. If this was by design and if they are anticipating our arrival-"

The Major interjected, "If they get in our way, we'll send them a message. Command, come in."

Jonathon was curious and moved closer to Alexavier. "What do you see?"

"The layout of the buildings and the scarcity of open areas is real visual disadvantage is a perfect ambush scenario, even if we're not the first ones to ambush.

Enter Alexavier

Since this is the only building we could land on, it would make sense they could ambush us." Alexavier turned to face Jonathon. "We're going in blind. It's a guessing game, and I don't think we know this area well enough to be careless. If anyone gets separated, they could be in real trouble."

The Major started yelling, "Come in command!"

Feeling quite concerned, Jonathon decided to take up further discussions with the Major. "Alex has a good point. Maybe we should take a second to re-evaluate this."

"I've looked things over," the Major barked back. "With our intel, and the fact that we're taking the offensive means we have the advantage. Now if we can only contact the complex. Come in, command!"

"Should we do something?" the doctor asked.

Jonathon eyed the buildings in the distance. "He's not going to listen. We need to be ready. We may have to play catch up if this goes bad. What's with the static in our Coms?"

"Anyone, do you read me? What the hell is wrong?" The frustration finally hit the Major, knowing he's now become helpless.

#

The wave of heroes began to swarm the buildings and open areas below, heading to the one building that had thought to be The Terror Tribe's hideout. Wally was the first to get close, hovering overhead. "Major? Come in. Can you hear me?"

A shattering blast hit the wall of the building below, sending shrapnel whizzing by his face. Looking back, several members of The Terror Tribe mounted an assault on the position of the team below. Instantly, his team intercepted the oncoming villains in an all-out brawl of super powered beings. Punches were thrown. Energy blasts were shot. Nothing was held back. Killus pulled out his knives, swinging at anything that moved. Hank looked to plunge his mace into anyone. For all of the intense combat currently going on, everything was not going their way. Dave was in need of backup, but quickly realized he needed to ask for it, "Major! I need some help!" But a wall of static in his ear made for another realization. "Damn it! Hey, guys! Communications are out! We're on our own!

#

"We need the chopper! Maybe the problem is with our Com-Links, and their radio still works." Major Constantine tried waving his arms, hoping to been seen by the pilot.

"With our Coms out, there's no way to talk to him." Jonathon reminded him.

The Major forcefully shouted, "No kidding! And extra arms in the air couldn't hurt! You might need to get on the elevator shaft to be more visible!"

Alexavier caught Jonathon walking by. "This is wrong. We need back up more than anything. I should be on the ground helping the team."

Jonathon turned to the Major. "Shouldn't we-"

"Get to the top of the elevator!"

Jonathon pleaded, "We need to get Alex-"

Major Constantine marched over to Jonathon. "Don't you screw with me! Not now! We need the helicopter back here to use the radio! Where the hell is that chopper?" Jonathon backed down and walked away with the Major pacing back and forth in a furious rage.

Alexavier turned to Dr. Dennis, "This is all wrong, and he doesn't even see it."

With the worried look on her face less than reassuring, Alexavier decided that the time for action was now. Looking around the rooftop, he eyed a couple of water

Enter Alexavier

drainage pipes hanging over the other side of the building. Alexavier raced toward the edge as Dr. Dennis watched on helplessly. In one fluid move, Alexavier jumped over the edge and disappeared from sight.

Enter Alexavier

CHAPTER 18

Emerging from the top of the building, Alexavier grabbed onto the cascading pipes and gained speed with gravity's help. His route ended only four floors down, when the pipes returned to the inside of the building. He kicked hard and jettisoned away from the pipes. His outstretched arms grabbed onto the lower rail of a fire escape ladder. Spotting the vertical ladder attached to the wall, he placed his feet to the outside, held on and began the quick slide down that stopped as the ladder ended at the second floor. Nearing the last rung, he squeezed his hands slightly to slow his descent and let go as he dropped safely to the ground.

Alexavier stood up, checking for signs of movement. Having his glasses would have been helpful, with the capabilities of infrared and other vision enhancing features. For now, he pulled his hood over his head before setting off to help, using caution while moving quickly to the corner of the building.

Poking his head out, the coast was clear all the way to the war that was being waged. In a full speed sprint, he charged for the battlefield. Little time passed before the sounds of combat were joined by the presence of conflict. The struggle between good and evil presented many opportunities to use his vast skills. But just as he headed to help Dave in his fight with the very large, overweight bad guy known as Glutton, a shocking sensation caused his muscles to spasm, and it dropped Alexavier to his knees.

Looking back, the man responsible for the attack stood his ground. Bolts of

Enter Alexavier

electricity shot out his arms and hands. His smile was as obvious as his powers and his name. No words needed to be said, as Alexavier remembered Mega Conductor from their previous encounter. This former Program recruit had a score to settle with any heroes from The Program. And for more than one reason, he was glad to make Alexavier his next victim.

With the furious crackling of electricity like a six foot Tesla coil, Mega Conductor slowly closed the distance but came to a realization of recognition. "You again! Oh, I can't wait. Unlike the first time, this should be fun." A storm of bolts intensified, resulting in another shock that sent Alexavier face first to the ground. Forcing himself up, another attempt to advance his position was met with more electricity and more pain.

Alexavier flexed his muscles, hoping to get them to respond to his mental commands. The twitched faded, long enough for him to run over to one side and try a tactic previously used to get the villain off his game. "Nice try, Electrode." He could only get a few feet before another debilitating jolt from a very angry Mega Conductor had him on his stomach again. The uncontrollable gurgling noises that came from his mouth became the sound of desperation, as each attack took more out of him.

Alexavier knew that he had to make his next effort count. Unfortunately, a leap to the side did not get him out of the path of the next electric shock. The voltage slamming his nervous system put him down in the dirt, but right where he wanted to be. As Mega Conductor laughed, thinking the dodging did his adversary no good, Alexavier lifted his head to see his target, a baseball sized rock within grasp. Placing his hand on it and holding tight, a quick pop up to one knee allowed a perfect throw that sent the rock colliding with Mega Conductor's stomach. Stumbling around doubled over, Mega Conductor lost all of his charge and opportunity for another attack. Seeing his chance, Alexavier rolled forward to his feet. And with all the force he could put behind it, he thrust his foot upward, connecting to Mega Conductor's

Enter Alexavier

head. The resulting head snap and unconsciousness had Mega Conductor's body twist around with him hitting the dirt with an uncerimonious thud.

A huge sigh of relief was followed by a moment to assess his physical condition, before going back to his duties. Grabbing a couple of industrial zip ties, he walked to his incapacitated opponent and began the ritual of securing his first capture.

Unfortunately, that is when gravity ran wild. The intense pull brought Alexavier down, his hands barely able to hold his face from the dirt. The thunderous sound of concrete, cracking and breaking, cascaded through the entire area. One of the buildings behind him started to collapse. Each floor fell in on the one below. Concrete and steel twisted together in a mass of destruction. The rippling effect eventually sent a cloud of dust into the air. A single blast of light energy shot skyward as the building finished its impromptu demolition. Just as it had started so quickly, the intense gravitational pull finally stopped.

Major Constantine witnessed the increase in gravity and saw the cloud of dust. At the same moment, he realized the static from the Com-Links was gone. "Anyone hearing me?"

Wally responded, "Loud and clear, Major. The Coms are back."

"We're behind the eight ball with this mission. We need to assess where we're at. Was anyone in that building? I need people to report in!" the Major demanded.

"I'm several buildings away, in a fight!" Michael replied.

"I need everyone to the building now!" the Major shouted. "Who's got eyes on it?"

Percy called in, "I can't see a thing."

Although his arms were weak, Alexavier focused hard, bringing himself to his feet. The devastation left from the fallen building was a shocking sight. Voices could be heard in his Com-Link, and he realized communications had been restored. "I'm near the building that collapsed. I got one Tribe member down. I'm tired, but safe. I could use backup."

Enter Alexavier

"Get to the building and see what happened. Has anyone seen Beacon or Killing Machine? I need a call out for an extraction chopper. Jonathon, get with command," the Major ordered.

"Until the dust settles, I've got no line of sight to the collapse," Percy stated. "I could get to a better vantage point, maybe check for Tribe members making a run for it."

"Do it!"

Reluctantly, Alexavier made his way over to the building. His balance was affected slightly, but slowly cleared up with each step. He called in to the team, "I'll be at the building in a few seconds."

"Good," Major Constantine replied. "Where is Beacon?"

"I'm helping Hack fight off Freak Show and Terrorcide," Michael responded.

"I'm on my way back," Wally interjected. "I chased an unknown, flying bad guy, but I should be back in a few minutes."

The Major turned to Dr. Dennis. "Stand ready. Wave Rider, the doctor is here and waiting. Pick her up and bring her to the battlefield. Anyone need the doctor?"

"Be there is a sec." Wally said, flying as fast as the wind would push him.

Dave called in, "I'm good."

Almost everyone chimed in as Alexavier made a slow trek toward the downed building. He kept his eyes on the surrounding landscape in case of an ambush. Only seconds after leaving Mega Conductor behind, he noticed a face he recognized from pictures back at the complex emerge from around a nearby building, as Bobbie quickly ran over to him.

"You're the new guy. You're called Dread, right? Boy, am I happy to see a friendly face. I saw a couple of stray members of The Tribe heading toward a different building and decided to follow them while waiting for everyone to arrive. I was tracking them when I felt the rumbling. What happened? This building is the one where I spotted Infamous and The Tribe."

"I don't know. It just fell. The Major wants me to head there to check it out." Alexavier called in. "Major, I'm with Booby Trap."

"What's her condition?" the Major asked.

"I'm fine, Major."

"Continue to the building," the Major said. "I need info on what happened. I'm guessing that gravity fluctuation was part of the reason it went down, and I'm guessing it originated from there. Where's Killus?"

"No clue," Percy responded.

Alexavier carefully entered the field of debris ahead of Bobbie. "The building is totaled. I'm not sure what happened. I don't see any signs of life here. I need back up. The Tribe could be nearby waiting for us."

Major Constantine continued directing, "I need Precision Shot to get to a better position to watch Alexavier's back. I need Hack and Mecha to the downed building if we need to remove debris."

"I'll back him up. I can stay and keep an eye out for The Tribe," Bobbie replied.

"I'm on my way," Michael responded.

"Did someone call for a chopper? Jonathon!" the Major inquired. "Someone get me a line to central command!"

"It's already on its way," Jonathon confirmed.

The maze of cement boulders had Alexavier stumbling over the outermost pieces. A dip in the terrain made him realize that a crater occupied the center of the remains. Barely able to see through the smoke, he continued to climb toward the center. Each step was difficult, slipping on loose rubble. His descent finally ended with an uncontrollable slide that provided a sight he hoped never to see. A white glove with golden tips on its fingers and part of a white cape were protruding from the center of

Enter Alexavier

the crater. His eyes stared as his heart dropped. "I need Hack 'n Maul, now!"

"Where are you, Alex? What's going on?" the Major asked.

Reaching the area where Beth was covered, Alexavier yelled out, "It's Beacon! She's trapped in the building! The debris is too large, and I won't be able to move any of it!"

"What?!" Dave shouted.

"Everyone to the collapsed building!" the Major shouted.

Wally started flying faster. "I'll get the doctor and be there as soon as I can!"

Bobbie rushed to the outer edge of the crater and stopped. "Oh my god." Her jaw dropped. "We need to get her out quickly before-"

A large explosion catapulted pieces of the building everywhere. Bobbie slipped and tumbled back from the edge of the crater. Alexavier turned away, protecting his face. The shrapnel settled, and from the dust cloud emerged Natural Disaster with a dark figure following behind and another racing away. Natural Disaster turned to see the white glove and exclaimed, "There she is."

Noticing the aggressive stance, Alexavier grabbed the nearest rock and threw it, smacking Natural Disaster in the side of the head. Staggering back, Natural Disaster pulled down his hand covered in blood and turned his attention toward Alexavier.

Realizing how vulnerable Beth was, Alexavier rushed forward as best he could among the debris. "Where is Hack? I need backup! I've got Tribe members at the downed building!"

"I'm working on getting there!" Hank exclaimed.

Michael yelled back, "I'll be there in a minute!"

The Major inquired. "Who's close to Alexavier?"

"I am, but we've got Natural Disaster!" Bobbie made her way through the rubble and ran to help. Natural Disaster saw the charging hero and shot an energy blast,

Enter Alexavier

spraying rubble into the air and all around Bobbie. She ducked, running for cover.

Seeing an opening, Alexavier jumped up to attack. Natural Disaster unleashed another blast. This time, the wave surge hit the hero, throwing him toward the outside of the crater. Before Alexavier could get his bearings, another blast of energy sent large pieces of debris towards him. He leaped away, rolling with the momentum and out of danger.

Raising his head up, Alexavier saw the ominous villain advancing towards Beth, readying to finish the job. "Stay away from her!" He could not sustain diverting Natural Disaster forever. Seeing the dark figure left alone, Alexavier found an iron rod in the rubble. With a strong throw he hurled it through the air like a javelin. Natural Disaster noticed the projectile and spun around, blasting it away with a powerful blast of energy. Hoping to seize the opportunity, Alexavier jumped up and advanced toward the cowering figure in the background. The dark figure slowly retreated, making Natural Disaster turn around and take up a defensive position. Hoping to stop Alexavier's progression, Natural Disaster shot several random blasts, but the explosive impacts did little to stop him. Alexavier leaped over a chunk of debris and noticed large pieces of broken glass. Finding a sizable piece perfect to throw, he launched it. Natural Disaster generated an energy field, encapsulating the two retreating villains. The glass shattered into a million pieces without doing any damage.

Seeing Alexavier grabbing more shards of glass and knowing his role had become more of a bodyguard, Natural Disaster scanned around for a safe escape. Drawing in a massive charge of energy, he blasted the rubble around him into a devastating storm of cement and concrete. Alexavier tried to dodge the deadly onslaught by twisting and turning his body, but his luck finally ran out. A chunk of debris ricocheted off of another just as Alexavier turned away. Instead of the projectile crushing his skull, the glancing blow knocked him down and almost unconscious.

Enter Alexavier

With blood running down his pounding head, he could barely think. He tried to hoist himself up using a small bolder, but his vision started to blur. Several voices continued to call out to him, but he couldn't distinguish any of them. After taking a few steps, his staggering ended with a hard fall to the ground. Each moment brought a fuzzier and darker view of the world as he tried one last communication. "Where's Hank? Beth… is still… down…" The last thing Alexavier saw before passing out was the white glove of Beth, sticking out of the rubble.

Enter Alexavier

CHAPTER 19

The light was getting brighter as Alexavier slowly opened his eyes. His head was not very clear, and his thoughts were hard to process. The vision he saw was a blur, masked by a white light's glare. Blinking several times brought more detail to his surroundings, which he recognized as The Program's medical unit and Dr. Dennis. He began to stir, asking, "Is she alright?"

Before he could even attempt to get out of bed, the doctor tried her best to keep him restrained. "Lay back and relax. You need to rest."

"Where is Beth?" Alexavier asked, struggling to sit up.

Dr. Dennis hesitated. With a severe head injury, she wanted to keep his stress level low. She decided to circumvent the subject. "If you don't rest, you won't be able to see anyone."

"I need to know if she's okay."

Mike noticed the commotion in the room from outside and came in to help. "Hey! Take it easy! You've taken a pretty good hit to the head."

"Please, just tell me…" Alexavier's head got heavy. His eyes rolled back, and he laid his head down from the strain.

Mike knelt down. "Easy there. Your head took quite a blow, and it's bruised pretty badly. The doctors are worried that you could have swelling or bleeding in your brain."

"I don't care about me. What about Beth?"

"You need to stay calm. Your blood pressure needs to stay down with your head injury," Dr. Dennis pointed out.

"Is there anything you can do?" Mike asked.

Dr. Dennis turned up his morphine. "He should be more manageable in a minute."

"I don't need drugs." Alexavier attempted to get up again.

"You need rest," Mike pleaded.

"Please tell me, is she alive?" Alexavier's arms got heavy, so Mike laid him back as the drug started to settle him down.

Mike backed away, allowing a view through the glass wall into the next room. "She's fine and resting thanks to you. Now, you need to rest too."

Alexavier was relieved to see Beth, but his heart stopped when he saw her hooked up to several pieces of medical equipment and a tube down her throat. Her face was bruised and bandaged. Wally and Dave were standing by her side. When Dave looked over and noticed Alexavier awake, he poked Wally. They hurried over with Dave the most excited. "Welcome back, dude. You did it, man. That took pure guts to take on Natural Disaster one on one."

"I guess the new guy really proved himself," Wally proclaimed.

"Guys, he needs to relax. Don't get him too wound up," Dr. Dennis stated.

Alexavier settled back into the pillow. "She's alright?"

"Alive because of you, pal." Wally pulled up a chair.

"What happened?" Alexavier wondered.

Dave sat on the bed. "You held them off long enough for Michael and Hank get to your location."

"While Hank removed the rubble, I raced to get the doc. We got there just as Beth was uncovered," Wally said.

Enter Alexavier

Dr. Dennis leaned over, checking Alexavier's pupils. "I was able to stabilize her, but the damage was severe. It took everything out of me, and I nearly lost her. We would have if it wasn't for Mike."

Alexavier looked to Mike. "How-"

Mike sat up on the edge of his chair. "I got the call from the command center that communications had ceased almost immediately, and the team was cut off from the source. I had a tour going on with some young recruits from other complexes. And since part of the tour had to do with seeing our operations in action, I didn't want to leave them unattended. I quickly prepped them for a flight. One of the kids had the power to sustain living organisms, and another to generate a protective energy field, I took the chance that they could be of help if the situation turned bad and boarded a jet copter with them. When we arrived, you were down, Beth was in rough shape and everything was in chaos. Luckily, Forrest Lifeson, the recruit who could sustain life, was able to keep Beth from deteriorating any further until we could stabilize her. Dr. Dennis did the rest."

Percy walked in the room. "But if you hadn't held off Natural Disaster, she wouldn't be alive right now. Got to admit it kid, you made me proud."

"Amen to that," Wally said.

"After coming back to life, I got there, and it was a pretty scary sight to see. She was crushed, literally flattened. She had no way to defend herself. Thank God you were around," Dave stated.

"Yeah, absolutely. When we arrived, she was barely alive with a weak heartbeat. She had no chance for survival except for you, which made all the difference," Mike proclaimed.

"She looks worse than she really is, especially with where her health was when we dug her out. She will fully recover, given enough time and rest, which you need as well," Dr. Dennis said, as she left the room to check on Beth.

Enter Alexavier

Percy stood over the injured hero. "That was impressive. Most kids come in and have no idea what it means to be here. You're truly a hero."

Alexavier let out an exhale in relief. "Thank God. I almost-"

"You almost got her killed." The voice of Harvey echoed throughout the room.

"Dude, shut up!" Dave yelled.

Harvey walked over to the bed. "What? He wanted the truth, and I'm not going to deprive him of that."

"You sure know how to support your team," Wally barked.

Harvey stared down Alexavier. "The truth hurts. He disobeyed orders. He took it upon himself not to follow the Major's commands. Maybe if he would have listened and signaled the helicopter, Beth wouldn't have hoses down her throat right now."

Wally walked up to Harvey, standing nose to nose. "Maybe you could have been there to help or even save her. And you weren't, but he was and did. Disobeying those orders probably saved her life."

Harvey backed away. "Any of you notice that since he's been here, things have started going downhill?"

"Oh, and like you haven't been a part of that?" Mike asked sarcastically.

"I've been the only consistent thing about this place in the past five years," Harvey stated.

Dave pointed out, "Yeah, a consistent pain in the-"

Harvey raised his voice. "Don't get me started on being consistent. I've captured more criminals than anyone else, even heroes out of The Program, including Sam."

"If it wasn't for someone's directions, you wouldn't have gotten those chances." Dave pointed to Mike.

"Really?" Harvey responded. "Where were you this time? Still can't handle the reality we live in, huh? Not that you mattered anyway, because the only person that matters is me. I'm the one who's going to get Infamous. I'm the one who's going to bring down The Tribe. The only thing Alex is going to do is get everyone hurt or killed. He may bring the rest of us down with him."

Percy stepped up to confront Harvey. "I think you better leave, or I'm going to put you through that door myself!"

Harvey realized that the threat was real. His silence signaled an end to the confrontation as he slowly walked to the door. Feeling brave entering the hallway, he shot back, "Once you understand that he is the cause of all our problems, I'll be the one to take care of things, just like I always do!"

Harvey vanished from sight as Wally stated, "God, I'm really starting to hate him."

"What do you mean starting?" Dave added.

Mike turned to Alexavier. "Let's forget about him and his childish behavior. He can feel sorry for himself all he wants. We have more important things and people to attend to. Make sure Alex doesn't do anything except stay there and rest. I'm going to check on Beth."

With one last look at her, the realization hit Alexavier. Beth could have been killed. With only a little variation in any number of circumstances, she would be dead right now. That hurt worse than the blow he took to his head.

Enter Alexavier

CHAPTER 20

The shades were drawn, and the lights were low. Major Constantine did not want anyone to bother him after the fiasco that was the mission. Some success was had, but at a cost, which he did not want to hear about. There were a couple of knocks on his door, but he ignored them, hoping those who were eager to talk to him would move on.

He's been buried in paperwork for months, appearing to never get caught up. And with every completed mission, that pile of folders on his desk received a new neighbor. Rather than add to the tall stack of work, he hurried to complete this paperwork and get it filed quickly so he did not have to answer any questions. The fact of nearly losing a recruit still stung pretty badly. But maybe getting this behind him and not having to explain things would ease his anxiety.

A ring from his phone disrupted his thoughts. Worse yet, the number was from Sam Nelson, the legendary superhero, not to mention one of the leaders of this particular segment of The Program. Each ring became one more knife thrust into the Major's eardrums. Knowing that the ringing might end, but would start right back again, he reluctantly answered the phone.

"Yeah. Hi Sam… They just finished the Session with Manny, and the doctors have moved him back to his room awaiting further evaluation. I'll keep you updated as soon as they let me know anything else."

The mood of the phone call quickly changed. "Yes. I know... I know… Things

Enter Alexavier

didn't go perfectly... Nothing's changed on Beth's status... Look. I don't think that's accurate... We followed protocols during every second of that mission... I understand that... But there wasn't time... I sent the team out, in a predetermined fashion. We attacked their front line fighters with force... Of course, nothing different than usual... Sure, it wasn't the best location for a frontal assault. We did come in hot and put the pressure on them right away... I feel we matched up well. Even if she was separated from us... Yes. You're right."

A long silence followed. The Major's demeanor changed with each passing second. It was a conversation he would rather not have. "Okay. It's your call. I'll expect you soon... And that will be fine... We can do that... Bye."

Fuming from what felt like an almost one-sided conversation, Major Constantine placed the phone on its cradle rather aggressively. The report that needed to get done, no longer mattered. He picked up the phone, dialed a number and waited. Soon a voice answered on the other end. The Major was in no mood for pleasantries. "I need Jonathon and Dr. Dennis to come to my office right away. Tell the doctor to bring her examination equipment. I need to know if Alexavier is cleared for action."

#

Mulling around his room, Alexavier became antsy. The downtime to recover from his bruises did little to scratch the itch of getting back to crime fighting. The only thing he could think about was being prepared. He had organized his gear twice already, but decided that a triple check could not hurt. Every weapon was clean and spotless. His belt, gadgets and glasses were all neatly positioned. Although, ten minutes would not go by before he stared at his outfit. Although this time, he stared at it a little longer. The fact that was hung up on display bothered him. If he was not wearing it, he was not taking on the bad guys, especially those who hurt Beth.

Enter Alexavier

His eyes were diverted when the sight of the human train that was Major Constantine, Jonathon and Dr. Dennis appeared in the corridor across the hall. Needing a break from the monotony, he watched with hope that they would be a needed distraction. His wish was granted as they came right to his door and entered into his room. The Major was all business, eyes buried in his papers and never locking onto Alexavier. "Doctor, please give me your assessment of Alexavier's health status and recovery."

Patting the desk for Alexavier to sit, Dr. Dennis began looking him over. "So, when Alex got back, he was in pretty rough shape. The injuries were extensive, although somewhat superficial. Some light burns were scattered about due to Mega Conductor's powers. Those appear close to being healed. The bruising from the flying cement is almost gone too. Now, the black and blue from the head trauma is better, but it's the possible concussion that's the worry. Let me check you over."

As she gave Alexavier a thorough examination, Jonathon walked closer. "What are the symptoms of a concussion?"

Dr. Dennis explained, "There's a long list of symptoms or effects that could reoccur or show up at any time or even odd intervals. He could have headaches or migraines, dizziness, light headedness, vertigo, confusion, lack of coordination, memory loss, nausea and/or vomiting, ringing in the ears, fatigue, sensitivity to light and sleepiness. And any of these could happen weeks from now, even months depending on how or what he does, especially if anything more happens to his head. How long they last is another thing. Some people have shown concussion symptoms for a week to a few months, while others always have them, and it never goes away. Each person is different, and the varying levels of trauma can also determine how bad things might be or if they don't get any at all."

"That's not what I want to hear," Major Constantine responded with a sigh.

Jonathan asks, "I guess the first thing we should ask is if you've had any?'

Enter Alexavier

"I did have a headache yesterday. I drank extra water like the doctor said, and it went away after a few hours. I haven't had any problems since."

"Document his headaches, just in case there's more in the future," the Major ordered.

"Yes, sir. Well, the swelling has gone down." The doctor moved aside Alexavier's hair. "There's only a slight discoloration from the bruise left. How does it feel when you touch it?"

"A little sore, but it's not anything that would keep me from training again."

"What about quick head movements?" the doctor inquired.

Alexavier shook his head and paused. "Everything is fine."

"How about if you stand up really quick?" Jonathon wondered.

Alexavier hopped off the desk, crouched down and stood up fast. "Nothing."

Jonathan put his hand on Alexavier's shoulder. "Don't overdo it. We don't need you accidentally hurting yourself before you're cleared."

"So then, what is Alex cleared to do?" asked the Major.

"He can participate in any activities he feels he's able to do," the doctor informed them. "A mission might be questionable depending on how sore he feels, as long as nothing hinders his performance or safety. Having been well documented, Alexavier displays unusual healing abilities of a somewhat heightened nature. Since we've never had him suffer such an injury before, knowing exactly what the results will be is unclear, but should be positive. In the end, if he feels up to it, he can do it."

"Alright. Let's get to the matter at hand." Major Constantine puffed out his chest. "Where did you get the thought about running off on your own during the mission?"

"The situation didn't feel right. How the buildings were laid out didn't suit anyone making any kind of offensive charge. They'd have us split into small groups that would've had us at a disadvantage instantly. I knew my help was better served

Enter Alexavier

assisting the team."

"But my instructions were for you to stay by me and wait. There's a reason for what I want. I have a game plan that I need everyone to follow. We go into almost every situation having little clue to what we might encounter. I have several things to consider while we're all in danger. And if something is out of place, I might miss a detail that could prove deadly."

"That's one of my areas of expertise. I was trained to notice slight details in every situation I'm involved in."

"Which is fine, but you should let me know and not act on them. That would be fine if you were on your own, but not when I'm leading this team. I've got the entire team's lives in my hands. It's my job to take what you see and determine the best course of action. My decisions are critical to keep everyone safe. What you try to do without my say so could jeopardize everyone else."

"The only thing I was trying to do was what I was trained for."

"And I don't want you to do anything but that. The other thing I need is for you to be a team player and do what's best for the team, even if it's not clear. So from this moment forward, you are to listen to me and follow my instructions, understand?"

"Yes."

"Good. Now, be ready. You've got a workout scheduled for tomorrow. It's important you're at your best."

"I'll be ready."

Feeling the need to clarify his position, Major Constantine walked over to his prize recruit and spoke a bit softer. " Whether you realize it or not, you are one of the most important pieces of this puzzle. Your high-level abilities, particularly in combat, make you something special. I see this team being a huge success with you as a part of it. I need you to excel like no one else. These workouts are your time to shine. Show the others why you're the future of this Program."

Enter Alexavier

"Tomorrow will be the best you've ever seen, sir."

With an approving smile, the Major moved away. "Well doctor, if you're through, I'd like you to update me on the healing of our other recruits from the mission." Dr. Dennis gathered her things, escorting the Major out the door.

Jonathon stayed behind. "It's nice to see you're healing up and feeling better. And now you get to show off those talents the Major is so excited about."

"I hope so. As mad as he was to begin with, I wasn't sure he would want me around."

"You're important to the Major. He's been trying to make this team into something special. Graduates go on to The United every so often, causing issues with the Major's plans. The timing has been perfect with you. The Major feels the right pieces of the team were slowly falling into place, but the one thing that's been missing is a recruit with supreme fighting abilities. Your fighting skills put you in a rare category. We have Bobbie, but she more stealth oriented."

"But if we're talking about categories, I'm just a Non-Meta. My fighting isn't as powerful as so many of the best heroes who've been through here. Why wouldn't Union, Intergalactic or even Mr. N. Sayen's indestructibility be better for fighting The Tribe?"

"The Infamous One," Jonathon stated.

"How is my ability to kick people's butts going to help with a guy who can blend in with shadows?"

"The reality of The Infamous One is different than what most people and our government know. What most people think of him is an evil person who happens to beat everyone by hiding in dark places until he gets the jump on them. Almost no one knows the fact that The Infamous One beats people by hand-to-hand combat. Even if we send in a Meta with outrageous powers, he somehow finds a way to beat them. The only people to ever come close to taking him down have been Sam and Bobbie.

Enter Alexavier

Sam's had the opportunity to face The Infamous One on several occasions, but each time came up short. Bobbie nearly had her hands on him once. But he was about to shoot her, so she fled. That's why we need you to perform well in the workouts. You showing your abilities and dominating during each encounter will have you on the first plane into battle. The Major believes you to be the only recruit in the entire system of The Program to be able to take down the worst criminal alive."

"Wow. I didn't know." Alexavier bowed his head, rubbing his head.

Jonathon walked over to the door. "So have a good dinner and get a good night's sleep. You have the workout in the morning to prepare for. Go out there and show everyone what you can do."

"I'll be at my best." Alexavier watched Jonathon leave, having much to think about. There was determination on his face. He began psyching himself up while gathering his gear for tomorrow. But one thing still crept its way back into his thoughts. Even though it was a very short distance, the walk seemed like a journey that would never end. When it did, he looked through the glass to see Beth, still lying on the gurney. There seemed to be a quiet that overwhelmed everything as he stood there, as if the rest of the world didn't exist. And for this young hero, nothing else mattered.

Enter Alexavier

CHAPTER 21

His night was filled with plenty sleepless moments. Alexavier tossed and turned, never truly getting comfortable. Not only was Beth on his mind, but also there was another workout scheduled. And the day had arrived for him to once again show what countless years of training and massive amounts of government dollars had done to perfect his skills. The planned workout would put him where he had excelled hundreds of times before. Enough time had passed since the mission that all the necessary healing had taken place, so being sore should not be a problem.

Setting his duffel bag on his bed and thumbing through the contents to assure that all of the necessary equipment was already inside, he noticed one of his boots was missing. This seemed quite odd, having made it a point to keep his entire world as much under control as possible. He scanned the tables and looked around the desk on the floor, but it was nowhere to be found. Alexavier sat on the edge of his bed and let out a deep sigh. This was not how he wanted to start what he hoped was his first opportunity to impress everyone.

As an awkward feeling hit him, Alexavier saw movement from his peripheral vision. Not wanting whoever to know that he was aware of their presence, he continued to sulk, waiting with the intent to surprise his guest. With a suddenly move, he reached out, but no one was there. What was there and in his hand was his other boot. He got the feeling that this situation was not quite as odd as it would have appeared. "Thanks, Jennifer. Just what I was looking for."

Enter Alexavier

His mysterious guest began to materialize in front of him. Jennifer sat on his desk, still transparent. Her physical form seemed to fade in and out. "How did you know I had it?"

"Wild guess, actually."

"Crap!" she exclaimed.

"It was a pretty good try. I almost didn't know you were here."

"You're still cute, even though you suck at lying." Jennifer giggled as she faded away.

Alexavier stuffed the boot in his bag and headed out of his room with a content smile on his face. Dave and Wally were casually walking by, so he joined them. "Looks like I'm not tardy for class."

"I'm not worried about me being tardy," Dave said. "I'm always late."

"Hey, sometimes it's better to be late than not arrive at all," Wally joked.

Dave nodded. "True."

A slight breeze started blowing. Wally quickly jumped in the air, using it to fly above the corridor full of people. "Last one there gets to shave the Major!"

"Crap. You gotta hate Metas so early in the morning," Dave said.

"Aren't you a Meta too?"

"Don't remind me. You heard him. Last one there..." Dave took off running. Realizing there was no way of getting there ahead of either of them, Alexavier took his time to enjoying the stroll, as well as Dave and Wally's playfulness that really helped to lighten the mood.

Having finally made it to the W.A.R. Room, Alexavier saw that everyone was already there, except for Major Constantine. He looked for a bench for his bag full of gear, eyeing an open spot right beside Dave and Wally.

Dave was grinning from ear to ear. "Guess who sucks today, Wally?"

Enter Alexavier

Alexavier opened his bag. "Rumor has it your boyfriend is good at that." Wally started cracking up laughing, falling all over Dave.

"Do you see any boyfriend here?" Dave asked.

"Yeah. He'd be the one with his hands all over you."

Wally was leaning over, draped on top of Dave and still laughing. They both suddenly realized how close they were, and Wally sat upright awkwardly. Calmly and quietly, they continued putting on the last of their gear. Wally tried to speak up, but Dave quickly turned to him and cut him off by pointing his finger and shushing him. Wally closed his mouth and finished getting ready. The silence was deafening between them, but there was no need for words. The smile on Alexavier's face spoke volumes.

The chaos that was a dozen or so heroes preparing for the workout unfolded as everyone moved about the room. Major Constantine entered and made his way over to the table closest to the front. He noticed Senator Steinberg standing just outside the doors. "How has Washington been treating you lately?"

The Senator stepped into the room and replied, "The rhetoric doesn't agree with my stomach. Plus, listening to the daily squabbling back and forth of childish politicians makes me want a vacation."

"Then why not quit the rat race and sign on here full time?"

The Senator responded, "I would love to join you, but my political, Jewish brothers have a duty that I must keep in light of the destruction of Israel. One day, when the turmoil stops and the political stars align, I will join you. But I cannot help with the development of these heroes any more than when I can get away from Congress."

"Understood. But do you think we are making enough progress to satisfy Washington's greedy little hands?"

The Senator walked closer to the Major so he could talk softer. "What COSHAD wants is irrelevant. We are in charge of these kids' futures, not to mention lives. Our decisions are what matters, not theirs."

"What if your decision is wrong?" the Major asked frankly.

"I will pay that toll when I come to that bridge. Don't you forget who is funding this program." The stinging comment from the Senator appeared to agitate the Major.

The W.A.R. Room was buzzing with activity. People were warming up, stretching or honing their powers. Some members sparred, while others compared information, while Killus' group stayed secluded in the back. Jennifer was fooling around as usual, and her intended target was a common one. She appeared from behind Wally, blowing on his hair. He waved at his head thinking there was a bug. Turning around, he saw Jennifer half-visible through the wall. She quickly floated away. Using the circulating breeze, Wally gave chase.

Dave saw them laughing. "They have too much fun. I'm dying to find some chick to fool around with." He quickly looked at Alexavier. "Well, I mean figuratively, not literally. I mean literally, not… boy. I could die right now. This I mean literally. See, I die, but come back to life. That's my bread and butter here."

Alexavier replied, "You get shot, and poof, back to life. Run over by a truck and good as new."

Dave looked at him with a slightly dumbfounded expression. "How did you know that? What? I got a stalker now?"

"No." Alexavier chuckled. "You came from the Philly complex. I did too."

"I swear your face looks familiar, but why don't I remember you?" Dave asked.

Before Alexavier had a chance to enlighten Dave, Major Constantine walked toward the door to close them. "Everyone to the stairs! We've got work to do, and we have very little time to do it in!" The unceremonious gathering at the steps did not end the chatter. "Enough with the blabbering! Let's get organized and bring down the noise!" Finally, a quiet fell over the room. "Today is a workout evaluation. We will specifically concentrate on our newest member, Alexavier. Let's get to the training. I believe Sam has arrived."

Through the door appeared a man who was the mirror image of Uncle Sam from the posters and pictures from World War 2. It was Samuel Nelson, the most legendary superhero who ever lived, most famously known as The Patriot Warrior. The sight of him had Alexavier's heart racing. Every boy that had gone through The Program, and millions who had dreamed of being a superhero, wanted to be him. So too did Alexavier. Sam was his idol.

"Is that really him?" Alexavier softly asked.

Dave leaned over. "Yeah."

"Good morning." Sam walked over to the Major, setting down a jacket and metal briefcase. "I see we have a new addition to the squad. I am Sam Nelson. Welcome, Alexavier. If you have not done so, please make him feel comfortable. Everyone has been given a handout with all the necessary information." Alexavier responded with a small nod and a big smile. "We have the updates, if the Major can oblige me." Major Constantine handed him a clipboard. "Thank you. Let's see. There are some issues to address as well as getting some intel back. Nice work on the Cleveland case, guys, especially Beth. Nice capture of Max Towers. We really needed that. Where's Dwayne?"

"He's not here."

"I can tell that Major. Is there an issue?"

"We can talk about that afterward."

"Fine." A little annoyed, Sam flipped to a specific page and stopped. "Jennifer, we need to have you re-evaluated." He looked up, scanning for her in the crowd. "I'm scheduling tests for tomorrow. I expect you to be on time." He scanned the room as an image of her became recognizable.

"As you wish, chief." Jennifer's body faded away.

Enter Alexavier

"It looks like Manny is recovering nicely from his Session. He will still be out of it for a few more days, and should have no permanent, negative effects. We'll know more soon. You will see the results posted when we get them. If any of you have a moment to help him along, please stop by his room. It would be greatly appreciated."

"The big news is that Major Constantine's staff have finished going through the information gathered from The Tribe's hideaway that was taken down, and there are some interesting things to report. Apparently, the financial crimes perpetrated have gotten bolder and bolder lately. What makes this important is the fact that The Tribe has also targeted warehouses and facilities that are for science, medical and chemical production. Everything points to something big on the horizon. What that is we clearly don't know, but history has a couple of clues for this puzzle. The logbooks that were recovered show non-monetary items being stolen of things that are very mechanical in nature. It is perplexing at the moment. Usually, The Terror Tribe is all about monetary gains. We need to step up our efforts and hit them hard at every turn. The Major and I will work to set up new teams for recon and deployment right away. If we can slow or stop their gathering of funds, we might make them a bit desperate or even careless. Just know this and be ready. Is that clear?"

A general nod from everyone was sufficient for Sam. "Alright, we are going to get in some combat exercises before briefings on recon assignments this week." He handed the clipboard back to the Major. "I think Alexavier can start by showing some of those skills that have all the brass in an uproar. You can show me personally." Sam removed his shirt.

The look on Alexavier's face was total surprise, having just been introduced to his idol, and now he had to spar with him. He had thought a small demonstration might have sufficed, not full contact combat. Carefully, he weaved through everyone and down the steps.

Sam put his shirt next to the metal briefcase, making his way over to Alexavier and

Enter Alexavier

putting himself about three feet away without saying a word. Sam stood ready for whatever his young opponent might try. Flooded with emotions, Alexavier hesitated.

"Well?" Sam said, hoping to spark some life from the new recruit. It did not. Knowing the standoff was counterproductive, Sam reached out to grab Alexavier. Just as quickly, Alexavier moved out of the way. Sam was mildly surprised and held off, trying to get Alexavier to follow up. To his dismay, again nothing happened. The hesitation forced Sam to attempt another move. He tried to take a sweeping leg kick, but Alexavier lifted his leg easily.

Each new move was met with little counter attack, just defense. Sam kicked, and Alexavier blocked. Every left jab or right punch went by with no result. The more Sam attacked, the more Alexavier dodged them effortlessly. Sam's attacks quickly became more aggressive with every missed attempt. The hope for a demonstration in hand-to-hand combat techniques became an exhibition in futility.

The consecutive attempts, added with the subsequent misses forced Alexavier backward, where he was quickly running out of space, becoming too close to the wall. Hoping this might be the moment that jump-started the young hero, Sam reached out with his right arm, which Alexavier blocked away, bending Sam over. Alexavier twisted and pushed off the wall, rolling over Sam's back and landing on his feet. Sam saw his advantage vanish in the blink of an eye, but did not want to give his young adversary any breathing room. With Alexavier only several feet away, Sam used the momentum and wound up for the hardest swing he can muster. As he turned around using his entire body to land a blow, Sam stopped mid-swing, noticing his adversary's unusual state. As Alexavier staggered around with a dazed look upon his face. Sam only needed but a second to filter the events and determined the cause. "Harvey!"

"What?"

Sam rushed over, standing face to face with Harvey. "I don't need your interference!"

Enter Alexavier

"He wasn't even trying to fight back!" Harvey exclaimed.

"That doesn't mean you can take things into your own hands!" Sam saw Alexavier drop to one knee. "Stop the Brain Drain, now!"

Harvey gave a small look toward the prone Alexavier, releasing his hold. "There."

Sam inched closer. "Every time I walk in this building, all I hear about is what trouble you've been stirring up! I try to be understanding!"

"Look, I was-"

"I've given in to your childish behavior on the advice of some of the doctors, but not anymore. Effective immediately, you are suspended and are to remain in this complex, no longer allowed to go on missions! Now go!"

Sam's proclamation brought a collective silence to the room as Dr. Dennis hurried over to attend to Alexavier. Sam motioned over to The Elitesmen Guard, who were standing just outside the door. "Take Harvey to his room. No leaving unless it's necessary. Even then, I want an armed escort by one of you. I will be in charge of further punishment." Sam directed Dirk Henderson, the head of The Elitesmen Guard. "Make sure he's secured and wait for further orders from me."

"Yes, sir!" Dirk followed Harvey out the W.A.R. Room.

Whispers continued among the group as Sam asked, "How is he?"

Dr. Dennis looked up. "He's good. It was minor, but he should take it easy."

"Take him to his room," Sam instructed. "Check back on his status and update me."

The doctor nodded as she finished examining Alexavier, who remained seated on the floor. Dave and Wally made their way to them as Killus and his band of cohorts laughed.

Dave came closer. "You okay?"

Alexavier looked up. "My head is foggy."

Enter Alexavier

"You should take a break," Wally suggested. "It's not every week someone gets worked over by Harvey."

Dr. Dennis added, "I think Alexavier might do better somewhere else."

Alexavier chose first. "I think I'll go to my room."

"He'll be fine there, as long as you escort him," the doctor advised.

Wally and Dave reached down to help Alexavier up, although he protested a bit. "I'm okay."

"Maybe you are, but we're helping you back anyway." Dave stated, as he and Wally guided Alexavier through the doors and out of the W.A.R. Room. Many eyes watched. The one set that mattered was Sam. His were full of wonder as to whether the young hero that had been brought before him truly had what it took to ever become a hero.

Enter Alexavier

CHAPTER 22

The door opened to his room, and Alexavier walked in under his own power. Wally went to the bed and pulled back the covers. Unfortunately, it would not get used, as Dave escorted Alexavier to the desk, where he took a seat. Wally gave his friend a weird look before joining them. Reclining back and exhaling heavily, Alexavier stared at the ceiling. A prolonged moment of silence finally ended with Alexavier exclaiming, "I messed up."

Dave placed his hand on forlorn hero's shoulder. "It happens to all of us. It's not the end of the world."

"It could be the end for me."

"I doubt it," Dave replied.

"I think all of us have failed at one point or another." Wally tried to be reassuring. The look on Alexavier's face said otherwise.

"Yeah. Just ask Wally about his."

Wally objected, "Not just me, but Dave. You've crashed and burned more than any of us."

"I thought we were trying to help Alex here?" Dave pats Alexavier on the back, smiling.

"I appreciate you guys trying to make me feel better, but that's going to be kind of hard. I had a chance to impress the one person I look up to most. And what happened?

Enter Alexavier

I failed."

"You'll get another chance," Dave said reassuringly. "I'm certain of it. And next time, you'll knock the socks off Sam, literally and figuratively."

The words did little to light Alexavier's spirits as he brought out his journal. "I hope you're right."

Seeing the worn cover to the journal, Wally walked closer. "Do you need some room to study?"

"No. I just write down what happens every day. "

"That's an interesting idea. Does it help?" Dave wondered.

"More than you know."

"How much do you write in it?" Wally asked.

"Just about everything. Having Sessions taking away what all of us remember, I've found it easier doing this."

"That's smart," Wally stated.

"Why aren't we doing that?" Dave wondered.

"Apparently we're not as smart as he is. How long have you been documenting everything?" Wally inquired.

"Since I was about ten. I realized that after every Session, I was trying to remember things that seemed like I should just know. It frustrated me, so I got this large journal and have been putting my thoughts and memories in it ever since."

"Really?" Dave said. "Any secrets that you'd be willing to share?"

"Dave! Actually, why would I expect anything different? You know what? Should we be letting you rest?"

Alexavier continued to flip through the pages of his journal. "I'll be fine. I can take it easy and sit here for a while."

"Hey, we can just take a seat-"

Enter Alexavier

"Okay, time to go." Wally pushed Dave from behind, removing him from the room. Alexavier looked over, and seeing Dave getting escorted down the hall made him chuckle. A few seconds pass before he remembers his journal and what now must be written in it. Reliving the previous moments of the workout is not going be pleasant or enjoyable, but it had to be done.

Suddenly, he stopped. Getting up from the desk, he left the room and headed down to the medical ward. He had made this trip several times, sometimes more than once a day. His journey ended when he could look through the glass at Beth in her unconscious state. He stood there in silence for several minutes until Dr. Dennis saw him outside. She walks by Beth, placing her hand on Beth's shoulder quickly before going out the door. Once near Alexavier, she asked, "Do you want to see her?

"Yeah." Alexavier followed the doctor in, pulling up a stool next to Beth. For the next hour or so, he stayed by her side. He was not sure if it was helping her. But after the disappointing day he had, at least it made him feel better being near her.

Enter Alexavier

CHAPTER 23

Sam exited a conference room adjacent to the W.A.R. Room after a debriefing with some complex personnel. "This really isn't the way I was hoping today would go. If ever there was a time I hoped I had retired, it was now. Harvey could be one of our best operatives, close to making it to The United. If anyone ever wonders why he has not made it yet, today is a prime example. Everyone needs to know that if Harvey can be suspended, anyone can. No one is above the team." He turned his head to stare at the Major. "As of this moment, Harvey is banned from going on missions. I don't care what setback that might make for Harvey to graduate to The United."

The Major followed close behind. "Are you sure that's wise? He's possibly one of our best recruit to date."

"He's also half of the problems with this team, besides James Killus being a loose cannon. Harvey needs to understand what it's like being a part of a team before being a part of THE team."

"We don't need to be left in the field without one of our best guys, struggling to fight The Terror Tribe."

"What we don't need is for the others on this team to struggle, when they see one of their own allowed to do whatever he thinks is okay. We should be rewarding those who are doing right by giving them better opportunities and punishing those who don't. My decision is final. Harvey is to stay here. And I'll be the one to determine when and if he can go on missions. Is that clear?"

Enter Alexavier

"He'll be notified of the punishment." Not too happy with the decision, Major Constantine hoped to change the topic as he pressed the elevator button. "Not the impressive show of ability I had hoped for with Alexavier."

"Quite an embarrassing display, if you ask me," Sam said, adjusting his grip on his briefcase. "What was with the instructions? Grab him. Kick out his feet. Throw multiple punches. Grab him again. What were you planning for me, to look stupid?"

The door to the elevator opened, and the Major finally looked at Sam. "I was planning for an introduction that would highly impress you." Both men stepped inside, as the Major pressed a button, and the door closed.

"Are you going to get offended if I call your attempt a failure?"

"It's your prerogative."

When the door opened, Sam exited in a hurry. He entered Major Constantine's office, door already opened, setting his gear down at the window. A look of concern passed over his face, looking down on the W.A.R. Room.

"I thought you said he was ready?" Sam turned around and placed a metal briefcase on the table. He opened it and grabbed a syringe, inspecting it closely. "You talked about him like he's going to be something special, possibly the be all end all recruit."

"I'll have a couple doctors shot in the morning."

"Not funny! We don't know if Bobbie can assume multiple rolls, and it would be bad judgment to have her do double duty. Even with her incredible fighting expertise, we need her for reconnaissance and not providing combat support all the time. We need him desperately. And you assured me he was primed for action now!" Sam placed the needle at his inside forearm and punctured his skin. A hefty push of the syringe injected the blue liquid.

"The numbers from his progress beat anyone ever put through the Program. He is not a Meta, but achieved higher percentages of overall progress more than any Meta-

Enter Alexavier

Human. Quite the accomplishment as far as I'm concerned." Walking over toward the window, the Major looked down with Sam. "We still need to further adjust his diet to negate Harvey's powers, like we've done with everyone else."

"None of it means much now." Sam quickly pulled out the needle and stored the syringe back into the briefcase.

"I think it would be a great accomplishment if we had something to show for it." Senator Frank Steinberg walked in, becoming a welcome interruption for the Major. "Wasn't he the kid who had everyone talking about being the next, greatest hero?"

"His numbers are phenomenal," Jonathon replied, following close behind. "All levels increased by at least six hundred percent. His skill set is larger than anyone else. His knowledge and use of weapons, even improvised ones, is beyond compare. And his combat win ratio between Program training complexes is a perfect one hundred thirty-one wins and no losses."

"So…" The Senator hesitated. "What's the problem?"

"He had no urgency to take the fight to me," Sam stated, putting the briefcase on the floor. "I advanced toward him, and he backed up the whole time. At least with Bobbie, she came after me, but not the case with Alexavier. When he did do something impressive, it was to get away. He cannot be tentative. That's going to get him killed. We need to get him to be more aggressive. Infamous, Everyone or any one of those guys will take him apart if he shows the slightest bit of hesitation. I will not put him in any situation if I don't feel he's able to handle it."

"Does he need some more chair time?" the Senator wondered.

Jonathon looked his schedule over. "We have a Session set up for April."

The Senator glanced at Sam. "Can we switch and have the Session for Alexavier?"

"Just say the word, and it's done." The Major looked over to Sam from the corner of his eyes.

"What would you have planned? Do we need to increase anything?" The Senator moved closer to the Major.

"What do you have in mind, Frank?"

"If he has achieved so much under the continued regimens from before with so little in the way of side effects, could more bring him around even faster? Can we boost his abilities, but help reprogram him for his combat shortcomings?"

Sam spoke up, "He doesn't need reprogramming as much as he needs motivation."

"When was the last time we saw any credible results coming from a Session in here?" the Senator asked.

"Results are subjective, but these kids' numbers do increase given enough time from their initial baselines when they first enter the Program," Jonathon added.

"Most of these kids are now young adults and the numbers and improvements have decreased to the point of barely showing any increases or have stalled completely," the Senator argued. "We got gun shy, particularly because we didn't want any adverse reactions like before. We still can't tell if those results were because of Sessions or personal choices. When we start someone on the regimen, they begin slowly. Dosages are increased as time goes on, am I right? If segmented increases have historically shown significant results, why wouldn't it help in this situation? I know there's a plateau that everyone gets to and increases stop. From what I've read, he's still improving from every Session, unlike the recruits who are here now."

"It's a theory the scientists have had for a while." Jonathon flipped through some paperwork. "They believe that under extraordinary circumstances, certain individuals can take stronger levels of drugs, lights, radiation and so on. They haven't had a chance to test that theory yet."

Sam remained silent for quite a few seconds, until the Senator continued, "From what you've told me, he retains information, thoughts and memories unlike anyone before him. He would be the perfect candidate."

Major Constantine threw out an option. "Since this is your thing, whether or not to

Enter Alexavier

get approval to join this team, I wouldn't say that was a make or break evaluation. I still have confidence in this kid, but you're the decider here, Sam. We could send him back to Philadelphia for a few more months, maybe even years. Various Sessions and more training wouldn't hurt. Or we can do it here and watch the progress for ourselves, shaping this kid to how we need him to be. It's your choice. But whether you fail him and he goes back or we keep him here, he still would go through the same stuff."

Both men look over, waiting for any reaction from Sam, who had dreaded giving any kind of thumbs up for Sessions ever. But the logic was sound, and Sam knew it. Finally, he stood up and turned around. "Alexavier is cleared for testing with the Session. Make it happen."

"You know the last time they attempted something like this, it didn't go very well," the Major reminded Sam.

"Wasn't that when Julie Beckenstein, the original Beacon of Light, started going crazy?" the Senator inquired.

Sam looked highly annoyed as he softly growled, "She didn't go crazy."

The Senator motioned toward the Major. "From everything that you and the doctors had sent us, it looked like she had a mental breakdown."

"It wasn't a mental breakdown." Sam's scowl grew as he gathered his belongings.

"It doesn't matter now," the Major stated. "Now we see what our chair can do for Alexavier."

Before Sam exited the room, he held up at the door. "Just so you know. If this goes bad, I will rip that damn chair out myself!"

Enter Alexavier

CHAPTER 24

Another morning had arrived for Alexavier, and more entries into his journal were a certainty. Being his most prized possession, the journal had been with him longer than anything else he owned. His hand glided along the paper. The pen laid down the words, one after another. His thoughts were transformed from tangible thoughts into historical records of his very existence.

Usually, there was no deviation from his daily task. But today, he heard something outside. He heard laughter. Looking through the far windows, nothing seemed out of place. Seconds later, Dave Headley ran by yelling at the top of his lungs. "Get back here... ACHOO!" He quickly vanished around the corner. Alexavier had more than enough experience with Dave to know pranks followed him wherever he went. Sometimes, they unfolded as planned. Other times, they backfired.

Before turning around to finish writing, he saw Wally flying down the hall toward his room, laughing hysterically. Dave followed close behind, running, jumping and yelling like a mad man. "You can't stay up there forever!" Once they disappeared from sight, Alexavier returned to his journal, grinning widely.

Suddenly, Wally dove and swooped right outside Alexavier's door. Having a high ceiling provided Wally room to performing intricate aerial moves. Every time Dave thought he had Wally within reach, he flew up and out of Dave's grasp. "You have to come down sometime... ACHOO!"

"With all the hot air you're blowing, I could take a vacation to Europe." Wally weaved and dodged, finally heading to one of the wings of the complex.

"Get back here! If I had a fly swatter big enough, you wouldn't be laughing so hard! ACHOO!"

Alexavier closed the journal and slid it to the end of the table, enjoying the surprise comedy act that Dave always seemed to be able to produce. But an early morning workout was next on the agenda. Once done, it would be great to get a shower in and possible breakfast, before tackling the day at hand. He threw his bag of gear over his shoulder, pulled his hood over his head and headed for the gym.

He could still hear the guys off in the distance. That sustained his smile, until he saw Sam walking in his direction, carrying a suitcase in one hand and a briefcase in the other. Once Sam was near, Alexavier pulled down his hood and hesitated before calling out, "Excuse me, sir?"

"Yes?"

Alexavier used his most confident voice. "I want to let you know that no matter what happens, I will do whatever is needed of me. I am dedicated to becoming as great a hero as I can. You can trust me to do my best."

Sam paused to answer, "You shouldn't be worried about me. Worry about what your teammates think. Someday, they will need someone to watch their back. That person may be you. They need to know you can be there for them. It's their trust you need to earn. It's their lives that you may hold in your hands."

Alexavier watched his idol walk away, without giving a rebuttal about his performance. Sam disappeared from sight, leaving Alexavier to wonder if this would be the last time he might ever see the man he looked up to most.

Enter Alexavier

CHAPTER 25

Feeling bummed out about his face-to-face interaction with Sam, Alexavier thought to drown his sorrows in food. He made a detour to the cafeteria, rather than his room. Walking in, he got a surprise that most of his acquaintances were already enjoying something to eat. He studied the pans of food laid out in front of him, but the moment of contemplation ended with specific food being put on a tray for him. He reluctantly took it and headed toward his teammates.

Mike saw Alexavier moving between the tables and waved him over. "How's it going?"

"I saw Sam today."

"And?"

Alexavier settled next to Mike, setting down his tray and taking off his hood. "I tried to reassure him that I would do my best. He told me I should worry about what the team thinks, not him."

"Spoken like the man he truly is," Mike stated. "Take what he says to heart. There's a reason he is who he is. The brain in that man's head is incredible. Once he passes away, I bet the scientists in this place will want to study that brain for all his knowledge."

"Got it," Alexavier grudgingly acknowledged. "Still, I was hoping to get a more positive message from him about whether or not I'm staying here."

Enter Alexavier

"By the way, has anyone heard any news about Beth, about how she's doing?" Percy wondered.

"Nothing so far," Bobbie answered. "I walked by and checked today. She's still out."

"If I get the chance to take down any of those Tribe scumbags, they'll pay for hurting her," Percy angrily stated.

Wally grew angry. "I want a piece of any of them."

Mike agreed. "You'll all get your opportunity soon. How are you feeling, Alex?"

"Pretty good, actually. I haven't been hit that hard mentally in a long time. Usually during sparring I can get my own licks in before my head feels like it's going to explode."

"Lucky that you ain't no vegetable." Percy said.

Dave jested, "Dude! What's funny is how you can say the word, but you won't eat your vegetables."

"Do I look like a rabbit? Do you see any buck teeth?" Percy stated.

"Open up, let me see," Bobbie joked.

Mike joked, "Rumor has it Percy wears those baggy shorts to hide his fuzzy tail."

"Shut up, Mike. Don't you even..." Percy eyed him waiting for another crack.

The table chuckled as Wally changed the subject. "Too bad Harvey stuck his nose in. No one has been able to evade Sam like that. It was quite impressive, Alex. I don't know if he lashed out because of Harvey's interference or being frustrated by you."

"I really didn't mean for it to go that way. He charged, and I reacted... or retreated might be a better way to put it."

"I was impressed too," Jonathon chimed in. "What you did do was very good."

Alexavier smiled, "Thanks guys. I feel a little better about it now, but I should have done more. I hope I didn't hurt my chances of being here."

Enter Alexavier

Percy slowed the parade of praise. "Don't know if you're safe for the time being, but I'd worry about going on missions. The man didn't see any moves. If you're gonna get the nod from him, offense is what he wants to see."

"True, but it wasn't as if the workout was allowed to go the full time allotment," Jonathon added.

"They'll probably give you a couple of days' rest, and then you'll do it all over again. I wouldn't worry," Mike reassured.

"I just need to show Sam that I can be trusted to handle whatever you guys need me to do," Alexavier said.

Dave got excited with a thought. "You know, I can't wait to see you two go at it once more. It might be the first time in a long time that someone gives Sammy a run for his money."

"You're just sour because he had you folded like a pretzel in about three seconds," Wally joked.

"It was like 23 seconds, and he never explained the rules," Dave replied.

Bobbie added, "You knew the rules fine. You ran like a little girl the rest of the workout."

"I wasn't running," Dave replied unconvincingly. "I was multitasking. Your boy got in my cardio with some hand-to-hand combat."

Alexavier looked puzzled. "Do people usually not fare too well against Sam? Isn't everyone trained equally in hand-to-hand combat?"

"Everyone is, but he's just so good," Jonathon stated. "Plus, he so experienced that it's hard to do something he hasn't seen. Bobbie's been the only one to ever get his shoulders to the mat."

"It might have been for a split second, but I got those shoulders flat." Bobbie nods with a big smile.

"You know all those comic books, T.V. shows and movies that depict him as being able to fight that well?" Mike asked.

"Yeah."

"They aren't far from the truth," Mike explained. "His ability to beat villains, even Super-Metas is not only legendary, but true. He's captured nearly as many bad guys as everyone else put together. He's one of only two people to capture more than one bad guy in a single mission."

"Who's the other?" Alexavier wondered.

"Harvey did it twice," Jonathon noted. "It took them both a while to do it, although Harvey did it quicker, after only three years here. It took Sam a decade of crime fighting to do it three times."

Percy said with disgust, "Yeah. The brass loves Harvey for that. So even though he's messing with you, they won't drop the axe on him."

"When it comes time for him to deliver, he usually does," Jonathon added.

"The Major adores him. And with needing him in the field, I don't see this suspension lasting more than a few days." Mike said with a little frustration.

"It won't matter, dude. He'll be back here soon, and we'll all have to worry about mister poor attitude," Dave said.

Jonathon hoped to shift everyone's focus. "Harvey will bury himself sooner than you think. We all have our own projects to work on, and there are enough training sessions coming up. Keep your heads on straight and focus on what each of you needs to."

"Yeah. I don't need the Major coming after me anymore," Dave stated.

"Speak of the devil." Mike quickly buried his head.

And as if on cue, Major Constantine entered the room, which made everyone lower their voices. He stopped right in front of Alexavier. "We have a Session planned for you tomorrow morning."

"Okay," Alexavier cautiously answered.

"Just be aware that you will be the first recruit to be tested with a new regimen, including greatly increased doses of all relevant treatment options. Be ready by 0845. We will get you at 0900." The Major noticed Alexavier's plate of food. "Jonathon, see me later about his diet. We need to test him to change things accordingly for substitutions."

The silence from the table was deafening. With no one responding, the Major walked away, as they began to look at each other. It quickly became an uneasy contest to see who would be first to speak up.

Alexavier made it easy for them, "It's not the news I was hoping for."

"I'm sorry, dude," Dave sympathized.

Bobbie agreed, "That sucks."

"How can they do that? Alex just got here. Don't they usually have some kind of process and evaluation to do this?" Wally asked.

"They can do whatever they want," Mike stated.

"They've never done it before," Wally added.

Percy responded with an angry tone in his voice. "Sucks how they're always playing God."

"Mike's right." Everyone's attention was quickly fixated on Jonathon. "It's never been set in stone. Their guidelines have always been loose. They tightened things up after certain issues presented themselves. But even so, if it's felt to be necessary, they can schedule you at any time."

"I better get an apple for the Major's desk," Dave joked.

Wally inquired, "Can't somebody talk to him?"

"I've had many discussions about how they do them, to whom and when. I've never seen the chair because they believe it will affect me mentally. That's the same if your powers are mentally based. But if yours aren't and if they feel it's the right time, you're in the chair," Jonathon explained.

"We don't need you turning against us," Bobbie said.

"That wouldn't happen, even though they're scared to try. But really, my job is to follow through with whatever the Major wants," Jonathon explained. "My responsibility to this team is my first priority. If they want any of you to go through a Session, I will comply with that order, but your wellbeing is most important. Nothing else matters if you guys don't make it out okay from a Session."

"When did you guys last go through one?' Alexavier's question brought an awkward silence to the table, allowing one of the side effects of the Sessions to show its ugly head.

"I guess I don't remember much about mine," Wally said with a confused look, as he glanced at Dave.

Bobbie shrugged her shoulders as Dave agreed, "Me either."

"That memory loss is a part of the process," Mike explained. "Jonathon and I are excluded from Sessions because of the possible effects that could hinder our mental powers."

"What about me?" Percy wondered. "My aim is part of my brain. They don't exclude me."

"That's true to some extent," Jonathon explained. "They didn't know for sure how your ability to be so accurate would be affected. They had to try it once to see what would happen. Once they saw major improvements, they felt it was muscular."

"That don't matter!" Percy said emphatically. "Next time, I could hose all you all, and it's because of them."

"That'll never happen," Mike responded confidently.

Percy replied sarcastically, "You don't know, and neither do they."

"You're a teddy bear compared to a lot of these guys," Dave joked.

"Yeah, but I got M16s in my room." Percy pointed at Dave.

"You wouldn't do that. You love us, and you know it," Dave stated as Percy looked away as if to say yeah, right.

"I wonder what is behind their motivation for this impromptu Session." Mike wondered.

"I'd like to know what's up myself," Wally responded as the rest of the table agreed.

Conversation at the table drifted from one person to another. No one noticed the affect the news had on Alexavier. His mind was off into other worlds of contemplation. His hopes of leaving behind the chair and the memories of it were now broken. His day had turned gray, although there was one thing that could change everything. Running through the door and straight to their table, Michael exclaimed, "It's Beth! She's awake!"

Enter Alexavier

CHAPTER 26

Walking quickly, Alexavier passed people in the hallways like a racecar on the track. Nothing mattered, not even when he passed Dr. Dennis just outside her office. Arriving at the door to the infirmary, he paused to look inside. A warm feeling washed over him upon seeing Beth moving her arm, reaching for the cup of water. Quickly, he hit the button to open the door and walked in, grabbing the cup. He handed it to her, which made her smile. The quiet of the room, only broken by the sound of equipment monitoring her heartbeat lingered, as he did not know what to say.

Her injuries were extremely severe, having most of her body bandaged and casts on both legs and the other arm. What he could see of her face was bruised, but not too swollen. She was reclined, not allowed to sit up too far. Leaning her head to the side, she took a sip. Alexavier set the cup back on the tray. Looking back, she began staring at him, which brought out a bit of his shyness. Needing to break the ice, she joked, "Boy, you look like crap."

He let out a small laugh, relieving some of the tension. "How are you feeling?"

"Never better. When does the battle royal begin?" She had him giggling again. "A bit sore, considering what landed on top of me. The doctor has been mending me with her healing powers."

"You were unconscious for quite some time. The longer you were out, the more I was worried about you."

Enter Alexavier

Beth smiled again. "It's nice to know. Thank you."

He looked around, showing more of that shyness. "Did they say when you'll be back on your feet?"

"Given the doctor using her healing powers on me, I could be on the helicopter in a couple of days, if this leg heals properly. One was shattered pretty bad. Thank the Lord for drugs and the doctor's touch, because it's not as painful as it should be. Apparently, the healing is way ahead of schedule too. It was just my brain that didn't want me to wake up until now, I guess. Although, I still feel tired."

"You went through a lot. Take all the time you need to rest. I'll be here if you need anything."

"Good. I think I need a vacation... or a burger."

Awkwardness swept over Alexavier. He had to force himself to finally ask, "What happened inside the building?"

"As we found the hideout and engaged the Tribe, I saw someone in black running toward the building. Since I hadn't started fighting anybody, I thought I could chase them down. I wasn't going to wait to let everyone know and lose the opportunity to catch a villain, especially if it was Infamous. Unfortunately, the static started. And by the time I could call in, I couldn't get through to anyone."

"Once I heard the static, I knew something was wrong. So, I left the Major and Jonathon. When I got down there, I could see almost everyone, but I couldn't find you."

"By that time, I had probably made my way down toward the basement of a building. That's when I discovered Natural Disaster guarding the dark figure that had to be The Infamous One."

Alexavier took a seat next to her. "You saw him?"

"Only with a mask on, but we know he wears that black outfit to blend in with shadows. He tried hiding behind Natural Disaster, but I lit up the place so it didn't

Enter Alexavier

make a difference."

"It sounds like you had them where you wanted them."

"I thought so too, until I was attacked by Nib. He stabbed me with his energy blade from behind. I went down and couldn't move. I thought he was going to kill me with that blade, but they left me there while grabbing some stuff. Whatever it was had to be pretty important that they didn't worry about me. After a minute, I could move my arm enough to fire an energy blast that hit the wall near them. That must have startled them, because they ducked and started running around erratically. By the time I made it up to one knee, I noticed them huddled together. Natural Disaster then put an energy field around them, and that's when everything got heavy. I was pulled to the ground like I had no strength. Part of the ceiling started to land next to me. I realized the building was starting to come down and quickly generated my own field trying to keep the pieces of building from crushing me. The weight kept building pressure, and I knew I couldn't hold it. Within seconds, there was so much weighing me down that I couldn't hold it up. The only thing I could try was to blast it away, but I was too weak to do both. What I couldn't deflect finally came crashing down." She paused, looking straight ahead. "It was the most afraid I've ever been, both in a fight and for my life."

"When I got to the downed building, I saw the dark figure behind Natural Disaster. They were trying to move toward you. I did everything I could to keep them away."

"Thank you." She placed her hand on his, and he didn't know what to say. He just watched and waited, until she finally asked, "Can I get another drink of water?"

"Sure." He brought the cup over, aiming the straw towards her. Once done, he placed the cup back on the tray. "Is there anything else I can get you?"

"I'm really in the mood for some roast beef."

"Really? I can stop to cafeteria and pick-"

"I'm joking, you dufus. Why so serious?"

"You almost died. That scared the hell out of me."

Enter Alexavier

"It scared me too, but I'm still here. And I'm not going anywhere. This is just a speed bump that's slowing me just a little bit until I'm back up to full speed. I don't need anyone holding me back. I need someone who's going to run with me as I take them down. Everyone says they're going to be the one to take down The Tribe. I want that to be me. You can either join me or get left behind."

Both as an inspiration, as well as an ultimatum, it provided a boost to his mood that was much needed. "There's nothing that I would like more than to take them down, and while doing it with you."

She got another smile, but noticed he still wasn't acting the same. "Are you okay? It seems as if there's something else bothering you."

The silence that followed felt like an eternity, especially for Alexavier. Needing to not put any more stress on her, he decided not to inform her of his upcoming Session. "No. Just that being my first mission, I really didn't think anyone might get hurt. You always want your first one to be a success."

Beth winced. She reached for the button to get more drugs for the pain. "As much as I got hurt, it was successful. We finally found one of their hideouts, retrieved some valuable information and the best part being you captured one of them. No one has ever captured someone on their first mission! You're the first!"

"I only did what I'm supposed to do."

"Yeah, but quicker than anyone, even Harvey. It took him four or five missions to do that."

Alexavier bowed his head, looking at his hands. "Still, you getting hurt doesn't make that feel as great as it could be."

"You can make me feel better, which might make you feel better."

He looks up. "How's that?"

"I'm in the mood for some ice cream."

It took a couple of seconds, but it worked. He smiled. "Not sure if it's okay with

Enter Alexavier

the doctor, but I'll get two scoops."

"Well, that's enough for me. Weren't you going to get some for yourself?"

"I'll get a tub... and two spoons." He stood up and walked toward the door. A hesitation to think about her caused his smile to grow. With a clear avenue to the hallway, he exited and made his way toward the cafeteria. The farther he got away from the medical ward, the more the smile went away. Reality came back that in the morning he would be strapped into the chair that had given him nightmares. Hopefully, a couple of scoops of ice cream and some company can make him forget about it just for a little while.

Enter Alexavier

CHAPTER 27

After a night of tossing and turning, his mind was racing about the events of the coming day and had him wide-awake, lying in bed. He felt the dread of sitting in the chair and letting the doctors poke him with needles. The radiation treatments, the fatigue and nausea that could follow haunted his mind. He remembered hearing the non-stop assault of noise from the weird headphones they made him wear and wishing he would never have to hear those sounds again. There were countless other things that had been done to him in the name of advancing his abilities for the greater good of humanity, but Alexavier had come to think that this was all because of someone's insanity. The chair, along with the procedures, must be someone's cruel joke. He was still waiting for the punch line.

The ceiling had been his focal point for hours, moreover the small, unassuming bug that wandered the tiles above him. But he could only stare at the wandering bug so long and sat up resting his hands on his knees. Looking down, he saw a couple scars and some calluses. Many things had happened to these hands, which had also accomplished many things. Looking up to see his surroundings and taking in the little things, it was a moment he wished to remember. Because of the terrifying chair just down the hall, his memory could possibly be completely wiped away.

Sitting silently in the darkest corner of the room, Jennifer watched with concern. Her body was almost completely transparent, although everything inside her body felt for him. She wished that she could make him smile. Her image vanished completely,

Enter Alexavier

just as Alexavier turned his head toward that corner. With his mind in knots, his perception and intuition was not what they should have been. Seeing nothing, he turned back with a sigh. His eyes closed tightly.

An eternity finally ended with visitors congregating outside his room. Alexavier sat on his bed holding a journal. He looked down at it, studying the writings.

Mike stood outside watching the young hero as Dr. Dennis arrived. "Is he ready?" she asked.

"I've kind of let him be. He looks to be concentrating or meditating, so I figured I wouldn't interrupt him yet," Mike said, joining the doctor by heading into his room.

Both entered quietly, trying not to startle Alexavier. Once they were close enough to see him focusing, she asked, "Alex, are you ready?"

"As ready as I'm going to be." Alexavier looked up.

Mike tried to be reassuring. "It's just another day in the chair."

Dr. Dennis opened a folder. "Just so you're aware, we're going to be giving you a stronger dose than what you're used to, but you should not have much in the way of problems like the others might. Your recovery has truly been amazing."

"Yeah. You'll fly through this."

"It's not that." Alexavier continued to rub his hands. "Most everyone goes through a Session never remember what happened. I don't know why, but I remember almost every Session I've been through, whether it's good, bad or completely horrible. I can still feel the pain, the heat and the feeling of helplessness afterward. I was hoping to not feel like a lab rat anymore. I was hoping to never see that chair again."

"This is just another stepping stone. Each time you get the misfortune of that chair means you're one step closer to becoming a member of The United," Mike explained.

"But I won't be here much longer if I can't perform the way I have in the past. I failed miserably with Sam."

Enter Alexavier

"Becoming a superhero takes more than a cape or mask, or suit with cool colors. You have to believe in helping that particular someone in need. It's not about the biggest of deeds." Alexavier looked up as Mike continued, "I don't doubt you'll get through this Session. And after you recover, you'll show the world why you're destined to be a hero."

The words appeared to make their point with Alexavier. "That's all I want."

"Don't worry. You'll get there." Mike placed his hand on Alexavier's shoulder.

Alexavier nodded in agreement as Major Constantine arrived, as he did, taking part in every Session. But the fact that Mike had become involved, seemed to annoy him. "Nice to see you doing something. Why are you here?"

Mike stood back. "Just making sure he's okay."

"He's okay. Now let us handle this."

"Isn't this my job? Don't you want me to give a crap about these kids?"

"You can give a crap later. Go back to making me weapons." The Major took an aggressive stance, waiting for his word to be challenged. Mike appeared ready to accept that challenge, but never got the chance.

"It's alright. I'll be fine." Alexavier stood up and put the journal on the bed. He walked up to Mike. "Thank you." He put his hood on and left the room.

Upon Alexavier leaving the room, the Major turned to Mike. "You haven't been on a mission in forever, and this is getting old. I don't know what your deal is lately. Personally, I don't care. All I know is that you better get your butt in the game and make me forget the fact that certain people feel sorry for you." The Major hoped for a response. But since Mike disappointed him, he walked out of the room.

Letting his anger settle allowed the quiet of the room to erase the hostility in the air. Feeling slightly better, Mike looked around and spotted an intriguing item. Walking over to the side of the bed and standing over Alexavier's journal, he picked it up, scanning over the cover. A quick look around ensured no eyes were present and watching. Mike opened it, skimming through the back pages. Mike's expression changed as he scanned each page. Originally, there was curiosity. But the more that Mike read, the more he further understood the journal's purpose. He flipped through the pages heading toward the front. He arrived and skimmed the first several pages, realizing how the next few hours needed to play out. Understanding what had been written as far as instructions and how the journal would help Alexavier to remember what the Session might take away from his memories, Mike closed the journal and placed it right where he found it. Using caution to not attract unneeded attention, he exited the room and quietly closed the door.

"Things going alright?" Jonathon approached Mike from behind.

"Just swell," Mike expressed quite sarcastically. "I can't care about these kids without the Major being such a pain."

"Everyone here knows you care. Nobody doubts that. It just seems like the Major sometimes forgets that there are actual human beings in this building. Look, Alex should be fine. You know his prelim reports from Philly."

Mike let out a sigh. "Yeah, but I can't help looking out for them."

"And you will never stop," Jonathon said, patting Mike on the back. "That's why everyone respects you so much. Go get a drink or food or something. I'll join you after."

"Fine." Mike walked away, but Jonathon turned toward Alexavier's room, wondering why Mike had disobeyed the Major's orders.

#

Alexavier was led through a continually growing mob scene, with each passing open door. Eyes stared, and comments were made under people's breath. The spectacle brought out all the usual gawkers. James Killus and his crew certainly qualified, although April found sanctuary further away from the group. Feeling sorry for Alexavier, she hid her expressions by looking away.

The convoy reached its desired location, with Beth sitting in a wheelchair near Percy. She looked up at him. "He didn't tell me about his Session. I found out from Dave."

"You've got healing to do, not worrying. The kid was thinking of your health."

"But they're going to try the regimen that got banned."

"Sucks to be him," Percy said, placing a hand on her shoulder. "Dude is gonna be a serious mess."

One by one, each person vanished through the doorway, with Alexavier disappearing as well. As the last doctor's lab coat was unable to be seen, Beth looked down, unsure of what the next few hours might bring.

#

From the comfort of the observation suite high above, Major Constantine and Senator Steinberg watched the medical staff of doctors and technicians work like bees to ensure the Session room was prepared accurately. The Senator wondered out loud, "If this works, how many others will get the same doses?"

The Major casually replied, "The doses will have to be adjusted for body surface area, if I'm correct. Trials could begin immediately, depending on the individual and the cycle of each recruit." To the Major's surprise, when he turned his attention to the Session room, Alexavier was staring back.

"What happens if this doesn't work, and Alexavier is no longer of use to us?"

"We continue on, possibly even starting over to find that last piece of the puzzle. We're so close to having what it takes to bring down The Infamous One. It might all come down to the next day or so."

"But Alex is young and raw. He hasn't been through the system. How can we know that he's our ticket?"

Major Constantine quickly responded, "There's something about him. There's something special. He has to be it. If he's not, there's not another recruit in the whole system that will be the one."

Confused, the Senator asked, "You're not serious? You mean with the hundreds of kids working hard to develop their skills in every complex around the U.S., Alex is our last hope?"

"Yes."

#

Back in the Session Room, the ominous looking chair was nearly finished being prepped. Various technicians had been preparing the entire room since the day before, allowing for any needed last minute adjustments. Standing along the wall of the room, Alexavier took in the constant motion, patiently waiting for the commotion to die down and for someone to give him instructions.

Finished coordinating some data with a fellow physician, Dr. Dennis walked over to Alexavier. "Are you feeling okay?"

"As much as I could be, knowing what is about to happen."

"Don't worry. We'll take care of you." Going unnoticed to everyone else around, she placed her hand on his. The sensation was soothing, with a calm slowly washing over him. Alexavier gave a small nod.

Seeing Alexavier relax, she let go of his hand, needing to return to finish the final adjustments of the reinforced wrist and legs clamps. They were equipped with heavily padded inserts to insure there would be no bruising under the stressful conditions. Long and terrifying needles hovered to one side, connected to syringes contained with the powerful drugs. Several radiation panels and speakers had been aligned on both sides of the walls, filling out the look of an odd, yet futuristic torture chamber.

After a few minutes, Dr. Dennis called Alexavier over. He took his place in the chair and took off his hooded sweatshirt, handing it to the doctor. Other doctors came over and strapped him in and rechecked each safety restraint one by one. Dr. Dennis began rolling back the clamp on the I.V. tubing, allowing the fluids to snake down to insure that all air was properly removed.

Major Constantine turned on the microphone. "What do you have planned, doctor?"

Dr. Dennis looked up. "We have adjusted the levels for today from the medical files we obtained of the last known attempt at such a high treatment."

"How does this compare with his old one?" the Senator queried.

"We have a newly devised protocol that will expose him to a significantly increased amount of the drugs. The light and sound have been modified to match our three previous experimental trials of the banned regimen. We will be administering a couple of new drugs and monitoring their effects for future analysis. The radiation therapy will be targeted to specific tissues. All in all, the doses will be escalated slowly to observe the effect on Alexavier." She grabbed a chart. "In any normal human being, this targeted radiation dose would result in tissue damage. However, with his extraordinary healing abilities, we believe his body will recover without much long term damage, if his past results are any indication."

"Alright, please continue with your preparations. He is cleared for treatment whenever you're ready." Major Constantine stood up and folded his arms.

After finishing attaching the sensors to Alexavier's head, a physician adjusted the straps at the bottom of the helmet and secured it to the back of the chair. Another proceeded to put one of the fixtures with needles and syringes to Alexavier's right hand side. An attempt to place the needle in his arm resulted in failure. No matter how hard he tried, it was too difficult to penetrate the skin. Dr. Dennis noticed the struggle and went over to help. She grasped the syringe with a strong grip and forced the needle in. A rush of activity ended as several doctors gave the go ahead to clear the room.

Curious eyes watched from beyond the front doors of the Session room. It was never pleasing to know someone was strapped down in this monstrosity of a chair. Some even turned away while others had to leave. Beth and Percy continued watching until the outer doors began to shut slowing narrowing the window of their final glimpse of Alexavier. Slowly, the sight of Alexavier vanished. Beth leaned over, desperately trying to catch the last sight of him. Once the entrance doors closed and locked with an ominous clank, she requested Percy to help her back to her room. Percy slowly shook his head muttering, "Damn."

In the distance, a mysterious figure looked on from a dark corner. Mike's thoughts matched everyone else's at the moment. Turning back, he walked away to no one's eyes. Remembering the written words in Alexavier's journal, the look on Mike's face became more solemn with each step away from the Session Room.

#

The few remaining engineers fine-tuned the radiation banks inside the room. One by one, they left through the rear exit after completing their tasks. Dr. Dennis finished an adjustment on the helmet before makings a last check on the intravenous lines. She glanced over at Alexavier, who remained quiet. "You still with me?"

"Do I get ice cream when I'm through?"

She smiled, touching his hand, which eased him again. "I'll be close by. If anything goes wrong, I'll be right in."

Alexavier gave a small nod of acceptance and returned to facing straight ahead. She lowered the visor over his face. After one last check of all clamps and straps, she followed the last technician out the back door and into the monitoring room. She exited as the door shut with a tremendous metallic clank.

Finally, after all of the commotion, Alexavier was alone. The wait bordered on torture. Taking a deep breath, he began to divert his thoughts, with a vision of Beth slowly filling his mind. Her warmth almost magically transcended the image, giving the sensation of her comforting him right by his side. Slowly, his muscles loosened, and he began to relax. A calm feeling washed over him, giving way to an acceptance of his situation.

Suddenly, the calm and the quiet were replaced by the sheer terror of piercing sound and intense heat. The radiation targeted various desired body parts. The complex noise of various sound waves pounded his head. The lights started to flash in his visor, soaking his optical nerves and sending messages to his brain. His muscles constricted, and his body began to spasm. His enhanced physical strength and endurance was doing everything he could to withstand this onslaught, until the cold flow of drugs entered his veins. Even though he had gone through the treatment before, the bombardment of this stronger regimen had Alexavier in the first battle, of a possible many, within this torture chamber. It was a battle he appeared to be losing.

Enter Alexavier

CHAPTER 28

With the horror of the treatment behind him, Alexavier was wheeled down the hallway on a gurney. His physical condition was nowhere as good as anticipated. Several medical staff, including Dr. Dennis, followed The Elitesmen Guard, as they carefully guided him to his destination. Upon entering Alexavier's room, Major Constantine made his way past and picked up the journal. "Extra gentle please," the Major instructed, as those helping Alexavier allowed for a gentle landing on the bed. The Major set the journal on the desk. Alexavier's expression was one of confusion. He looked around, trying to piece together what was happening.

"Leave us and return to your stations." The Major's command had everyone except Dr. Dennis quickly file out of the room. "Just relax. You can take all the time you need. We'll come back later to check your progress."

The Major and doctor slowly backed away while keeping an eye on him as they closed the door behind them. Silence enveloped the room, letting Alexavier settle in and close his eyes. A couple minutes passed. The sound of the door opening had Alexavier slowly open his eyes. As the person walked around the room, Alexavier turned over to see who it was. He was greeted with a journal hovering in front of his face, placed there by the outstretched arm of Mike. "You should read this."

Alexavier slowly sat up. "I thought I was supposed to rest?"

"Sorry, new orders," Mike replied, setting the journal down next to Alexavier. "Read this and follow the written instructions at the front. Once you are done and feel up to doing so, you can come or go as you please. Also, you have a workout coming up. So be ready."

Before Alexavier could look up and inquire a little more, Mike exited the room and closed the door behind him. He walked around the corner, looking through the window. Alexavier continued to read from the journal, scanning each page thoroughly before starting to blink repeatedly. He followed the instructions he had written for moments like this. Satisfied to see Alexavier looking through the journal, Mike walked away.

#

Beth's healing progressed quite fast. Only minimal bruises were visible, although some of the major injuries had nagging, unseen effects. They may have bothered her, but she was more on edge over the day's events. Feeling anxious, she sat down on the floor in her room. The fact that Alexavier's first Session was so aggressive had her wound up and nervous. Taking a deep breath, she rolled a toy rubber ball across the floor.

Suddenly, a knock on the door diverted her attention. "Come in," she called out, hoping her mind could be distracted for at least a little while. To her surprise, standing in the doorway was Alexavier, pulling back his hood. She was caught off guard, not expecting him to be in any condition to be up and around. She cautiously inquired, "How are you feeling?"

"I'm doing better than before. I had to take someone's advice and do some reading."

She showed a bashful smile. "Care to join me?"

"Sure." With a smile of his own, Alexavier took a seat next to her on the floor.

The fact that Alexavier was there and looking surprisingly well lit her up, figuratively and literally. A slight glow radiated from her whole body. "I was worried that you might not be okay. They really hit you hard."

"I was just as worried. When they said it was going to be stronger, I began to question whether I wanted to do this anymore. In the end, I realized I've come so far that I couldn't give up yet."

"I'm glad you didn't give up."

He looked down bashfully. "I've got another workout tomorrow. I hope I'm ready."

"You'll do great."

Both now sported that bashful look, but before the conversation could go any further, a puppy emerged from behind a box and charged at Alexavier. Barking with cute ferociousness, he slid across the floor and into Alexavier's leg. With boundless energy, the young pup started to climb onto his lap. Alexavier could do nothing but laugh. "He's adorable. What's his name?"

"Morkie."

"Morkie? That's an interesting name."

"Actually, he's a Morkie, a cross between a Yorkshire Terrier and a Maltese. I liked the sound of it so much that it ended up being his name."

Confused, Alexavier asked, "How did you get a pet? I heard there were no animals allowed anywhere in The Program."

"Everybody here asks for a favor or two, but I've never asked for anything," she explained. "When I was on surveillance in Cleveland, I followed Mortemmer and Max Towers into a shopping mall a little south of there. When Max used his powers to grow large, he shattered the roof, which came falling down everywhere. Luckily, I stopped the debris from harming anyone and destroying businesses. One store happened to be a pet store. I went in to check to see if everyone was okay, that's when I saw the Morkie puppies. But as I was looking over the animals, Max returned, trying

Enter Alexavier

to give enough time to allow them both to flee. It only took a couple of shots of my light blasts before I had him down and out. It took a little fighting to get Morkie, but eventually the Major relented because this had been the first capture in quite some time."

Suddenly, she came to a realization. "You remembered me from before your Session?"

"It would take a lot more than that for me to forget you."

She smiled as Morkie jumped up, looking to play with Alexavier. They laughed as the puppy continued his playful assault. Alexavier enjoyed the moment for as long as he could, as he knew another Session could be right around the corner.

Enter Alexavier

CHAPTER 29

The sound of heroes training in the W.A.R. Room resonated down the hallway with the doors slightly open, allowing any passersby the opportunity to witness the flurry of activity. As Alexavier walked through the doors, he grinned, welcoming the sight of his colleagues. He strolled through the room and set down his gear on the steps. Suddenly, a figure appeared with her face poking out from the stairs, causing Alexavier to step back. Jennifer soared into the air and around the room. She giggled while Alexavier smiled. The room continued to fill with heroes, as Percy, Mike and Bobbie walked in. Dave strolled by, smacking Alexavier on the back. It was a nice feeling to have old friends around again, plus new ones with such fantastic abilities.

"Everyone settle in and find your places!" Major Constantine's voice and presence brought a shift of focus among the mass of recruits. A quick falling-in ended with a collective silence. Oddly, there were a couple of vacancies on the steps. Seeing the empty spots annoyed the Major, who sighed. His frustration was only partially relieved when Harvey casually walked in and took his usual spot. Everyone felt the tension, especially after what happened in the last workout.

Seeing no acknowledgment from the Major about Harvey's presence had Mike a little perturbed. "Do you think that's best to include Harvey?"

"He's a part of this team, so he should be here for any team activities," the Major replied, reviewing his prep work.

"But the last time we had them together, things went poorly. And at this point, especially with Sam's instructions, it might be best if Harvey wasn't here."

"Sam had his say, but he's not here right now. I'm making a decision for what's best for this team."

Mike turned to face the Major. "What's best for this team is a little more cohesion. That's sure not coming from letting Harvey-"

"It's what's needed to be done." Major Constantine turned his stare to Mike.

"Yet Dwayne isn't here, although he should be. What could have been done is-"

"This is not your place to question my decisions!"

"When it pertains to these guys, yes it is! That's because you made that decision when you appointed me watch out for these new recruits!"

"Well, not anymore. You're off your duties entirely. So get out of here!"

Mike looked over at Jonathon, but held his tongue. He obliged the Major and took his frustration with him, leaving the room.

Given a few moments of deep breaths and getting his thoughts together, the Major spoke up, "Do you have the report from our intel recovery, Jonathon?"

"Yes, Sir." Jonathon walked forward to address the room. "So, we've gathered the data from the building that was destroyed. Coupling that with some of Bobbie's great surveillance, there are some really good things to report. First, the building was indeed one of their hideouts. We've never found one while they were still actually in it. This was huge win! We've recovered buildings well after they've been abandoned, but not while The Tribe was actually occupying one. This location was highly significant, since all of the major players were there, including The Infamous One, Natural Disaster, Nib and Game Over. Things appeared not so good for them, as Bobbie witnessed some dissension among those top members. If Bobbie would care to elaborate?"

"Sure." Bobbie stepped forward to the front of the group. "They were arguing back and forth, with Game Over and Nib going at it pretty hard. Eventually, it got so bad

Enter Alexavier

that The Infamous One had to step in between them, but had his own words for Nib. I can't give you the details on what was being said, but the fighting appeared to be much more than a simple disagreement. They nearly came to blows at one point."

"Thank you, Bobbie," the Major acknowledged. "If they were unhappy before, taking down that hideout might really help to disrupt their operations much more. I'm also happy to report, we recovered a bunch of the money that they had stolen with their last bank heist. With that adding to their frustrations, we have to get back after them. We will be hitting various sites harder in the coming weeks. Maybe the added pressure will cause them to make a mistake we can capitalize on."

"What's Beth's status?" Wally wondered.

"With the doctor's healing powers, she's completely recovered," Jonathon stated. "In fact, she should be here any moment."

As if on cue, Dr. Dennis escorted Beth as she walked through the doors. Despite the tension in the room, having one of their own who had been hurt badly back in the fold brought a bit of relief. Clapping started and Dave shouted, "Beacon, Beacon!" She walked over to the steps and settled next to Alexavier, who gave her an approving smile of his own.

"Okay. Since we have Beth here and feeling better, I've been told you're ready for action?"

"She is cleared for duty. Just as we've discussed," Dr. Dennis stated.

"Good." Major Constantine pulled out some papers and took them over to Beth. "We're putting you in the field. Rather than have you sitting back and waiting for you to feel up to being field ready, we're throwing you to the wolves. Jonathon and I think it would be best to have you back and scouting some of the locations we've picked out. We don't need you to start being gun shy. Jonathon can fill you in on what you will be doing."

Clearing his throat, Jonathon addressed the group, "The Tribe left behind some important files when they escaped. We have some information that there are some bigger crimes on the horizon, with an end goal in mind. We're not one hundred percent certain as to what that is, but until we do, it's business as usual. We're having Beth doing some reconnaissance to rule out some possible locations of interest."

Looking directly at Beth, Jonathon continued, "There shouldn't be anything out of the ordinary, so this should be a cakewalk. Scout the locations and report back what you find. You should be gone no longer than three days or so. We'll follow up after the workout."

The Major took over. "Also, Sam wants to send out every recruit that is trained to do recon. We might be getting close to finding another hideout, so Bobbie will be checking out several New York locations. More missions are being put together now, so everyone is to be ready. At any time, you may be called into action."

Moving over to the sea of wooden posts, Major Constantine continued, "Since Beth needs to prepare, we're cutting today's workout short. I've got some important things to attend to. The only thing on the agenda is to have Alexavier retry the obstacle course. We need to collect post-Session data, so let's get started. Alexavier, you're up."

While he walked over to the closest post, Killus spoke up, "How will these numbers make any difference? He knows the course now. It's all familiarity."

"I don't believe that will be the case." Jonathon reached over, taking a sheet of paper from the doctor. "Alexavier doesn't adjust to situations after doing things once. He can adjust just by seeing what's in front of him. So, the first time he ran the course was as fast as he was going to do it. Any gains made by the Session will show up today."

"Plus, the hammers that fall on the return trip across the posts are timed to cause as much disruption as possible. Their timing changes based on the performance of the individual. If anything, the varied pattern would cause more problems." The Major

Enter Alexavier

turned back. "Now, get into position."

With ease, Alexavier hops onto the post. He turns back, pulled on his hood and waited for further instructions.

"The same as your previous attempt. You can hop on one leg down to the end, and however you want to get back." Major Constantine backed away. "Jonathon, you have the stopwatch?"

"I'm ready."

A hush fell over the room with the Major waiting patiently. The group's attention was squarely on Alexavier, who had not moved a muscle. He seemed very relaxed, as if in his element. When it became a call to action, even if it was nothing physical, that's where he excelled. Finally, the Major shouted, "Go!"

Alexavier erupted, jumping forward on one leg at a frenetic pace. He made his way from one post to the next, bypassing several along the way. In no time at all, he reached the far side. With a twist of his body, he sprinted across the flattened posts. As with his first attempt, the avenue to the finish became obstructed with swinging hammers that emerged from the ceiling. His path was direct, zooming by the first couple. Getting closer to the finish line, a random hammer swung close by, sending Alexavier off course. A mild correction had him aiming in the right direction, but one last hammer sent him flipping in the air. His hands planted firmly on the final post with his body weight distributed unevenly. Stretching his legs out instantly stabilized his position. As quickly as he could pull his body back into a straight handstand, the final hammer returned, swinging within inches of him.

The gathered heroes held their collective breaths. Everyone knew his time would be quick, but how quick. Alexavier twisted his body and dropped down to the floor, looking at Major Constantine. He turned to Jonathon, who was looking at his stopwatch. Calculating the numbers, Jonathon announced, "Alex went down in 14.22 seconds, and back in 7.84 seconds. That's an improvement of about a third of a second both ways."

As much as the collectively excited group wanted to bask in the great improvement, Killus again had to be a pain in the butt. "He ain't getting any better. It's all crap."

"You just don't like it that you can't do it," Wally responded.

Killus turned to face Wally. "I don't have to."

"You did, and you sucked when you did it. You don't have any times in the top ten," Percy stated.

Dave laughed, "Oh dang! Burn on you, Mr. Grumpy Pants!"

"Let's see how you like it when I take your pants-"

"Stand down now, Hank!" The Major gave a death stare to the whole group. "All of you!"

Jonathon explained, "For your information, various simulations have been tried with Alexavier over the years and he always performs at the same level from start to finish no matter if he's familiar with the exercise or not. His efficiency in all those performances changes, but only by a fraction of a second after going through the Session. This third of a second is considered a substantial improvement. Expand the distance out to a full mile, and he's nearly three seconds faster."

"The Session provided the data we needed." Major Constantine paced in front of the team. "We put you guys through them for a reason. Today is proof that it works. I believe everyone should be prepared for an upcoming Session. We will schedule everyone for their turn. Now, I need Beth to stay behind. The rest of you can leave."

The words started a race for the door, with several of them giving Alexavier a nod or congratulatory handshake, as he pulled the hood back. He appeared to be back on the Major's good side. If he can stay there is another question.

Enter Alexavier

CHAPTER 30

Most of the W.A.R. Room had cleared out. Major Constantine stepped out, talking with Jonathon about their plans for the upcoming reconnaissance. One of the last to leave, Alexavier put his gear back into his bag. The day was going great, as he performed well during the workout. Things were about to improve. Looking over, Beth saw her intended target. She had sneaked up behind him and poked him in the sides. He jumped and turned ready for action, but it turned out to be a nice surprise when he saw her trying to hide her laughter.

Alexavier set his gear down, not quite finished packing up. "It looks like you're back to normal?"

"Yup! Back to normal is right. My healing was so far ahead of schedule that it impressed the doctor. She can work wonders, although I'm not sure when I'll be cleared for missions."

"Aren't they sending you out shortly?"

"That's just recon and scouting. They have much tougher guidelines for being cleared for missions."

"What do you need to do to get cleared?"

Beth sat down on the steps. "Usually, the doctors and staff test any injuries to make sure you're healed properly. Then they check to see if you're suffering from any cognitive issues, especially after any traumatic head injuries."

"Will you go through these tests?"

"Probably, but not for what the Major has in mind. It's an easy recon mission. I'll be back in a couple days. He really doesn't like having any of us out for very long. It makes planning missions harder."

Alexavier noticed a few missing friends. "Dave and Wally didn't want to stick around?"

"They felt bad for Harvey, so they decided to hang out with him for a while. Maybe that's good, 'cause Harvey hasn't been the same lately. Jonathon said that it's causing issues with the Major and the staff. They don't know what's going on or if he's going to be effective if he's sent out in the field."

"I'm not sure what his problem is with me. I didn't do anything to him when I got here, but he acted weird right away."

"Did you guys ever have any interactions before living here?"

"None that I can recall. If I did, I'm pretty sure I'd remember it. If he has a problem with-" With his mouth wide open, Alexavier was interrupted with Major Constantine and Jonathon re-entering the W.A.R. Room, both stopping in front of Beth and Alexavier.

"How are you doing, Beth?" Jonathon asked.

"Great. I can't wait to get back to my normal routine."

The Major stepped closer. "Well, we had a meeting with Dr. Dennis, and she thinks you're ready to get back to active status."

"I'm ready whenever you are, but I haven't gone through-"

"As I mentioned, we've decided to throw you to the wolves, even without the necessary post injury clearance," the Major responded.

"What are you going to have her do?" Alexavier asked.

The Major pulled open a folder. "We're going to send you out for a reconnaissance mission to New Jersey, based off some of the intel we gathered during the Tribe hideout raid."

"This information doesn't really support anything substantial, but we think this will only be a short excursion to check off this off our list," Jonathon explained.

"Is it wise to send her out so soon?" Alexavier wondered.

The Major handed her some paperwork and pictures. "After some talks, we don't want you to get gun shy, so a simple operation like this would be great to get back in action. Your ability to manipulate and produce extreme levels of light is the perfect counter to The Infamous One's power to hide in the shadows. We need you out there and at your best."

"When do I leave?"

"After we go through a few more details of the plan, you can gather your gear and leave whenever you're ready. The helicopter is being prepped as we speak." Major Constantine moved closer and pointed to the files. "These are the areas that possibly contain intel. It's remote, plus these areas appear to have been abandoned some time ago. A couple of farms and orchards dot the landscape, so be aware of the possibility of locals. Scout them out and report anything you find. Once you've searched them thoroughly, we'll bring you back so we can plan our next move."

"Yes, sir. I'll gather my things right away." With some spring in her step, she headed toward her room. Jonathon smiled, patting Alexavier on the shoulder. He followed the Major out the door, leaving Alexavier to his thoughts and his worries.

#

Sorting through different jackets, which none seemed to fit her needs, Beth reluctantly chose a black, hooded sweatshirt. Placing it next to the bag, she turned for pants. Usually, she would have chosen the best match based on color and style. For the use during a reconnaissance mission, practicality was most important. Something light and waterproof was perfect, plus it needed to be black. Socks, shirts and even toiletries and essentials all were collected. With the table full, the next task was packing the abundant items into a purposeful bag.

She turned at the sound of a knock on her door, as Alexavier poked his head in, "Are you almost ready?"

"Hi. Did you get the clothes? The Major said you'd have some stuff they had ready for me?"

"Yup." Alexavier entered, waiting for the attack. "I don't hear any growling."

"Dr. Dennis is watching Morkie while I'm away. That way he won't tear up the whole room."

He handed her the clothes and gear. "I'd be glad to watch him. I'm sure once I give him a treat, we'll become good friends."

"Hey, you're not that special. He'll be anyone's friend for a treat." She began arranging her things neatly inside the bag.

"And I got you your favorite, just as you requested, a cream soda. Do you need any help?"

"I'm pretty much done, except for packing."

Alexavier handed her the drink, followed by various articles of clothing. Patting down the clothes for one last zip, she slung the bag over her shoulder. "You want to walk me to the chopper?"

"Sure."

She led the way, shutting off the lights. Once outside her room, he caught up to match her stride. They glanced over at each other with a cute shyness. Neither had the words to say. Finally, a giggle by Beth broke the tension.

"What's so funny?"

Enter Alexavier

"Just that you're such a shy guy, even though you're so good at being a hero."

"I'm not a hero yet."

She stopped. "You're a hero right now. It doesn't matter that you haven't made it from The Program to The United. You saved me. That's all that matters."

"But I can't save you all the time. You're going to be out there on your own in a few minutes. If something were to happen-"

"I'm not worried. Okay. If by chance I get in trouble, I'll make sure to yell loud enough that I'll wake you in your sleep." Beth continued down the hallway.

"That won't help, 'cause you never yell."

"I will if you can't keep up!" She smiled, continuing toward the entrance of the hangar. Already there, giving commands in preparation for takeoff, Major Constantine waved his arms with each order. Like a conductor in front of his orchestra, the processes and procedures happened in unison, resembling a harmony of activity with the music being the whirring of the helicopter blades. The Major checked and re-checked each item on the safety checklist, until he realized his next hero to enter the field for reconnaissance had arrived. After some last instructions to the flight crew, he put his full attention on Beth. "You've got all your gear?"

"Yes, sir."

"We're going to have you follow up on a couple of leads. They're not very promising, but this will get you back into the field." The Major turned and walked toward the aircraft.

She followed. "I can promise you, I'm ready to go."

"Good." The Major handed her a packet with the appropriate documents. "Make sure to blend in as a tourist, from the moment you check into the hotel. Stay out of sight whenever you're scouting. Report back often. Got it?"

"Yes, sir"

Enter Alexavier

"Get aboard. Call in once you're at the hotel, and we'll finalize any things that we might have forgotten."

"Yes, sir!" Beth turned back, looking at Alexavier. "You take care, rookie!"

Alexavier smiled, but only momentarily. Watching her image vanish up the ramp of the helicopter was hard to watch. The image of her glove in the rubble of a building was still fresh in his mind. While she's away doing some scouting, he could not be there to help in case she ran into trouble. The helicopter blades spun faster and faster. Soon, the doors to the roof opened, and sunlight rained down. Lifting into the air, the helicopter became smaller and smaller until the clouds blocked his view. He stared a bit longer, until the roof doors slowly closed, which made him let out a long sigh. He pulled his hood forward and walked to his room.

Enter Alexavier

CHAPTER 31

Between Beth out looking for Tribe members and something really bugging him about the Major, Alexavier needed to do something to get his mind off things, and his room did not provide any comfort. Eventually, he found himself outside the doctor's office. Peering through the window of the door, the only one inside was the doctor. Hopefully that meant that the procedure she had mentioned before could be completed without any interruptions. A knock on the door had it instantly open. Dr. Dennis turned around and smiled, seeing the young hero. "I take it that it's time to try that memory recovery I had talked about during your first visit."

Alexavier walked in and gave a tug, pulling back his hood. "Is it a good time though? Are you done with all your appointments?"

"I have a light schedule for most of the day. We have at least two hours before my next appointment." She pushed aside an empty tray and slid another one over, which was loaded with various medical tools and walked over toward her desk.

"I wonder if we'll find anything."

"We'll find out shortly. I've spent a couple of days going over the proper procedures, and I'm sure we'll have our best opportunity to recover something hidden away or what might have been thought to been lost." The doctor walked back to Alexavier placing a file on the tray. "Now, if you'll take a seat, we can give it a try."

Alexavier sat in the chair, getting as comfortable as possible. "So how does this work?"

"The first step involves mild sedation, which is made up of a combination of drugs to free up part of your subconscious. Depending on the amount, the sedation should provide the level of recollection. We can adjust the doses for best results if you decide to come back later to try it again. Second, we wait and see where your mind takes you. It's that simple, just the drug combination and your brain. Are you ready?"

"Let's give it a try."

With his approval she pulled out a syringe, uncapped it and verified the amount of drug. A careful placement of the needle next to his arm, just outside the extruding vein had her studying him closely. For a brief moment, he became a test subject, knowing that on his previous visit, she encountered a rough time penetrating his skin. Eyeing the insertion point, she slowly pushed in. Encountering the same problem, an increase in the force continued gradually until the needle finally broke the skin, and she began injecting the drugs into his vein. With the placement of an alcohol swab next to the injection site, Dr. Dennis withdrew needle and looked at her patient. He remained calm, blinking normal until the medications started taking effect.

His eyelids grew heavy. Within a few second, Alexavier slipped into a semi-unconscious state. The darkness overwhelmed his mind, allowing his brain to open up. Memories that were once tucked away came rushing back. For what seemed like an eternity, the blackness of his mind morphed into a spectrum of colors, until there was one single, solitary blob. It remained indistinguishable, no matter hard much he stared. But what was the known, the blurred image before him felt absolutely comfortable. He reached out, hoping to embrace whatever it was. As if on command, the vague images cleared up a bit, revealing his parents. He welcomed them, although nothing more came from them other than what he remembered. No matter how hard he stretched his fingers, they stayed back, only partially becoming visible.

With arms grasping for even the slightest of touch, both images faded. The

Enter Alexavier

resemblance of their bodies became less distinguishable forms. Soon, the familiar turned into an odd, piercing point of light. What began as a simple shimmer brought an increase in intensity with every passing moment. Once the brightness became so overwhelming that he had to use his own arms to deflect the light, an abnormal image of a woman's arm emerged as if exiting a still lake. It reached out. A hand turned with the palm open. The unknown of what was presented before him did not stop him from placing his hand in hers. She closed her fingers into a calming embrace. Her arm slowly retracted, pulling him into the bright abyss, which he gladly welcomed.

Descending into the extreme light, the world around Alexavier transcended to a different world. A world that contained a much younger version of him, standing in front of what appeared to be a younger Harvey.

But things turned weird when his younger self yelled, "Stop it, Harry!"

An angered Harry wound up for one big punch and swung as hard as he could. Alexavier ducked under, allowing Harry's fist to go by. Using Harry's follow through, Alexavier reached back with both hands around Harry's head, grabbing at his chin. Alexavier dropped down, pulling Harry with him with Harry's head slamming into the ground. He screamed in pain, as Alexavier stood up, shocked by his own actions.

But the world began to feel awkward with Harry screaming harder. The louder his cried, the stranger Alexavier felt. Something from the extreme noise bombarded his brain. Dizziness consumed him. As each second passed, his balance got worse. He struggled to keep himself upright. He staggered back and forth and finally fell to the ground. Alexavier laid there, losing consciousness to the sound of Harry's agonizing screams.

With a flooding of emotion, paired with a scream, consciousness came back to Alexavier. As his body shook and he gasped for air, the doctor reached for a syringe, placing the needle to his skin. His blood pressure had sky rocketed to an unsafe level, and it needed to be brought back down quickly. The needle wouldn't penetrate his skin, so she pushed harder. Strangely enough, when looking back at the blood pressure monitor, it had fallen back to a safe level, nearly back to normal. She pulled away the syringe, looking slightly confused as to how it could return so quickly. Alexavier looked around, focusing his thoughts after such strong and real visions.

"Are you okay? Your blood pressure spiked, and your whole body was shaking."

Alexavier gave one more mental check of himself before explaining things. "Yeah. I had a really powerful dream... or vision. I'm not sure which it was."

"Were you able to make anything out?"

"I saw my parents. It was the same vague vision of them. But suddenly, it was replaced by the same white light I sometimes see when I'm sleeping. The only difference is that a hand emerging, reaching out to me. It got extremely bright. Once the light subsided, Harvey was there, but weirdly, his name was Harry. I think he was bullying me, until I fought back. Then I took him down. But as he laid there, he started to scream, which got louder and louder. Eventually, I passed out. That's when I woke up."

"So, whatever was going on with this boy affected you somehow?"

"It felt just like what happened when Harvey attacked me during the workout."

"Interesting. Was there anything new about your parents?"

"No, same as before and only as I remembered them. But it was the other memory, which was new. I don't know why Harvey was Harry. You know, I think it was the first time I used my abilities."

"You don't have any other memories about your youth before that?" She put the syringe on a tray and sat back on her stool.

"No."

She grabbed for a pad of paper and quickly began writing. "I think this might be noteworthy. Are you sure you're okay?'

Enter Alexavier

"I'm fine. A bit tired, but I'm okay."

She continued writing while giving one final check. "If you feel alright, you can head out, but I think we should visit this again. Any thoughts?"

Alexavier stood up, straightening his clothes. "I'm not sure what to make of it all, but I think this was helpful. Maybe after I get settled, I can come back?"

"I'll have things ready for you. Any time you feel up to it, just stop back."

"Thank you." Alexavier slowly walked to the door, pausing just outside the entrance. The mildly confused look subsided a bit, and he put on his hood, beginning a brisk walk back toward the center of the complex. His mind raced faster than he did, processing the information before him. As his image blended with the people in the hallway, Dr. Dennis kept documenting the events that unfolded. Something important just transpired, and she is hoping it is something very significant.

Enter Alexavier

CHAPTER 32

Having made a beeline from the doctor's office to his room, Alexavier could not wait for the door to open. He quickly squeezed through when there was just enough space and walked over to his desk filled with anticipation. Quickly pulling out his journal from the top drawer, he dropped it on the desk and sat in his chair. Opening the cover and flicking through the first few pages, he stopped at one of the earliest pages. A pause allowed him to focus on just a very few words, 'I hear the screams, and then there's black.'

The episode with Dr. Dennis brought to light that these few words meant so much more, especially to what became of him and how his powers first manifested. With the vision still racing through his mind, he searched for a pen, picking up the nearest one and expanding on those simple words. He started to scribble just below them, providing the story to what in the journal that had now become a title.

#

Like daily clockwork, the Major entered his office, tossing the papers he held in his hand onto the desk. His preferred method of relaxation came in a bottle. Multiple bottles and flasks adorning his cabinets housed various types of alcohol. This day had been bad enough that he headed straight for his prized whiskey. Nothing else mattered

Enter Alexavier

until he finished pouring a full glass and took a large gulp. He lowered the glass, closed his eyes and paused to take in the much-anticipated effects.

A knock on his door was unfortunate. But for a man in his position, it was not unexpected. A press of a button to open the door gave way for Dr. Dennis to enter. Making her way to the desk, she placed a report in front of him.

"I hope this is good news. Dealing with Dwayne is becoming tiresome."

"What's going on?"

The Major sighed. "For disobeying nearly every order we give him, Dwayne has yet to participate in events, workouts or keep any appointments. For that, I'm going to have to have him confined to his quarters."

"Actually, he's trying to seclude himself most of the time. This is only feeding into that."

"Then I'll have to force him to become a part of this team, even if that means Dirk will have to escort him back and forth everywhere."

"I see the next few weeks are going to be rough." She placed her hand back on the folder. "Alexavier stopped by my office today, and we attempted to retrieve some possible lost memories. We didn't get what we were trying for, but I think we made a breakthrough."

"What kind of breakthrough, doctor?"

"If you skim through my report, the first portion doesn't provide anything other than what he experienced previously, except maybe a hand that appeared. What did come back to him was the possibility of the first time his powers manifested. This is significant, especially with his high level of retention."

"Interesting." The Major browsed the paper. "I'd say this was a success. If he can recall additional memories, ones that can be used for our benefit and his, you should have him back for more as soon as he's able."

"I'll make it happen." As she turned away, leaving his office, she continued, "By

Enter Alexavier

the way, Alexavier's last vision also showed Harvey as a child being a bully who picked on him. What was odd is that the bully's name was Harry. That information is detailed at the bottom of my report as well."

"Thank you, doctor. If I have any questions, I'll let you know."

With an unwavering stare, Major Constantine kept an eye on the doctor. His fingers thumbed through the pages, not sure what to make of the folder. Right now, the only sure thing for the Major happened to be that his glass was still half-full.

Enter Alexavier

CHAPTER 33

Taking a break from doing the Major's bidding of customizing weaponry, Mike took a stroll. With no specific destination, he headed across the complex, eventually walking by the weight room. With a quick glance inside, he noticed a determined Alexavier, vigorously pumping iron. Pausing for a moment, he looked around to see if anyone was watching. With nobody of importance paying attention, he walked over to the entrance. "Hey! No need to be angry at the weights!"

Alexavier placed the barbell into its cradle and sat up. "Beth is out doing recon, so I thought I'd do something to take my mind off of her being out there alone."

"Somebody need a friend?"

"Just trying to focus my energy until she returns. I thought the Major said you couldn't do anything with us recruits?"

Mike entered the room, looking back at the doorway. "Well, he kind of doesn't know I'm here, if you know what I mean. I heard you met with Dr. Dennis."

"She tried that memory recovery thing. It was quite weird."

"Did it work?"

"Yeah and no. Nothing new came of my parents, but I think I remembered the first time I used my abilities."

"That's good, isn't it?"

"I guess. I'm not quite sure what to make of it. We're going to try it again soon to see if I can bring back more."

"Sounds like it's starting to help. How did the workout go?"

"Pretty good. The Major said my small increase was significant. It was a third of a second."

"A third of a second total?"

"A third for each run."

"Wow!" Mike eyed the hallway. "If you take a third of a second both ways and extrapolate it out, that's huge."

"I don't know. I didn't feel any different when I was out there."

"Trust me. It is pretty big. Just give it a couple more Sessions, and you'll start to notice the gains overall. Those are gains rarely made by some of the best that have been through here. The Major must be feeling as giddy as a schoolgirl. He's going to want to give Sessions every other day."

"Just what I need, more chair time. I think I'm fine with Sessions for a while."

"I wouldn't get too worried. They can only plan and run a Session about once a week. So, if they decide to put everybody through it, you're looking at probably another four months or so before having to think about it."

"All I'm thinking about right now is Beth out on her own."

"I heard she was sent for a small intelligence gathering mission."

"Yeah, and the Major said it wasn't anything, but she's by herself. Last time, we were all there with her and look what happened."

"I know you guys have always been close, going back to Philadelphia. And what happened with the recent mission scared you. Heck, it scared everyone here. So, I understand your concern. But if there's one thing I know about Beth, it's that she's one of our best and most determined recruits. She's not going to stop until every bad guy on earth is taken down. She brought back Max Towers on her own. If there's anyone

Enter Alexavier

who can handle a tough situation, it's that spunky hero."

"But The Tribe almost killed her. That has really bothered me. I swear. As soon as I can get out in the field, they're all going to pay for what they did."

"Don't let that anger mess with your judgment, especially when you're out in the field. That can get you hurt pretty bad. Several recruits have paid a high price due of their emotions. Stay in control. Use that head and those amazing skills you have for justice. Revenge is a road I'm not sure you want to venture down."

Alexavier gave a reluctant nod, picking up one of the dumbbells. "I'll never get the chance to go after The Tribe if I can't figure out this problem in training that I had with Sam."

"Nearly everyone who's been through here has had a rough start, Union, Riva, Intergalactic and even Sam. We're all human. No one knows what this place is like when you first get here. It's a lot different than the lower level portions of The Program."

"Still, it's the one thing I've been trained for. It has always been second nature to me. I don't understand why I would freeze up." Alexavier put down the weights and let out a sigh.

"Have you ever had this issue before, in or out of The Program?"

"Not that I can remember. I mean not like that. One time, Dave and I had to spar, and it kind of happened."

"Dave Headley, Dead Head?"

"Yeah. We were matched up and supposed to take each other on in combat games. We were always on the same team, because were we friends. One day, a doctor got the idea to split us up. Just so happens that it was hand-to-hand exercises."

"So, you froze up the same way?"

"Kind of, but not that way. It sort of happened, until Dave punched me in the face. After that, I beat his butt. He was mad for a week."

Enter Alexavier

Mike chuckled. "Let me mull this over and pick it apart. I'm sure I can come up with something to help you. I'm not sure what your status is right now. But in the end, Sam is the one to ultimately approve your admission to this complex or send you back. Maybe we can come up with a plan to get his approval, before someone decides to send you back. We'll keep this between us."

"Okay." Alexavier gave a reluctant nod, looking at the clock.

"Still can't stop staring at the time, can you?"

"I'll feel better when she gets back safely."

Mike put his hand on Alexavier's shoulder. "Hey, Beth will be fine. If anything happens, we're not that far away. You'd be there for her in no time. And don't worry about going after the Tribe. You've got all the time in the world to find them and bring them down. Just do what you need so you can get that opportunity. You know what's needed. There's something special going on with you, so don't doubt what you think, know and that weird feeling you get. You're here to be a hero. Go show them."

Alexavier grinned, "I will. Thank you."

"Anytime." Mike poked his head out the doorway, carefully surveying the hallway before exiting quickly and quietly. Alexavier turned back to the weights on the bench. It couldn't hold his attention as he once again looked at the clock, still counting the time until Beth would return.

Enter Alexavier

CHAPTER 34

Finished with one location, Beth carefully moved to the next location on her target list. Just two more areas to investigate, and she would finish her first assignment back. One of the locations was simple to visit. The building was close enough to a major town and easy to get to. It had been abandoned long ago and a quick walk-through provided no information. The next location was much different, being further from the city and among the rolling hills. A cab ride was necessary, although it looked weird be dropped off in the middle of nowhere. This location would be a great place to stay off the radar. The only thing remotely near was some kind of farm in the distance. There appeared to be an old overgrown road making its way back, but she needed to stay inconspicuous. A small hike among the plants, trees and weeds brought the building in question into view. Hiding to study this particular building was not the easiest, but the grassy and elevated areas that surrounded it were camouflage enough to stay hidden.

Time passed without seeing any signs of life. After a half hour or so, Beth sighed while crawling back away from the ridge. Once far enough down the hill and being blocked from view, she crouched down and moved quickly toward the other side of the building.

The wind was blowing slightly, masking any sound she made while moving through the foliage. Enough trees dotted the property, allowing for segmented hiding spots. The path to a new viewing point was long, but made necessary for being able to

Enter Alexavier

see inside a few small windows that were on the far side of the building. Her dark outfit contrasted the vibrant green plants in the light of day, each move was very careful. Edging slowly to the plateau of a hill covered in two-foot tall weeds, Beth pried them apart to peak through.

The building was weathered and old, but not falling apart. A feeling of lifelessness exuded from the dull concrete walls. The condition was slightly better than the surrounding landscape, but not by much. Having spent some time already surveying the property meant she only had to watch for a brief time more before moving closer to fully investigate. But boredom slowly crept in. The inactivity from the building made her antsy. Backing down to find a path that would keep her hidden as much as possible, Beth progressed further toward the back of the building and its door.

The wind blowing through the trees shifted, allowing the sound of movement through the tall weeds around her to be heard. She quickly ducked, scanning for cover. A patch of reeds near a low land area rose to towering heights. Making a dash to them, she dropped to one knee once well inside. Listening intently, the movement continued toward the building. Not able to differentiate what could be making the noise, she inched forward until the reeds thinned to the point of having a clearer view. The sound faded, as if whatever it was had moved away, but she was not sure where. Curious as to the source of the movement, she separated the weeds, but did not see anything. Deciding to find out what it was, she scampered along, hoping to catch up to it. Once the next ridge came up, her eyes found no sign of what had walked by her.

Animals were sporadic, but populated the entire area. It would make sense that either deer or something a bit smaller could be around the perimeter. But the shuffling sound through the leaves returned, louder and from multiple areas. Scanning for a place to hide, nothing was remotely close, so Beth backed up against the flatter side of the hill, waiting for it to emerge. Taking a defensive stance, her wait didn't last long as Silver Shockwave appeared. He started to produce an explosive silver sphere. Beth

Enter Alexavier

beat him to the punch, blasting him with a condensed beam of light that knocked him down. Gathering up enough to shoot again, she was hit by a wall of energy that could only come from Natural Disaster. She landed on her back, turning quickly to shoot at him. He produced a field of force energy that deflected her blast, but weakened him significantly. A large tree weaved back and forth from over a hill. It fell down, but slowly came closer, being dragged by Game Over. He did not get the chance to use it as a baseball bat, because of a well place light blast from Beth that splintered the tree into a thousand pieces.

Needing some room to breathe, she sprayed all the villains with a more intense and focused beam. The maneuver worked, providing a few seconds to call for help. But when she tapped her Com-Link, she was only greeted with static. Knowing the problem could not be fixed right away, she continued the offensive efforts of shooting any villain in front of her. But the problem was the villain behind her. An intense pain shot through her back and into her chest, as a red energy blade pierced her sternum. All of Beth's strength was instantly taken from her. Standing over her prone body was the smirking Nib. He held both his hand up with energy blades, finally putting both hands together to create an intense crimson blade. Upon raising his hands high for one final attack, a voice rang out.

"Quench your death blade!" The Infamous One made his presence known. He climbed over a nearby hill, staring down Nib.

"She's a problem that needs to go away," Nib stated.

Game Over pulled himself back to his feet. "I agree. As much as I think Nib is a feminine hygiene product, she's a problem as long as she's breathing."

The Infamous One walked over and stood between Nib and Beth's prone body. "For the purpose I have, she's to be brought back alive."

A disgruntled Nib walked away. The rest of The Terror Tribe stood over her. She gradually lifted her head. Gathering the strength in hopes of possibly mounting one

Enter Alexavier

last desperate offensive, her chance to escape ended as Natural Disaster's fist rendered her unconscious.

Enter Alexavier

CHAPTER 35

The command center for The Program is usually buzzing with activity of some sort. Right at the moment, things were down right crazy. An operation was underway and had taken a turn. People were talking over each other, as well as those manning the chaotic phones. Rarely does anything happen that causes this much chaos. Rarely does everything fall apart.

Like a charging bull, Major Constantine marched into the room, followed by Jonathon. Neither of them was in a good mood, and no one was immune from their wrath.

"What the hell is going on? I need updates, not jaws on the floor!" The Major's stare did not discriminate.

A Sargent spoke up first. "We have nothing, sir. And we haven't for the last half hour."

"That's not the answer I want!"

"What can you tell us?" Jonathan asked.

"About a half hour ago, Beth's Com-Link went black, and we haven't heard from her since," the Sargent replied with his voice cracking.

A communications tech spoke up, "She was last heard heading into an area outside of Trenton, New Jersey. Soon after, communications went silent, but we only thought that she was keeping quiet so as not to get discovered. The possibility was that she might be close to engaging a villain."

"When she didn't become available, did you attempt communication again?" Jonathon inquired.

"We did," the Sargent stated. "But without any disruption that we could detect, we chalked it up to her needing radio silence."

"How long before it became obvious that something had happened?" Major Constantine started showing his angry side. "Did the thought arrive in anyone's head that continued radio silence meant something was wrong?"

"We're sorry, sir. But-"

"I don't care about excuses! We have protocols for these kinds of moments!" The Major looked over to Jonathon. "Take the lead on this. Start tracking her positions for the last two hours."

"Will do." Jonathon went to the nearest console.

"I need everything you can tell me, and I need it yesterday. Call out to the team. I need them at the chopper in five. Meet us in the hanger when you're done." Jonathon nodded as the Major exited the command center in a hurry, leaving the assembly of military suits to handle the necessary preparations.

Enter Alexavier

CHAPTER 36

No time was wasted in preparing the jet helicopter. Every technician and mechanic the complex employed moved about the hangar quickly and efficiently. The rush of loading combat essentials through the back of the chopper ended with the crew clearing out to allow the pilot to warm up the engine and prep for the flight. With the propellers beginning to spin, the overhead doors to the hangar slowly opened, allowing sunlight to flood the landing pad. The air swirled throughout the hangar. Anything not held down and of very little weight began to get blown around.

First to run in was Alexavier, fully clothed and prepped, glasses in hand. As usual, his turnaround being at lightning speed had him waiting. He stood, staring at the ramp leading to the cargo area of the helicopter with a wanting to just climb aboard. Each second ate away at him. He was ready to go, unlike the aircraft and his team.

Not the sight he wanted to see, but Harvey was the first to join him. Harvey took a spot next to Alexavier, waiting for instructions. No words were exchanged, as the dirty looks they gave each other were all that was needed.

Every hero that could be ready for battle began to arrive. They all lined up waiting alongside Alexavier and Harvey. Within seconds, Major Constantine, Jonathon and Dr. Dennis walked in. They stopped in front of the group with the Major moving in closer. He did not take his eyes off them, particularly Alexavier. "Both of you get aboard and in a seat. I'll update everyone once we're airborne."

Alexavier looked puzzled, not sure how Harvey could be allowed to go after being

Enter Alexavier

suspended. Not needed to get in trouble himself by arguing, he took the lead, running up the ramp and taking a seat toward the front. Harvey walked up, entering at a deliberate pace. He stopped about halfway, seeing Alexavier at the front and decided to retreat and sit near the entrance. Others began boarding, finding a seat of their own. Percy, Dave and Wally located themselves near Alexavier. Everyone gave Harvey an odd glance as they walked by. Killus and his crew filed in, but April sat near the end closest to Alexavier. Once situated and looking up, Killus began to stare her down. She became uncomfortable and moved toward the center of the cargo area. Alexavier noticed, giving his own death stare back at Killus, who just smiled.

"I thought Harvey was not allowed to go," Alexavier said.

Dave didn't even flinch. "Yeah. I figured that wouldn't stick."

"You mean this has happened before?"

"It ain't going to stop any time soon," Percy responded.

"That doesn't make any sense."

"Welcome to The Major's Program," Dave said sarcastically, putting on the last of his blue, red and black gear.

With the final members of the team strapped into a chair and secured, Major Constantine took up the rear behind Jonathon and the doctor. He made his way to the front, right next to Alexavier. Everyone turned his or her attention to the Major as the door lifted and sealed. A display lit up, showing a map with highlighted areas.

The Major looked everyone over before starting. "We are flying into a rural area outside Trenton, New Jersey. It's the last known point of contact for Beth. We will be coming in hot and in stealth mode. There's likely no one around for us to worry about interfering with this operation, but there are some unknowns. First is the scant knowledge of the population in the surrounding area. Satellites currently show limited houses where we shall be, but not much more than that. The only major structure is a building that was repossessed years ago by some banks and also a cattle farm with

Enter Alexavier

slaughterhouse. There's no aerial evidence of the building in use. But the cattle farm has been very active, particularly the slaughterhouse. Our landing point will be between these two, far enough that neither site will be disrupted or know of our arrival."

"Are we going to be checking out one over the other?" Percy asked.

"With no apparent activity at the building, we will use the farm as our cover for their operation. We will land and spread out to set up a perimeter at about 50 meters. We will approach the farm silently, but with as much firepower as possible. Take down anyone in your path, until we find Beth."

Alexavier looked concerned, but continued to listen.

"File out quickly to your designated spots and wait for my commands. Keep radio chatter to a minimum, unless you're contacting me."

"How soon before we land?" Killus wondered with devilish smile.

"With the helicopter at full speed, we should arrive in less than a half hour. We have all surrounding airspace cleared, so it should be smooth sailing."

Jonathon saw the look on Alexavier's face. "What's up, Alex?"

"When were the surveillance pictures taken of the building?"

"Today," the Major replied.

"No. What time of day."

"About 10 minutes ago, around 7pm."

"Were there any taken before that, particularly at night?"

"If you're asking about being able to see light from the electricity, there's no power going to the building from the electric company and no sign of vehicles in the pictures. The only activity around is at the cattle farm."

Major Constantine gave a glare, daring Alexavier to go on. Satisfied by the silence, he continued and pointed to the monitor. "The farm is situated toward the southeast of

Enter Alexavier

the property, closest to where we will land. This will make access easy, especially the slaughterhouse, which is where we should concentrate our efforts. When we hit the ground, everyone will be going by his or her code names. I'll give the signal to charge the compound. It'll be dark, but you'll see the lights in the distance. Harvey and Dave are to take the lead once Michael sends his missiles close enough to make an entry point. No direct hits. I don't want to take the chance of injuring Beth. Just give the team access to the building. I want Wally to carry Hank to head the entry. Killus and Alexavier to take out anyone in their way once inside. Everyone else can follow behind and engage as needed. Any questions?"

Alexavier held his tongue, but Wally could see something bothered him. The Major passed them, heading to talk to the others toward the back, giving Wally the opportunity to inquire. "Is there something that the Major doesn't see?"

"The farm would make sense for body disposal, especially with the slaughterhouse. But to use as a daily hideout makes no sense. People would regularly come by, which might blow their cover. You have a better option with a whole building that everyone believes is empty."

Wally thought for a second. "I guess that's true. But there's no activity at the building."

"And what of the fact there's no electricity?" Dave asked, still getting his final pieces of gear on.

"That just means there's no vehicles around at the moment of the picture. And as far as electricity goes, a night time picture would show whether that's correct, especially because they had someone who produced electricity."

"That's true with Mega Conductor." Dave stated.

Wally looked at the map. "It's far enough from any people and daily city activity. You don't go that far out without committing to the building"

"An if they've invested in the building for much more..."

Enter Alexavier

"They wouldn't want to lose whatever it is they have there." Percy studied the map. "But the building is at enough of a distance that you might not even see it, even if they have power. And I don't know if even my scope will allow me to see through the hills and landscape."

Dave looked down toward the Major. "There's no way he'll let you check it out."

"Maybe he doesn't have to." Alexavier leaned in to speak softer. "When we exit the chopper, move toward the perimeter in the direction of the building. I'll see what I can using my glasses' night vision."

"Are you guys getting ready or socializing?" The Major strolled by, surprising them.

"Getting ready," Percy stated.

Dave agreed, "Yup, Mr. Major."

"Good," Major Constantine approved, but with a bit of hesitation. "I hope you're ready."

"Yes, sir." Alexavier kept an eye out, as the Major walked past, making sure he had no clue of their discussion. They buried their heads and continued to prepare for the inevitable. It was only a matter of time before they hit the ground and needed to be ready for anything, even if it was not exactly what the Major had ordered.

Enter Alexavier

CHAPTER 37

The world slowly returned to Beth. Her head was a bit foggy. But her mask had been removed, and she could tell she was chained to a wall. Listening to the Com-Link that was still in her ear, she could only hear static. Its tiny size made it hard to notice, and it was her only hope at this point. She pulled on the chains that held her tight against a wall. Looking at her arms, she noticed that she had been wrapped in a paper thin, covering. The thought had come to her mind to burn away whatever it was and heat the chains to where she could break them and escape, but a deep voice stopped her.

"If you're thinking of using your lovely heat and light abilities, let me be the first to inform you that what you have covering your body is a unique substance that has a low flash point and will ignite easily, but burns at several thousand degrees. The slightest heat will not only catch it on fire, but you as well." The Infamous One slowly came closer, still with his all black outfit on. He had a swagger about him that exuded confidence. What he did, he did with purpose. Several members of The Terror Tribe, including Natural Disaster, Cavalio, Game Over and Nib, also joined him. They were all in their full outfits, as if ready for a confrontation.

"Maybe I'll catch us all on fire."

"Sorry to inform you, but the burning will only happen to you. Once the paper lights on fire, it will burn fast, hot and hurt you and only you to the point you'd wish you'd have died. I do not wish that, so please refrain from using your powers."

Enter Alexavier

"I can keep her from using her powers permanently." Nib walked near, glaring at her.

The Infamous One placed his hand on Nib's shoulder. "Rushing to terminate this young hero will do nothing to help our current situation. Things may get worse if her friends come looking for her. We must prepare accordingly."

"Why are we wasting time keeping her around if we're not going to have a little fun?" Game Over asked, waving a long pipe in the air that nearly hit Beth.

"Why don't you shove that pipe up-"

"I can shove this right through your skull."

Raising his arm as if to heave the pipe in her direction, The Infamous One caught Game Over's bicep. With a tight grip and not letting go, he stared him down. The war of wills only took a second before Game Over backed down. He dropped the pipe and started walking away, glancing back to give her a dirty look. She smirked, knowing she annoyed him even more.

Cavalio walked closer to their prisoner. "Do we need her?"

"She is not a necessity, but we need not kill her right now," The Infamous One replied.

"I'm not needed like you're no sweetheart."

The Infamous One held back Cavalio before turning to his captive. "Trying to provoke the aggression of my comrades is not a wise move. I can only contain them for so long."

"Then kill me now."

"I'm not one to disappoint a lady and her wishes," The Infamous One responded. "But this one I don't think you want granted."

"You don't know how much of a disappointment you really are."

"Dear girl, you have no clue as to the reality that is this world."

Enter Alexavier

"I don't need to know reality. I know the truth."

"All I know is how bad I want to shut your mouth," Nib barked.

"That can be arranged," Game Over agreed.

"So can a cell that you'll spend the rest of your lives in once you're taken down. You're a bunch of terrible human beings with no regard for anyone, not even your fellow Tribe members. You're all a bunch of criminals on the run or hiding. It's only a matter of time. You can't run forever. They're coming for me, and they're coming for you."

"Your opinion, just like your powers, doesn't really matter right now," Natural Disaster taunted.

With a screaming yell, Beth produced a blast of light shooting from her mouth that glanced off the shoulder of Natural Disaster. Game Over rushed to check on him as the Infamous One made his way around the machinery, grabbing a hood made of that same quick burning material Beth already had on her and placing it over her head. Nib went to head toward Beth, but was cut off by The Infamous One and dragged away. Nib calmed a bit and was finally allowed to go on his way. The Infamous One checked on Natural Disaster, who was angrier than he was hurt. Natural Disaster turned quickly, wanting to hit her with an energy blast, but was held up by his leader.

"Let me go!" Natural Disaster pulled away.

"Your need for retribution is not worth the check you'll have to cash."

"She'd be better in the ground than disrupting us like this!"

"Your anger would be better served in securing the important things at this facility. Finding her so close to our location has compromised this operation." The Infamous One leaned in. "She will be dealt with very appropriately, but that time isn't now. She's currently not a threat to us, but those who want her back are."

"Then, let them come."

Nib joined the conversation. "If I can't carve her open, then bring it on."

Enter Alexavier

"It would be unwise to invite heroes into your home when you don't need them," The Infamous One advised, looking at Nib. "This is your investment. You stand to lose more than anyone, more than your freedom."

Nib reluctantly backed down, returning to help gather documents as The Infamous One motioned to Cavalio. "Take those containers and head to the safe house with your ladies, who I believe are on lookout upstairs, right? We should be right behind you."

She acknowledged by kissing him on the cheek, gathering the desired materials and heading toward the door while tapping the mic button on her earpiece. "Troublemaker, prepare to leave."

Sweating under the black hood started to irritate him more than anything. Taking off his mask revealed a middle-aged Caucasian male. The Infamous One's face had a look of confidence, although that confidence started to show some cracks in its foundation. He knows the longer they are there, the more vulnerable they are. He proceeded to wiped his forehead and return to packing folders into the file boxes for removal.

Enter Alexavier

CHAPTER 38

Circling overhead, the pilot dropped the helicopter down below the clouds. It swooped in to search the area of Beth's last known location. A couple of passes allowed Major Constantine to survey the area, which resulted in disappointment. She was nowhere to be found, and the terrain only allowed for one secure drop off point. The pilot brought the helicopter slowly in for a landing. It touched down softly in a grassy field of weeds that moved in waves from the wind generated by the spinning blades.

"Masks and helmets on!" The rear door slowly lowered to the ground. Heroes stepped out with Killus and Hank leading the way, weapons in hand. The rest of the heroes followed, spreading out to secure the area with Alexavier heading in the direction of the building. The Major was last off with Harvey staying with him. Turning back, the Major motioned for Dr. Dennis to stay on and signaled the pilot to close the rear door. Walking around into the pilot's view, he gave the gesture for the helicopter to take off and stay safe in case of any villain attacks.

With the helicopter high enough in the air and the sound subsiding, the Major started directing the team. "Stay out at about 50 meters! Wait for further instructions before moving forward! Harvey, you take the lead near Hank."

Alexavier looked around as he stood his ground next to Dave. Both searched the furthest points either could see. Not satisfied, Alexavier pulled down his modified glasses onto his face and turned on the night vision. Something interesting came into view, but he was not sure if it happened to be the building in question. In the distance, he saw a very dim light that flashed a couple of times and shouted, "Hey, Dead Head!"

Dave ran over. "What do you see?"

"It's very hard, but way out there in the direction of that building was a light that shined briefly. We're too far away for normal city lights, so it could mean something or someone is there."

"Should you let the Major know? I mean, if you've truly found something." Dave went back to his spot on the perimeter.

Alexavier tapped his earpiece. "Major, I saw a light in the distance, but only for a few seconds."

"Do you see it again?"

"Not since then."

"It's probably a distant light source that was shining through the trees that are blowing in the wind. Keep a look out for anything else."

"But Major-"

"I said let it go! Now keep on the lookout! I want Wave Rider to..."

Alexavier gave Dave a frustrated look, who shook his head, not able to do anything. As Dave headed back to his appointed position, Alexavier walked forward to look again at that area. The view stayed dark, which was disappointing. But just as he began to turn away, the same small flash happened once more. Zooming in, the point of light appeared to be moving.

"Precision Shot should be over to that highest hill for any sniping that-"

"Major, I just saw the same-"

"Whatever you're looking at is not important, understand? You are to stand your ground, maintain radio silence and wait for my instructions! Killing Machine, circle

Enter Alexavier

the perimeter..."

Frustration enveloped Alexavier, especially when the light appeared one more time. But this time, with his eyes squarely focused on it, the light appeared to flicker. He knew there was something in the distance that needed to be investigated, but did not want the wrath of the Major. Fortunately, the Major began shifting everyone over in the direction of the cattle ranch. Alexavier stood back, waiting for everyone to be far enough in the distance before heading off into the night to check out the unusual light.

Continuing to set up the team while he could evaluate the area where Beth was last known to be, Major Constantine completed his orders for the team and began assessing the outlying areas. A tiny dot moving along the horizon caught his attention. It quickly changed directions, heading right for their location. Having a bad feeling, he called out, "We have something incoming from the southwest by air. Be ready in case we're spotted. Hello? Can anyone hear me?" Static was the only sound coming through his Com-Link, causing the Major a moment of panic. He yelled as loud as he could, "INCOMING!"

Before the blob in the sky could reach them, The Terror Tribe attacked. The team took the offensive and charged the villains, while the Major ran for cover. The Terror Tribe's first move was to take out Killus, their deadliest member. A massive energy bolt slammed into Killus' chest, knocking him backwards. April pulled out extra arms and attached them to her side while running to tackle Glutton. As more villains made their way from the plant-covered hills, the Major continued attempting to shout instructions in vain. The battle created such high noise levels that his efforts were useless. Watching was the only thing he could do. Frantically scanning the field, he was searching and searching, but not seeing all of his heroes. With sweat breaking out on his forehead, panic set in. Alexavier was missing.

Enter Alexavier

CHAPTER 39

Sitting on top of a plant covered outcrop and hidden from view, Alexavier studied the building in question. He could hear the fighting behind him, but it had no importance. His ears blocked out the sounds of battle, while his eyes focused on the target structure in front of him. Switching modes on his glasses to night vision, the grounds were empty of living creatures. The road to the building was open and clear to view, so he needed to follow a less conspicuous path.

A steady progression through the pitch-black night toward the back of the building had brought him upon an area that had a solitary man, a few hundred meters from the building. He was alone, waving around a single flashlight to help him see. The dark of night made moving among the trees, plants and hills quite easy. But the distance was still significant enough that identification of the villain was not possible. With not knowing whom he might be dealing with, the best course of action happened to be stealth.

Sneaking slowly without making any sound, Alexavier crept along the taller plants, ducking when the light was flashed in his direction. The villain appeared to be skittish, jumping at various noises caused by the increasing winds. No other cover was possible between where Alexavier's final hiding place and the villain. The distance was still too great that he could be seen before intercepting him.

With the villain scanning the darkness with a flashlight, the only way to get to him would have to be a distraction. Feeling around, the grassy ground there were no stones to throw. Then, a thought popped into his head. All Alexavier had were some small items on his belt and his glasses. He took off the glasses and heaved them just beyond the skittish bad guy. The sound startled him, causing him to shine the light in the opposite direction. Darting through the night, Alexavier generated as much speed as possible, jumping on the villain from behind. Alexavier transitioned to his back with his legs wrapped around him and arms across his throat, choking him. In desperation, the villain instantly moved to another place, taking Alexavier with him. But in doing so, Alexavier felt a mental drain that caused slight confusion. Still struggling, The Tribe member dashed once more, in hopes of wearing down whoever was on top of him. The mental fatigue was much worse, but Alexavier squeezed tighter. One last jump had both of them closer to the building, but the villain ran out of oxygen. A worn out Alexavier released the villain who slumped to the ground unconscious.

Taking a second to clear his cloudy mind, Alexavier picked up the flashlight. Shining the light down revealed a villain he was not familiar with. His recollection of the ability to dash from one place to another and affect people, both physically and mentally, made him believe the villain's name was Dasher. Knowing the villain might regain consciousness soon, he brought out the zip ties, securing him for extraction later on.

"Major, come in." The Com-Links only produced static. Knowing he would have to go it alone, he scanned the ground with the flashlight. With a sigh of relief, he located his glasses, which were still intact and working properly. Putting them on and turning off the flashlight, his next target was the back door to the building. The fighting going on in the background gave assurance that focus would not be on him, as he silently made his way to the door. A pull of the handle resulted in disappointment, as the door was locked. There was no card reader, just the standard dead bolt. Reaching into the side pocket of his belt, he pulled out a lock pick set. As

Enter Alexavier

with almost every lock, it only took a few seconds, and Alexavier was able to unlock it. Placing the tools back in his belt, he slowly opened the door. He listened first, taking a second before peeking inside. The entryway was devoid of any Tribe members. Quietly, he opened the door enough to slip in and shut it.

The building was lit up with many corridors, especially in the back leading to the private offices. Quietly sneaking from office to office, not a soul could be found. The rooms looked like they had not been occupied in years. Moving past the group of offices, the building opened up into a two-story area that housed a plethora of racks, cartons and boxes. With a couple of floors above that, he guessed the purpose of the building was warehousing, Alexavier began to search the file boxes in front of him. The labels on the outside gave no clue, and there was no paperwork anywhere. Where the offices seemed inactive, this staging area did not. Some of the boxes and crates placed near the dock appeared to have just arrived. There obviously had been items coming and going, but what and why was a mystery.

Suddenly, that weird sensation flooded his brain, and Alexavier leaped out of the way of a huge guardrail crashing down where he stood. Before him stood Game Over, with guardrail in hand and cocky smile on his face. His powers to lift objects much heavier than him made for a dangerous match, especially at distances. If he had something enormous in his hand, he was good to fight. "Looks like the puppets have been sent in. Aren't you going to introduce yourself? I always like to know whose butt I'm kicking."

"Me? I'm Dread, and I'm here for a girl who vanished."

Game Over twirled the guardrail. "Is that supposed to scare me? I mean, seriously?"

Alexavier circled behind a palette of boxes. "That doesn't matter. She's a friend of mine. If you know where she is, tell me now."

"Well, if you're not going to ask nicely..." Game Over swung the railing, barely missing the containers, as Alexavier rolled away to keep his distance. The large piece of metal was more than Alexavier could handle out in the open, so he headed for the racks filled with boxes. Ducking and slipping between boxes, he looked to lose the aggressive villain among the clutter throughout the aisles. Game Over obliged the chase, weaving through everything on the floor. Keeping his eyes toward the places that could be used for hiding, he was startled to see Alexavier charging forward. A swing of the guardrail missed its mark, as Alexavier leaped to the side. Rolling with momentum to his feet, he blasted Game Over in the chest with both hands. Game Over fell back hard, landing on the ground and losing control of the guardrail.

For the first time, uncertainty crept into Game Over's mind, along with a feeling of embarrassment. Angrily, he picked up a palette full of boxes and threw the entire thing in Alexavier's direction, before running toward the far side of the dock. Alexavier easily dodged the incoming projectile and began giving chase. Reaching the wall where the exit was located, Game Over slammed the door behind him, locked it and proceeded to head downstairs. The door had reinforced glass, so breaking it was difficult. Pushing on the door, Alexavier felt a stronger locking mechanism. The lock however, was still standard in nature and easy to pick. It took only a few seconds before the door was opened. Entering the stairwell, he saw it descended to only one exit. A quick jaunt down had him staring through the small glass window of the door. A quick listen to the Com-Links only gave more static and disappointment.

The lower level of the building was a more industrial area consisting of boilers, heaters and other machinery. Toward the back, several of The Terror Tribe gathered various papers and items, throwing them into any boxes or containers that were close by. Game Over went running up to them, pointing back toward Alexavier's position in the stairwell.

As Alexavier pushed the door open, he saw for the first time what the headquarters of a super villain team might look like. It was nothing too amazing for such a high-

Enter Alexavier

level organization. Many computers lined the back tables, but their hard drives were being pulled out. Several file cabinets lined the back wall, which were opened and being emptied. The lack of newer technology made this part of the building feel outdated.

Then, for the first time, he saw Beth, chained up and covered with something. It was an unusual sight to see that her upper body was not visible. He proceeded to run toward her until a blast of force energy threw him back toward some machines. It did not stun him, but it did knock him off balance. Looking up, Natural Disaster stood in front of all of the villains, waiting to attack again.

Pulling his mask over his face, The Infamous One gave the commands for others to continue grabbing more stuff, as he walked closer to Alexavier. "We have a guest. What is your purpose here?"

"Let her go!"

"I cannot do that." The Infamous One walked closer. "I have bigger things that cannot be interrupted, not by her or you. How about you reconsider your position with The Program and join us?"

"That'll never happen."

Joining them, Nib extended his fingers and produced a blade of energy. "What'll never happen is you getting out of here alive."

The Infamous One put his arm out in front of Nib. "Now, now. We don't know anything about our guest. Maybe if you enlighten us, we can come to some kind of understanding."

Alexavier realized he was outnumbered and at a serious disadvantage. "The only thing you need to understand is that I'm here for her. And if you've hurt her, I'll make you pay."

"I say we bury them both," Natural Disaster suggested.

"I like the idea of playing with him first. Can we keep him dad?" Game Over

Enter Alexavier

joked.

The Infamous One waved his hand, shushing his troops. "Why don't we all settle down for just a moment? Those who think rashly, usually end up hurt. I believe we all can get proper satisfaction from this situation. Let me start by saying, we want to make an exit without any interference. Our timely exit would allow a chance for you to walk away."

Alexavier continued to survey everyone. "I want you to back away and let her go."

"You're in no position to make demands, young hero," Natural Disaster growled.

"Actually, I will take his demands into consideration." The Infamous One responded quickly. "We do not want our first meeting to be unproductive."

Nib stepped forward. "Productivity means killing this little pain in the ass."

The Infamous One pushed Nib back, "That is not the way to start this relationship. Now let's see. If you give us a moment, we can figure this out. You want her, but we want to exit here without incident. Maybe we can come to an agreement?"

"You give her to me, and I might think about it."

The Infamous One smiled. "I think there might be a breakdown in the communication. Maybe you need to understand us a little better. We are not looking for trouble. Physical confrontation will not bring about resolution. We have numbers on you. These numbers are a devastating statement of what has been accomplished and the trophies we have taken. You can give thought to the offer we have put on the table. It only makes sense for you to take it. Otherwise, you can contest this arrangement with my comrades."

The situation appeared pretty grim. Battling most of the fiercest villains all by himself did not mean a happy ending. Worst of all, he did not believe the sincerity of The Infamous One. Alexavier could feel The Infamous One having an ulterior motive to the conversation. The longer they talked, the more that various Terror Tribe members gathered more items. It became obvious that once they had removed

Enter Alexavier

whatever they needed, he and Beth were expendable. The time was now to act.

Sprinting ahead, Alexavier dodged and weaved. Large mechanical objects were picked up and thrown by Game Over. Natural Disaster released energy blasts. Nib charged, swinging his blade. Alexavier engaged them all, except The Infamous One who ducked into the shadows. Alexavier rolled out of the way of consecutive attacks. Each time Natural Disaster would fire a blast, Alexavier leaped out of the way just to find cover for another object being thrown by Game Over. Their attacks were careful to not target Nib, who moved in for closer combat. Nib would sneak over, wait for the attacks on the hero to happen, then strike. That strange feeling kept flooding Alexavier's mind with each attack.

As the battle ensued in the semi-open area, the possibility for injury was greater for Alexavier. He ducked behind some of the machinery, hoping to throw his attackers off. The energy blasts stopped followed by an odd silence. He knew that they were stalking him, and that there were limited places he could go.

That feeling hit him again, and he jumped away, just as The Infamous One sent shots towards his hiding place. Alexavier charged the man in black, landing his shoulder square into the mastermind's stomach and driving him into a set of pipes. The Infamous One dropped his guns, screaming in pain. The sounds carried, alerting the other villains to his location. Quickly, Alexavier slipped behind more machines, weaving his way while dodging things flying through the air toward him. Stepping out into the open area, he felt that sensation again, but was too late. Taking a full blast of force energy from Natural Disaster, Alexavier was thrown through the air and landed against the wall. Game Over grabbed a few wood pallets and heaved them toward the downed hero. Alexavier made it to one knee before the projectiles smashed around him. One came too close, having him shield himself with his arm. It slammed hard, knocking him back on his posterior. Nib suddenly emerged, running up with his arm raised and the red energy blade slicing through the air. With a quick

Enter Alexavier

twist of his body, Alexavier rolled away as the blade smashed into the ground. Another twist and he kicked Nib's legs, sending him stumbling backwards. Alexavier scrambled away, but not before his hand grabbed a wrench lying on the ground. Finally having a weapon, he jumped up and threw it toward the easiest target, Game Over. The wrench smacked him in the leg, causing him to yell out in pain, sending him to the floor.

Seeing his disciple hurt, The Infamous One realized he had much more to lose over this. "Gentlemen! We're leaving now!"

Natural Disaster backed up to Game Over, helping him toward the back of the building. Nib followed, retreating quickly. The Infamous One slowly walked away, only looking back to make sure the hero would not follow. Alexavier did not give them a thought as he rushed over to Beth.

Pulling the paper-thin cover from her face, she breathed a sigh of relief. "We need to get out of here!"

"First, I need to get you unchained. Why couldn't you shoot your way out?"

"They put this hot burning paper all over me that would ignite and burn me alive if I used my powers."

He quickly removed every piece. "Now it's gone. What about the chains? I don't think I can break these."

"Give me a second. I can heat them up." Beth grabbed the chains on her wrists and concentrated, turning the steel red hot. With a hefty pull, they bent enough for her arms to be freed.

Suddenly, a thunderous boom could be heard, and parts of the building started to fall around them. Several massive pieces of concrete came crashing down blocking their path toward the back of the building. Alexavier grabbed Beth by the hand, guiding her towards the stairs he came down, which happened to be the last possible exit. Only making it half way there, more chunks of the building smashed several pieces of machinery that blocked their only escape route, leaving them with no place to go.

Several more thunderous booms were heard. "Are they blowing up the building?" Beth asked.

"Yeah. I think that's Natural Disaster blasting away. If they had imploded it, we'd be dead by now. We need to find another way out."

Seeing an aisle heading off to the other side of the building, Alexavier grabbed Beth's hand and started to run, hoping that it could lead to an exit. Pieces of the building continued to fall around them, littering their path. They sidestepped one after another, moving as quickly as they could. Unfortunately, a section of the upper floor the size of a semi-truck crashed in front of them.

"We're trapped!" Alexavier exclaimed. "Can you shoot them away?"

Beth aimed at the concrete block, hitting it with a concentrated beam that caused it to break up slightly. She took aim again, but by the time she could try again, more had fallen on top of that piece. Faster than she could clear it way, more portions of the building collected around them. The sound of cracking above had a piece of the upper ceiling fall. Alexavier yanked Beth's arm, moving them from getting crushed. With each passing moment, more debris landed around them, as they covered their heads. A large section began falling directly above them, and Beth put up a concentrated field of energy that deflected it away. Finally, enough of the building had fallen to corral them into a small area. Beth continued to hold her deflection field to protect them from fragments of the ceiling. Unfortunately, the continued downpour of concrete had them buried, and she started to struggle. "I don't know how long I can keep this up!"

"You can do it! Keep your focus on the shield!"

"It's draining my strength!"

Finally, enough debris had fallen that the noise of destruction subsided, creating a cavern under the rubble from above. Yelling no longer became necessary. "You're doing great, Beth. I think everything has finished falling."

"The pressure is pushing too hard. We need to call the Major."

Alexavier tapped his Com-Link. "It's still just static. I can't get ahold of him."

"I'm sorry. I can't hold it."

Alexavier flipped up his glasses. "Yes, you can!"

"I don't think I have the strength to keep this up very long!"

More cracking sounds were followed by the rumbling of concrete that put more pressure on Beth. Her shield slowly collapsed closer to them as her strength drained. A shift in the debris sent a thunderous crunch of noise reverberating all around them. Her arms began to shake as her muscle began to tremble.

Alexavier looked around quickly. "Okay. So, what about blasting our way out?"

"I tried that last time and it didn't work. That building was only three stories! This one is five!"

"Can you generate the field using only one hand?"

"I've never done it before, but maybe I can!" Beth pulled her arms together, pointing straight up. Slowly she brought the one arm down.

"Are you able to hold it?"

"I think so!" The look on Beth's face said otherwise, as desperation set in.

"Can you focus that same beam of energy like you did before, but out of your free hand?"

"I should, but that won't clear it all. The rest will fall on us."

Alexavier moved in closer. "Let the shield come in around us, until it's right on top of us."

"Okay."

"Then, bring your other arm up and give everything you've got to blast straight up."

"I'm not sure I can do this." The strain was much more visible the closer she let the shield get to them. With the strain, the shield began to shake, losing its stability.

"When I say go, I want you to project that light beam with your free hand like your aiming for the moon, okay?"

Beth struggled with the words just to reply. "Yes!"

"Then I need you to bring both arms together quickly, giving it all you can to send all the light possible skyward in all directions."

"The shield is coming in, and I'm losing energy. I don't know if I can!"

"I know you can! You're the only one who can save us! You're the only one who can do this! Bring that warmth. Bring that energy. Channel it straight up through your arm."

Still becoming weaker, she brought up her free arm and sent out a small, compressed beam that slowly tore through the concrete slabs on top of them. Her face showed the pain that grew stronger with every moment.

"You're doing it! Great Job! Now, I need you to gather every ounce of strength that's left."

"I can't!"

"You can do it! Listen to me! I want you to take all you have and send it out in all directions like you're shining a light for the whole world to see. Show them with that light you're a fighter, and that you're going to fight to survive! I want you to FIGHT!"

The sound of battle was made silent by a thunderous blast emanating from the distant building. The massive explosion stopped the battle happening across the vast field. Heroes and villains alike ran for cover from pieces of the building that came raining down all around. A few seconds passed before the shower of concrete ended and confusion set in. The Major shouted loud so his heroes could hear him, "Somebody get to that building!"

Enter Alexavier

Taking that as his cue, Wally rode the circling winds to make his way there. Searching from the skies, the devastation was unbelievable. He found it inconceivable that anyone could possibly survive. Landing just outside the debris field, he looked over the rubble in awe of the destruction. Incredibly, through the dissipating dust cloud, an image slowly appeared. Wally focused hard, trying to make out what it could be. To his surprise, it was Alexavier helping a very weak Beth walk across the scattered remnants of the building.

Enter Alexavier

CHAPTER 40

The explosion sent cement raining down on the battlefield and confusion through The Terror Tribe, who halted any combat and fled the scene immediately. Major Constantine looked over his team the best he could, having been spread out to fight the villains. Not sure of Wally's status, the Major was about to send heroes to search for him when all of a sudden the Com-Links began working again. A voice yelled through everyone's ear, "I've found Beacon and Dread! They're alive!"

Everyone called out, jamming the Com-Links. Needing to clarify what Wally relayed, the Major shouted, "Everybody, I need silence!" It took a few seconds, but the team complied. "Wave Rider, elaborate!"

"I'm where the supposed empty building once stood. I found Dread helping Beacon away from the center of the rubble. Dread said they were buried, but Beacon was able to get them out."

"What happened to the Tribe? Are there any villains that we need to worry about?" the Major inquired.

"Negative. They must have fled while trying to drop the building on them. I scanned the perimeter as I flew over and couldn't find a sign of anyone."

Major Constantine motioned to his team. "We need to evacuate now. Get the chopper down here. I want Hack 'n Maul, Killing Machine and Precision Shot to secure the building. You are to remain there until we can get a tactical team to take

Enter Alexavier

over. Guard it with your life. There may something of value to us."

"I'll be setting up on a nearby hill to scout with my scope," Percy said.

"I'll be landing in two," the pilot replied.

"Good. Everyone, be ready for extraction. What's Beacon's condition?"

"She's unhurt for the most part, but very tired," Alexavier responded. "It took a lot out of her to get everything off of us. I'm not sure what we could give her to improve her strength."

"We've got the doctor and some fluids on the chopper," the Major stated. "Appendage, go help to bring her back."

"Yes, sir!" April pulled out wings from behind her, attaching them to her back and flew toward the building.

The Major continued directing the team. "If anyone sees any Tribe members, it's shoot to kill at this point. We've got some things to attend to and don't need any distractions. Wave Rider, patrol the skies. I want Mecha to escort the chopper back to our position."

"I'm downwind from you. I'll be there in a minute." Mecha put his arms out. The metal plates on his forearms opened, displaying wings. His calves produced jet rockets that ignited, sending him skyward.

Major Constantine turned, looking in the distance to see Alexavier and April helping Beth. He started walking, and his pace quickened. Once close enough, he began to yell, "What the hell were you thinking running off?"

"She's really exhausted," Alexavier responded, changing the subject. "Is there somewhere that she can sit down?"

"The chopper will be here shortly. What happened?"

Alexavier helped Beth sit on the ground before facing the Major. "I took down one of The Tribe, as he was guarding the perimeter. I think his name is Dasher. He was

Enter Alexavier

tied up back near the building. I made my way inside where I held off The Tribe until they decided to leave. They tried to bury us alive, but Beth blasted our way out."

As the wind picked up with blades of the helicopter, it descended to a soft landing. The noise disrupted the Major's opportunity to further berate Alexavier.

Alexavier leaned over to check on Beth. "How are you feeling?"

"Mostly tired. Can I get some water?"

The Major pulled out a bottle of water he kept in reserve. "There's more stuff on board." The Major turned to April. "I want Alex and Beth on the chopper now! Tell Dr. Dennis to set up for an I.V. as soon as possible! And both need to be checked for injuries!"

The Major looked pointedly at Alexavier. "We will talk more later."

April took one arm, as Alexavier took the other, escorting their wounded comrade onto the waiting helicopter. Once placed on one of the pull out beds, Alexavier sat down in a seat next to her and took off his hood and mask. Dr. Dennis made a quick check of her vitals before starting the I.V. in her arm. April pulled out some water and energy drinks, looking to re-hydrate them both. Beth began sipping some water, while taking a deep breath. The preparations for extraction moved along at a steady pace as Alexavier and April waited by her side. Beth lifted her arm and put her hand on his. He smiled cautiously. She was out of trouble, but he would not let his guard down. Until they were back at the complex, she would never be out of his sight.

Enter Alexavier

CHAPTER 41

Back at The Program complex, the team exited the helicopter, led by Major Constantine. He was a slightly subdued, considering they just saved Beth and took down a Terror Tribe building. He did not stay behind, but directed Dr. Dennis. "There's a few bruised recruits that need healing. Beth will need to be completely checked out."

Dr. Dennis nodded, staying with Beth, while the Major headed toward his office. His hopes of secluding himself and not being interrupted were brought down like The Terror Tribe building when Sam walked up. "I heard the basics over the radio and got here as soon as I could. Give me the details."

The Major looked back, seeing Harvey sneak away unseen from the helicopter. "We came in hot, but shortly after landing we were met with resistance. Our team engaged, but Alexavier ran off, leaving us a man short. Luckily, we were able to handle The Tribe until we got the better of them, and they turned and ran."

"Where did Alexavier go?"

"He disappeared, apparently going to the building we had determined to be of unimportance. Alex said he took out Dasher before entering the building, but no one could locate Dasher. Shortly thereafter, the building came down, but Beth was able to blast away the falling debris enough for them to escape. We found them near the building that had been brought down."

Enter Alexavier

"So, he saved her?"

"I guess. He's lucky to not have killed her. This is the second time he's disobeyed a direct order."

Sam stopped in front of Major Constantine. "Maybe Alexavier did the right thing, and that's why she's alive."

The Major was fuming and needed to change the subject. "Well, beside her being alive, the positive thing is the building we found happens to be a warehouse for goods and supplies for The Terror Tribe. Most everything they had, which appears to be millions of dollars in goods, is now either destroyed or in our possession."

"How was the intel gathering?"

The Major stepped aside, continuing toward his office. "It's early, especially since most of their important items were located on the lower level and are now buried, but it appears we were able to gather a couple of computers and some files that were left behind. We did get enough of their files to see a portion of their current activities. Also, a majority of the money not recovered from the earlier bank robbery appears to be in the rubble. Preliminary findings also indicate credible intel of illegal gains of a wide range of chemicals and chemical manufacturing sources."

"Were the items found consistent with that?"

"So far? Yes. But, as much as we found, there's also evidence of equipment used in nuclear labs. Not much of it was salvaged or yet removed from the collapse. But what we were able to locate was clearly identified by the few serial numbers we could find."

Sam paused before offering, "Could they be looking to weaponize material for a nuclear device?"

"You know from personal experience what happened in New York. We could be looking at another threat to millions of people."

Sam looked down while walking. "We can't let that happen again. We need to know for sure. From this moment on, all our efforts are to find out if The Terror Tribe is looking to build and detonate another nuclear bomb. I want every recruit trained to do so, out doing recon to find The Tribe before something terrible can happen."

Major Constantine slowed down, watching Sam rush off toward the command center. For the foreseeable future, the Major's life was going to get even more complicated and very busy.

Enter Alexavier

CHAPTER 42

Every hero who went on the mission made his or her way through the infirmary, one by one. The only exception was Beth, who had been brought in first to be evaluated and treated. Dr. Dennis assessed each member of the team, and they were prioritized by the severity of their injury. Luckily, everyone only had minor injuries, even Alexavier who was last to get checked, since he wanted to wait by Beth's side. Dave gave one last look and nodded before heading back.

Dr. Dennis finally called over Alexavier. He hopped onto the exam table, still looking back at Beth. The doctor saw his preoccupation and tried to redirect his attention. "Any broken bones? Do you have any bruises?"

"No."

Seeing the many cuts and scrapes, the doctor rubbed her hands over them, slowly starting the healing process. "Are there any really painful areas?"

"Just some minor pain in my back and my left arm. I'm sure it's nothing."

"I'm going to check them out anyway." Dr. Dennis lifted his shirt, seeing significant bruising to his whole back. "Do these hurt when I touch them?"

He winced. "No." She put pressure on them, and he winced again. "They really don't hurt much."

She walked over to the medicine cabinet, pulling out a bottle of pills. Coming back, she handed him one. "Take this. I'll have these added to your regimen for the next couple days."

Alexavier took the pill and a glass of water, swallowing the pill. "Thank you."

The doctor placed her hands on his bruises for one last healing session. He closed his eyes, letting the sensation flow over him. After a few moments, the doctor took her hands from his bruises, going back over to check on Beth. Alexavier pulled his shirt down and waited, still feeling the healing energy. He hopped off the chair, making his way back over to where Beth was sitting and put on his black costume's sweatshirt jacket. He waited for the nurse attending to her to finish. Once the nurse left, he moved another chair closer.

Beth looked up and smiled. "Hi."

"Are you doing okay?"

"I'm fine. You actually have more injuries than I do from fighting the entire Tribe. You were giving them quite a fight."

"I'd fight them all many times over if necessary, just to save you."

"You only need to fight them once. Just beat them the first time, then you don't have to get patched up so much."

He rubbed his arm. "It's not that bad. I think Game Over has worse to worry about."

"What happened? I heard him scream."

"He kept picking up large objects to throw at me, so I threw something back."

"What did you throw?"

"A wrench."

"A wrench! Really?" She giggled a little.

"It was the closest thing to me, so I picked it up and aimed at Game Over's leg. I figured, if he couldn't stand, then he couldn't get to the stuff to throw at me."

"Wow! That's smart. But why did they leave?"

Enter Alexavier

"I noticed The Infamous One doing a lot of talking, trying to stall to get their stuff out. I didn't want them to get away with all of their documents, so I started fighting them all. I guess that forced them to leave early and abandon whatever they couldn't get to. They were hoping to bury us, so we couldn't tell what we saw. That's when they tried destroying the building. Because of you, they didn't get the job done. Now, It's my turn. I'm going to hunt each one of them down and make them pay for that."

"Take it easy, big guy. They'll get what's coming to them. You'll see."

"That can't come soon enough. I'm going to ask to be placed on all recon and standard missions so I can be ready when we find their hideout."

Beth grew concerned. "Are you sure you're alright?"

"Yeah. Outside of a couple of bruises, I'm-"

"I don't mean that. Your anger isn't normal. You've seemed so level-headed since you got here."

"Look at what they've tried doing to you. Twice now, they've attempted to bury you under buildings, and this time with me in it!"

"But, we're alive. We're back at the complex, ready to go out and take on any Tribe members that might pop up next."

"But we almost didn't. They came close to killing you, and I'm not going to let that happen."

"You already showed me that, when you saved me again."

"The problem is, I didn't have an exit strategy when I got inside, and I had no backup. The only thing I could think about was finding you. Once I did, my fighting instincts took over. I didn't think about what my next step. I didn't use my expertise in strategic planning. My only thought was to hurt them, and in the end it almost cost us our lives. Even if I did make it to you, I would have never made it out of the collapsing building if you hadn't saved us."

"But that's where you're wrong." Beth stood up. "You were the real hero. You did

Enter Alexavier

use your skills. You used your stealth and combat training to take on nearly the whole core of The Terror Tribe, and you got to me. You forced them to retreat. The only reason I was able to blast away the falling debris of the building was you. Your encouragement and your belief in me were what made it possible to do what I did. I could have never done that without you."

"Yes, you could have. You've done it before."

"How? What do you mean?"

"When we were back in Philly, one of the exercises they had you doing was to use a shield to protect yourself while shooting away things they'd throw at you. It was a very basic exercise, but it showed that you could use your powers to do more than one thing at a time. That was a few years ago. So I figured with the improvements that had to have been made over the years increasing your powers, you might have been able to pull that off. It was the only thing I could think of."

Beth paused, looking down. "If you hadn't saved me-"

"I will always be there to save you."

Beth smiled, moving closer. "That might be more difficult than you think."

"How is that?"

"I'm not stopping. I'm going after each and every one of The Tribe."

"And I will always be there."

She kissed him on the cheek. "Then you're going to have to follow me wherever I go, no matter what." Walking away and looking back, Beth left the medical ward and headed back toward the complex. Alexavier was shocked, but in a good way. He sat there, not sure what felt better, the drugs, the doctor's healing touch or the fact that she had just kissed him for the very first time. He looked around the room, still soaking the moment in when he noticed the doctor staring at him. He focused his attention on her, wondering why she was watching. Finally, the doctor said, "She did say to follow her." Alexavier realized Beth had long left the room. A little embarrassed, he quickly

Enter Alexavier

got up, racing to catch up with her.

Enter Alexavier

CHAPTER 43

Settled in at a café on the streets of Trenton, New Jersey, both Nib and Game Over enjoyed a morning coffee. The villains' costumes were gone, replaced by jeans and khakis. The casual environment would have been a perfect place to enjoy a leisurely bite to eat or latte, but the atmosphere at the table was not as brisk as the air swirling around them. Considering the animosity between them, it was no wonder that hardly a word was spoken. Even though they were teammates, they were usually at each other's throats. And with losing one of their prized warehouses, neither was in the mood to socialize. The silence was eventually broken when The Infamous One and Natural Disaster strolled up to them, also dressed in regular attire.

"So what's with this place? You know that a guy with a hurt leg can't walk too far? I had to scrounge for change just to get cab fare." Game Over pulled his bum leg from one of the chairs.

"Infamous didn't want any undue attention. Plus, I think he wanted you to suffer a little," Natural Disaster replied.

"Yeah. That's as funny as your face." Game Over pointed at Nib, showing a sarcastic smile. "I can't wait 'til you have to walk forever on only one leg after taking a bullet."

"It was a wrench," Nib stated. "And it didn't even break the skin."

"It hurts just the same," Game Over expressed. "I gotta get to Suture when we get

Enter Alexavier

back so he can heal this up."

A waitress strolled over to the table. "Can I get you guys anything?"

Natural Disaster kept his head down. "Nothing for me, thanks."

The Infamous One ordered, "I'll have an Earl Grey tea if you have it?"

"We sure do." Game Over and Nib shook their heads. "I'll be back in a couple of minutes."

As the waitress walked away, The Infamous One lowered his voice. "Our anonymity is most important. We have settled in well, but I would like to keep it that way. We have now lost two secluded locations. That anonymity is possibly compromised."

Nib sat up in his chair, resting his elbows on the table. "Any word on whether we were successful?"

"It's a negative on all fronts." Natural Disaster informed them.

"What the hell?" Game Over exclaimed.

The Infamous One leans forward. "Beacon of Light survived along with her savior. They almost apprehended Dasher. And worst of all, some of our most important information has made it into their hands."

"Well, I got punked by that new kid. He and I have date coming up very soon." Nib produced a small energy blade from his extended fingers.

The Infamous One grabbed the back of Nib's hand and closed it, extinguishing the light. "We need no undue attention right now. Our exploits have made the news. Planning and strategy needs to be of the utmost importance. We have been put at a disadvantage by their new member."

"Who is he?" Nib asked.

"My sources tell me his name is Alexavier," stated Natural Disaster.

"That's it? What a dumb name for a hero," Nib exclaimed.

Enter Alexavier

Nearly rolling his eyes, Game Over replied, "His code name is Dread. I found that out when I confronted him upstairs."

"Is that a joke?" Nib laughed. "With a name like that, am I supposed to be afraid now?"

"You should be less worried about his name, than the fact that your voice carries," The Infamous One explained. "This unknown hero took out Dasher before Dasher could blink. He entered our complex by himself. He stood before the best of us, took what we thought was our best effort, on his first try, saved his teammate and survived a building implosion. You should be very afraid at this moment. We're just lucky to have rescued Dasher before we left."

Game Over burst out in disbelief, "You're kidding!"

The Infamous One motioned. "Lower your voice."

"Tell me you're kidding. Me, be afraid?"

"Is he powerful?" Nib wondered.

"He's a Non-Meta with enhanced physical abilities and fighting skills," Natural Disaster explained.

"Piece o' cake, my friend," Nib assured.

"We have firsthand knowledge that he is not to be taken lightly," The Infamous One stated. "You should respect his abilities."

"Sorry, there's that earn thing you're forgetting when it comes to respect," Game Over seriously joked.

The Infamous One stared down Game Over. "He has mine."

"What do we do now?" Nib inquired.

Surprised, Natural Disaster asked, "I thought you were only for hire?"

"I owe the brat one. I had a boatload of change invested in that operation. Because of this new hero's interference in my business, I'm in for the duration," Nib

Enter Alexavier

proclaimed.

The Infamous One leaned forward. "Your allegiance is most welcome. Now, we have another target to hunt. Prepare your knives and sharpen your swords, gentlemen. Show no mercy when your hand is raised, ready to strike. Make sure he is all but a memory."

Game Over sported a devilish smile. "Fill me in. How is this Alexavier going to die?"

Enter Alexavier

Glossary

Those involved with the program:

April Dandridge (Appendage): Has extra limbs, including arms, legs, wings and even a tail, that are hidden on her body that she can pull out, attach to her body and come to life as her own.

Alexavier Vankendreh'd (Dread): Has increased physical abilities, including strength, speed, and agility and healing. Is skilled in all forms of combat, with or without weapons. Also possesses a unique 'feeling' that warns him of dangerous situations and people that causes him to react unknowingly to stay safe.

Beth Breckenridge (Beacon of Light): Has light based powers that can be intensified to become used as heat and impact abilities and weapons. Can create a nearly indestructible defensive shield.

Bobbie Terpstra (Booby Trap): Touches objects that become traps to distract enemies. Is highly skilled in various forms of combat, stealth and reconnaissance.

Brad Stryper (Broadstripe): Body turns in waves of color and light to travel short distances or escape dangerous situations.

Brian Haveman (Brindlehaven): Possesses very limited mystical abilities.

Dave Headley (Dead Head): Has the ability to return to life after apparently being killed.

Dirk Henderson: Leader of The Elitesmen Guard.

Dwayne Cygnus (Sickness): Inflicts various sicknesses and diseases upon making contacting with someone's skin.

Frank Steinberg: U.S. Senator and financial backer of The Program.

Glen Euw (Glu): Secretes sticky substances from his pores and mouth.

Enter Alexavier

Harvey Stringer (Heart Strings): Has a limited magnetic control over small iron particles, particularly in someone's bloodstream. Can cause anything from dizziness to complete stoppage of blood flow throughout the body.

James Killus (Killing Machine): Maniacal psychopath who has no regard for human life. Appears to have no powers, but also no fear. Is highly skilled in combat, particularly with weapons.

Jean Dennis: Doctor who possesses various healing abilities.

Jennifer Xiaohan (Syphon): Draws energy from her surroundings, which can be used for electric bolts. Can become transparent, fly and move through solid objects.

John Constantine: Major, retired, who is the head of The Program and coordinator for The United.

Jonathon Bender (The Time Bender): Uses a field of energy that appears to change whatever it comes in contact with into

Manny Batista (Human Battery): Can absorb or draw energy from various sources, which can be used for various forms of energy weapons or shields.

Michael McKnight (Mecha): Has skin that can turn into flexible, yet tough metal plates. Metal plates can open and transform, revealing many mechanical items, including guns, rocket launchers, wings, booster and tools.

Mike Mackinaw (Mr. Machine): Has a high level of understanding and expertise in all things mechanical, electrical and computers.

Percy Shottenheimer (Precision Shot): Has uncanny level of accuracy for anything he throws, shoots or aims.

Sam Nelson (Patriot Warrior): Technical advisor and consultant for The Program. Has a high level of increased strength, speed and endurance, which includes limited invulnerability.

Wally Ryder (Wave Rider): Uses various sources of energy to obtain flight.

Villains:

Cavalio: Girlfriend of the Infamous One. Establishes a mental link with persons who obey her every wish. Is highly skilled in various forms of combat.

Dasher: Uses a blink of the eye movement to go from one spot to another and drain enemies of their energy if he makes contact during the dash.

Game Over: Makes whatever he touches become feather-lite, allowing him to pick up massive objects with ease.

Glutton: Able to swallow incredible amounts of things safely that don't slow him down or affect his mobility.

Mega Conductor: Formerly known as Electrode, draws from the Earth's electromagnetic field to produce bolts of electricity.

Natural Disaster: Son of Major Disaster, who can produce massive amounts of raw energy to use as blasts, shields or to propel him short distances.

Nib: Creates an energy blade from his hand that drains an enemy's stamina and disorients them. Putting both hands together creates a death blade, which can kill.

Silver Shockwave: Produces small metallic spheres that grow in size and explosiveness, which he can detonate at any time.

The Infamous One: Formerly Known as Midnight Thief and current leader of The Terror Tribe, can blend into areas that are shaded or have shadows to become nearly invisible. Has been considered one of the most intelligent people on the planet. Is highly skilled in all forms of combat, including weapons.

Made in the USA
Monee, IL
13 November 2020